FRIENDS
DON'T
TELL

FRIENDS DON'T TELL

NADZ & GRACE

HODDER CHILDREN'S BOOKS
First published in Great Britain in 2022 by Hodder & Stoughton

1 3 5 7 9 10 8 6 4 2

Text copyright © Grace Francis and Nadia Mendoza, 2022

The moral rights of the authors have been asserted.

*All characters and events in this publication, other than those clearly
in the public domain, are fictitious and any resemblance to
real persons, living or dead, is purely coincidental.*

All rights reserved.
No part of this publication may be reproduced, stored in
a retrieval system, or transmitted, in any form or by any means, without
the prior permission in writing of the publisher, nor be otherwise circulated
in any form of binding or cover other than that in which it is published
and without a similar condition including this condition being
imposed on the subsequent purchaser.

A CIP catalogue record for this book
is available from the British Library.

ISBN: 978 1 444 96437 0

Typeset in Adobe Caslon by Avon DataSet Ltd, Alcester, Warwickshire

Printed and bound in Great Britain by Clays Ltd, Elcograf S.p.A.

The paper and board used in this book
are made from wood from responsible sources.

Hodder Children's Books
An imprint of
Hachette Children's Group
Part of Hodder & Stoughton Limited
Carmelite House
50 Victoria Embankment
London EC4Y 0DZ

An Hachette UK Company
www.hachette.co.uk

www.hachettechildrens.co.uk

NADZ – For James and the 'Maddy Mendozas'
GRACE – For Sunny

CHAPTER 1

JADE

I never thought there'd be this much walking! Don't get me wrong, I love the great outdoors. Mother Nature, what an icon. Get me out in the morning sun for some yoga or in a gong bath amongst the trees and I'm in heaven. But ask me to drag a sledge piled high with a weekend's worth of supplies through a field? I'd rather swerve it.

Yet that's exactly what I appear to be doing now.

My burnt-orange flared trousers cling to me as the breeze tickles my brown belly. The sun beats down stronger than I'd expected and the yellow-tint lenses of my flower-shape shades don't do much to stop its glare.

'C'mon!' Lexi yells, fidgety and excited, bouncing from foot to foot like she's prepping to return a big tennis serve. 'We're gonna miss the good tent spots!'

I haven't seen my bestie giddy like this in, well, years!

The sledge I'm pulling sticks, crunching on a pebble. The string that's slung over my shoulder digs in a bit deeper while I heave it over the latest obstacle.

We used to use this thing to go careering down the 'hill' around the corner from my house during snow days when we were little. The hill, a tiny mound of grass, felt like Everest at the time. We'd squeal as the sledge flipped over at the bottom, then we'd race back up the mound on repeat . . . until the sun went down and we dragged it home, freezing cold and voiceless.

Lexi struts along in front of me, a 'backpack on legs', making more ground than I could ever dream of. She's Hadid-esque in stature, while I'm more of an Ariana Grande in the height department. So, where she leads . . . I follow.

Today, I think she might be leading us round and round in circles, cos I swear I've seen that exact Get Lost poster before. We're flanking a gigantic fence that towers over the two of us! You could stack three Lexis on top of one another and she still wouldn't reach the top. There's green gauze covering the metal mesh fence and occasionally the gauze is switched out for posters of the festival that display the line-up for the weekend, headed by the Get Lost logo. There are also massive band and album posters, brightly coloured, in my face. The energy here is huge, different to home. Not just different – the complete opposite. It's not calm and cosy, it's jittery, edgy, like we're waiting for an explosion or something. A good explosion though! Like a glitter bomb.

We stop for a moment to take a look at the Get Lost map that lives in the small plastic pouch swinging around Lex's neck. She unfolds it and presents it to me.

'Pretty sure we're here.' Lex stabs the map with her finger a little more aggressively than the paper can handle and it crumples on the crease left by the fold. 'Oops!' She giggles mischievously, popping it back the right way. 'We need to be here.' She moves a finger on the map, more gently this time.

'Okay, so how long do you think it's gonna take?' I ask, sliding my shades back up my sweaty nose.

'I dunno,' she replies, 'this place is massive, isn't it?' And I can see excitement bubbling up behind her eyes.

She's not wrong – it's gigantic. I feel like a tiny ant, scurrying around in search of my home. I nudge a little closer to get a proper look at the map and see all these zones – different coloured blobs. I guess they must be for all the stages or whatever. There's a solid line that encloses all the colourful splodges and runs through the green field that all but covers the page. The word *BACKSTAGE* is emblazoned on the line, along with some little cross-hatched blocks reading *CATERING, PERFORMERS CAMPING/SHOWERS, BUS PARK*.

'But wait, Lex,' I say, 'hardly any of it's for us! Look, half of it's backstage.'

'Guess the VIPs have a festival of their own back there,' she replies.

I spot the lake on the map and feel the colour drain from my face. I squint to see how close our campsite is to it. I do not like water.

I look away and try to forget about it. I should focus on the good things about this festival. After all, we've been counting down the days since Lex decided it was time for a summer of fun back in January. We'd been spending less and less time together cos of Lex's detentions. Mrs Hake refused to let me sit in with her – but shouldn't it be my choice? What if I want time to centre myself and meditate the stress of each day away before I go home?

We had to frantically save up for Get Lost – I waited tables in the café down the road and Lex washed pots. According to Steve, the manager, she 'lacks the patience required for customer service'. I think he decided that when she told a regular to 'quit lookin' at me, perv!' during our trial shift. In the customer's defence, he was trying to get her attention to pay his bill at the time. In Lex's defence, the customer gave off a very creepy energy *and* had been staring at her the whole day.

But it wasn't enough to be split up in the café. A few weeks later, Steve split us up on the rota too, putting us on different shifts after he kept catching me chatting to Lex when I took the plates into the kitchen.

It's like the universe was trying to push us apart or something, probably cos we're twin flames, platonically I mean. The cosmos will always try to maintain that original soul separation, but it never will – me and Lex will always find each other again.

It took countless hours of achy feet, pruney hands and the customer always being right, but we're here! It already feels so charging. The energy is reverberating around me now, like a hum, filling me with vibrations. Stopping my tablets the other day was the right call. I wanted to really feel it all, y'know? Every last little bit of this festival. I don't even think I really need them anymore anyway. I've got them in my bag just in case – Mum checked to make sure I had them. So if I don't feel right, I'll take one, maybe. I haven't told Lexi, I just want one weekend without anyone worrying about what I put in my body.

After walking and walking, dragging and dragging, and another couple of map stops, we can see a campsite up ahead. Little tent tops peek out over the grassy mound in front of us. We scale it with one final push of energy and finally collapse on the once green grass. I hear it crunch as my butt hits the floor and the hard strands prickle through my trousers . . . Mother Nature should really send some rain soon.

'Right, so we've got . . . six poles, twenty-four pegs, the outer, erm, tenty thing and the inner tenty thing,' Lexi says, hands on hips. She jumped back up almost as soon as her feet were off the floor to start on the tent. Her blonde-pink, wavy, shag-cut hair is tucked behind her ears and her fluffy eyebrows furrow as she reads the instructions. Is this going to be as serious as building flat-pack furniture with Dad?

'First, we need to assemble the poles,' Lex says, still looking at the manual.

'Assemble the poles?' I reply, confused.

'Yeah, right now they're in pieces.' Lex stumbles over her Doc Martens and picks up a floppy non-assembled pole. 'You have to slot the pieces together, so they make one long pole.' She hands me lumps of plastic threaded around cord. They're like the numerous friendship bracelets I made her when we were in primary school out of macaroni and string. 'I'll carry on reading the instructions whilst you do that.'

'Yes, boss!' I reply, saluting Lex before taking the pole

and shooting her a playful side eye. Though it seems my commander in chief is too focused to notice.

I place my macaroni jumble on the grass and reach for a can from a bag on the sledge. 'Hey, Lex, why don't we catch our breath for a second? Sit in the sun, have a little drink.' I wiggle the tin that's in my hand from side to side with a wry smile, trying to tempt her.

'Sure, I guess . . . there's no bands today – it doesn't start properly 'til tomorrow.'

'Yeah,' I reply, although I have no idea what days or times any of the bands are playing. I spent exactly a nanosecond checking the line-up schedule. 'I just wanna dance, Lex, all weekend! Oh, and visit the stone circle at least once! And we could go and visit the psychic – I heard there's one here. Maybe our girl will come through?'

'Jadey, that's not what we're here for. Festivals aren't about "the other side",' Lex says, deepening her voice to sound mysterious, 'they're about music!'

Lexi's idea of a good time is guitars and synths and crowd-surfing. Mine is dancing and candles and meditation. When Lex mentioned Get Lost, it sounded like the kind of festival that was all about connecting with people and yourself and having a little bit of freedom. It wasn't until we were working in the café that I discovered that it's famous for its massive headline artists. And even later I found out about its huge lake and the afterparties where people splash around in the moonlight.

A shiver runs down my spine at the thought of swimming. Lex meanders over to me and plonks her denim-clad bum onto

6

the grass. She unlaces her DMs, pulls her feet out and wiggles her toes inside their odd socks, her alabaster legs outstretched in front of her. I follow suit, tugging at my Western-inspired boots 'til my feet ping out one after the other.

'That's better,' Lex sighs, blowing her fringe out of her face. She reaches for one of the cans I got from the sledge before tilting her head back to worship the sun. She puts the drink to her lips and sips . . . Her face suddenly scrunches up and the liquid comes spraying back out.

'Jaaade!' She coughs, wiping the back of her hand across her mouth. 'What is this?' She looks between me and the can in horror.

'Oh, it's kombucha!' I reply with a grin. 'Amazing for the gut! And I was reading an article the other day about how basically if you keep your gut healthy, it's impossible for your whole body to be unhealthy or something?' I chatter away as I rifle through the stacks of deliciousness on our sledge. 'I bought these vitamin sachets – they're tasty too. You just drop them into water, and that way we'll stay super refreshed and hydrated all weekend in the sun. There are these cans of water that you can refill and seal back up too. Gotta save the fishes, haven't we!'

Lex flings her body backwards to lie on the grass.

'Jade! You had one job – bringing goodies.' She giggles, kicking her feet up and down like a two-year-old. 'I never thought you'd turn our festival into a health retreat!'

I lie down on my side, prop my head up on my hand and face her cheek.

'Want to see what else I've got!?'

7

'Ooookaay!' She laughs, now looking at me fondly, clearly resigned to the situation.

I start picking up package after package from the sledge proudly. 'Sweet potato wraps, loads and loads of carrot sticks, some pea and mint dip, hummus, peppers, tomatoes, rice crackers, potato salad and a bit of pasta bake that Mum made especially.'

Lex bops me on the nose with a long finger topped by a heavily bitten nail coated in chipped black varnish. She reaches for her backpack and wrestles it closer to us by leaning forward over her legs. Then Lex unclasps the clips and flips the lid open.

'Luckily for both of us, I did some packing of my own.' Her eyes light up and a cheeky little grin ripples across her lips. Inside the bag, all I can see are crisps.

Lex flings them onto the ground one by one. Skips, Quavers, Pom-Bear, Space Raiders, Monster Munch are flying through the air, crumpling as they land. Next up: sour sweets in every colour of the rainbow. Then chocolate bars, Pop Tarts – loads and loads of Pop Tarts – and fizzy drinks that would last for days.

As she flips the bag upside down, and a couple of rogue Refreshers fall onto the grass, it dawns on me that the backpack is now entirely empty. It contained nothing but snacks!

'Lex, where are your clothes!?' I ask, slowly.

She jumps up from her squatting position and gestures by running her hands down the outline of her body and flipping them outwards once her arms are fully extended, for a flourish.

'You're lookin' at 'em, babe. Denim shorts and a T-shirt or two from you. It's a fool proof plan.'

'Fool proof?' I reply. Although if I'm honest I did overpack on outfits.

'Right, we can't stand around drinking kombuchaaaa in the sun all day,' Lex announces with a smile. 'Let's get back to building Kylie and then we can go and have fun.'

'Kylie?' I ask, confused.

'Yeah, I figured the tent needed a name.' Lex reaches for my hand and pulls me to my feet. We wrestle with the macaroni poles until they form rigid lines that are more like uncooked spaghetti, then we feed them delicately through loops attached to the canvas. Kylie starts to take shape. We stamp metal pegs into the hard crumbling ground to be sure she doesn't blow away and unzip the door so we can start making her feel like home.

'Airbed time?' I ask and Lex nods.

Together, we pull the plastic roll off the top of the sledge. The heat has made it stick to itself so we have to peel it apart. I assemble the pump, and Lexi and I attach the two together. Soon I'm bouncing my foot up and down on it like the world's most enthusiastic barn dance attendee. Lex and I take it in turns and after what feels like hours, we stand back to admire our work, leaning into a sweaty embrace in celebration of our achievement.

It dawns on us (almost simultaneously) that Kylie's door is far too small for this monstrosity of a mattress to fit through.

'Noooo,' Lexi says, turning to face me. 'How are we gonna

get that thing in there?' I hold her gaze for a second before a brilliant idea strikes . . .

I run back around to the valve on the mattress, pluck out the plug and plonk my bum down on the corner to squeeze out some air.

'Woah-woah-woah!' Lex yells, running around to drag me off. 'We spent ages doing that! Put the plug back in!'

I squeal and roll away, as Lexi scrambles to stick the plug back in. I jump up and grab the now slightly flaccid mattress to race towards Kylie's entrance, like a knight on horseback with a jousting pole. I ricochet off the fabric on the first few attempts and stumble back a few steps before trying again. Eventually, Lexi understands what I'm going for and helps me to guide what will be the new floor to our tent. Bending it, the mattress fits inside lengthways. As we let go, it unfurls itself to fill Kylie's entire floor and push her walls out.

We belly laugh at both our foolishness and ingenuity before high-fiving.

'Perfect!' I announce.

'Perfect!' Lex agrees.

Lexi sets up the Bluetooth speaker as I start to unpack my outfits. The sun has dropped a little in the sky and it's a balmy evening. Despite the hundreds of people all around us, it feels as if it's just the two of us, which is how I like it.

I pull my orange, lilac and green items (my colour palette for the weekend) out of a bag. Luckily, I also packed a couple of black band Ts that Lex had left at mine last week. I unfold them and fan them out on her side of the bed whilst she sits outside in the breeze tucking into crisps and her kombucha. I think she's starting to enjoy it . . .

I light a white sage incense stick and leave it just by the porch, close enough to bring good energies inside but far away enough that it won't burn the tent fabric. I hang headscarves, belt bags, waistcoats and shades from the many tent pockets dotted around Kylie. Then I pull out my make-up bag. Inside lurks my chrysocolla crystal that calms me and I slip it under my pillow. There's a little gift for Lexi too. I saw it when me and Mum went to Brighton to visit the uni's Fine Art department. Mum thought I should do a summer school there before trying to get a place. I dig out the tiny plastic gift bag and place it next to Lexi's T-shirts before calling her in to inspect our new home.

'Lex, come see!' I shout over the music as I hang our torch to dangle from Kylie's 'ceiling'.

'Baaabe! It's awesome!' she replies, appearing in the doorway. She crawls in through the door and clambers onto the airbed, spying her Ts and the small glistening thing sat on top of them. 'What's thiiiis!?' she asks, giving me a cute sideways look before opening the bag.

'It's an amethyst crystal in a ring so you can always keep it close. It's your birthstone, but also it's supposed to bring peace and protect you from getting drunk!' I giggle.

Lex crawls over the bed towards me. 'You're nuts, but I love you and I love it, you big hippie!' she says, squeezing me hard before placing the ring on her middle finger. She scooches back out of the door to fetch us another drink and the pasta bake to share. My head is starting to ache a bit, maybe from these big vibrations.

I lie back on the bed, clutch my crystal in both hands and place them on my forehead, breathing deeply as I do. I'm sure it'll pass soon.

CHAPTER 2

LEXI

We used to cross off the days in our school diaries, before summer holidays or Christmas break, until there were none left. 'Just one more sleep,' we'd eventually say. We were throwing away time like old pennies we didn't need. I remember the countdown to Get Lost felt like forever! Now, I count up. It's 340 days. Nearly a whole year with Jade gone.

I stride along, wheezing from the upward slope, gravel crunching under my DMs. Fitness is my frenemy. I might be an expert in running away from reality, but I hold Olympic gold in Excuses for Getting Out of PE. The breeze on my skin makes my hairs stand on end even though it's sunny. I could do this walk blindfolded; Jade's house used to be my second home, now I hang out at her grave.

I reach the top of the footpath, then take a left onto a different walkway that leads to Jade. I keep my head down as I go, never wanting to see the messages written on the other headstones, especially the one always surrounded by helium balloons and colourful windmills for the girl who will forever be eight years old. It sends shivers into my bone marrow.

I carry on walking until I reach the willow tree, drooping like it's drunk. I step onto the grass and see a blanket of wilted red rose petals as I approach her grave. Someone else's visited since I was here last week. They're defo not from me – red was the only colour she didn't like.

I tried bringing flowers the first time I came here, a few days after the funeral. I spent ages picking the prettiest yellow ones I could find. Jade's favourite colour – she said the colour felt like sunshine. But it didn't feel right. I'd never have done that when she was alive. If I'd turned up at her house for a sleepover with tulips instead of Haribo she'd have checked my pulse to see if I was ill.

I take a few more steps and kneel by the headstone.

> *In loving memory of Jade Felix.*
> *Beloved daughter and granddaughter.*
> *Rest in peace.*

It makes her sound like she was 85. 'Beloved' makes me think of all the Shakespeare plays I've never read, and 'Rest in peace'? Jade didn't want rest. She wanted life. Or at least, that's what I thought. She'd have much preferred it to say something like . . .

> *Damn, it's dark down here. Lol.*
> *Bring an aura quartz next time!*
> *Rave in peace.*

Once on Halloween, we tried to do a Ouija board. When nothing happened Jade asked if we could use an aura quartz – apparently it helps you 'connect with the spirits'. She pulled the crystal from the top of her chest of drawers as I lit a candle and turned off all the lights. We sat back down and I asked if anyone was there. The upside-down glass moved towards the word *YES*. At first, Jade thought I was messing about but I swore on her life I wasn't. Then, when we asked the spirit to spell out its name and the glass shot over to the letter *E*, Jade jumped up and didn't want to carry on – even though it was her idea in the first place.

I fiddle with my amethyst, as if it holds all the answers. When Jade gave me the ring, she told me it was my birthstone. But the other day, the shopping channel was selling brooches with a gem just like it, and the presenter said it was to avert negative energies. Should I be worried that there might be 'negative energies' coming my way? I only saw it by chance as I flicked between channels after my Netflix show finished – there was no point starting a new episode when my pizza delivery was due any second.

I don't really believe in that hocus pocus, but lately I'm wondering if it was Jade trying to tell me something. Through the TV. Like, warning me to stay away from something. Or someone? I know that sounds mental, but it makes things easier. I can imagine her sending messages to me while floating around in a white dress, wearing a halo amongst the angels. It's better than the other option: thinking of her flesh being eaten by maggots while she lies in a coffin.

I wish we'd never gone to that stupid festival. Life would

still be *normal*! I would do anything to turn back the clocks and un-buy the tickets. I thought we'd have the time of our lives and I'd come back with incredible memories, not a dead best friend in a body bag.

God, I hate myself. For taking Jade to the festival. For promising we'd have the best time *ever*. For not being able to remember what happened. The not knowing has been driving me NUTS – for the last 340 days. Mum says I'd have 'closure' if I could remember, but right now there's nothing but a big black hole in my mind.

At first, when I saw Jade lying there . . . like that . . . my brain filled in the blanks. It was a tragic accident. She'd got lost at Get Lost. She hadn't been able to see in the dark and had fallen into the lake. But afterwards, when she was brought home, they had to do a post-mortem. I googled it and found that they do autopsies when deaths are suspicious, sudden, or unnatural. Then it made sense – it *was* sudden. Jade was sixteen.

But the autopsy people recorded Jade's death as an open verdict, and I got confused again. Open verdict? It sounded like a name of one of the mocktails we'd served at the café. Eventually, I got told it's cos nobody really knows what happened.

I can still see Mum sitting on my bed explaining, trying to avoid the s-word, as it clicked in my brain. They couldn't be sure if what took place in the water was accidental, or suicide.

Before that, when I'd thought Jade's death had been an accident, it had been simpler. I don't mean painless, but at least I could live with myself. But knowing she might've died by *choice*, I can barely breathe. It's as if someone is holding a pillow over my face. Like, could I have done something to prevent it? Were there signs I missed?

Was it something *I* did?

I keep staring at the amethyst, willing it to talk. It's as though all the secrets are locked inside – and they are, because the ring was with Jade when it happened.

Do you know what it's like to lose someone you love?

It's like having the life crushed out of you too. It's so much pain that your heart feels as if it's shattered into a gazillion pieces. It's not wanting to get out of bed, and I don't mean like wanting a lie-in on a school day, I mean like never wanting to get up ever again. It's having a bath and lying with your head underwater wondering if you should bother coming back up. It's bunking your entire Lower Sixth as you can't face sitting next to an empty seat. It's seeing the person every night in your dreams, only to wake and remember that they're dead. Every single day.

The nightmares are hard. Jade feels *so* real in them.

There's one where we're at Get Lost and someone starts to chase us. I try to run, but my body slows. No matter how hard I try to use my legs to get away, I can't. It's as though I'm on a running machine, in motion but not travelling forward. It's like I can't move on. Then I turn around and see the face, and it's me. I'm running from myself.

There's another nightmare, with a blue girl. Not blue like a blueberry, or blue like a summer sky, but a faded blue like jeans that have been washed too many times. The girl tries to tell me to escape but her words don't come out right – they're slurred, like she's underwater.

One of the hardest things about losing Jade is thinking what would've been going through her head in those final moments, that she might have thought there was no other way out, that this time the bad in her brain got too big to tell even me.

We told each other everything – I trusted her with my life. Instead of pinkie promise, we did heart-hugs. Anytime we told a secret, we'd both put a hand on our hearts then with the spare hand reach across and place it on the other's hand over their heart. We used to say we'd take each other's secrets to the grave. It's strange to think that's true now. She's six feet under with only my troubles for company.

It's mad lonely too. I reached out to Cassie a few times, but she's always so busy and takes forever to reply. The only time I ever hear from her is when she sends a message with details of the next event she's putting on for her coursework, which has clearly gone to everyone in her contacts list. I could try calling, but I'd rather be alone than a desperado.

I sit on the cold, grey marble, and take my rucksack off to unzip it. The Cherry Coke and citrus cleanse tea glisten into view. I place her drink on the grave and mine in my lap to open. The ring-pull snaps back and bubbles shoot to the top, then I cheers the cola against her tea. I take a gulp before resting my can down to dive back into my bag for Mum's old iPod and my mini speaker. I want to play Eva Skowl's new album to Jade! I do it this way cos if I use my phone it sucks the life out the battery. I don't like it one bit when that happens.

As I'm rummaging, I hear a *tssSSS* fizz and somehow my Coke is no longer standing upright. The can's on its side and the drink's hissing out. I reach for it quickly, but it's too late. The sugary liquid oozes like a sticky river away from me and towards the headstone, branching off from itself to create other streams.

I balance the can so it's steady again, taking the hoodie from around my waist to mop up the spillage. I know the sun will dry the liquid, but it feels like I've poured my drink all over Jade's bed.

I finish wiping the mess and I pick up the teddy bear that's been left by the flowers, wrapping him in the sleeve of my top to try to dry him. Poor little guy. Once I've absorbed what I can, I move to put him back next to the limp roses, but I feel something.

I bring the fluffy bear back towards my lap and sit him face-up, so we're looking at each other. A small card has been tucked beneath his miniature T-shirt. I slide it out and see that the envelope is sealed. I'd never, ever have read Jade's emails or her texts when she was alive, but does snooping count when someone's dead?

Apparently not – I find myself unpeeling the paper to undo someone's lick work. I pull out the card and see a picture of a candle with the words *My Deepest Sympathies*.

I open the card and read what's inside.

I'm sorry, R

That's all it says. Nothing else.

Who the hell is R?

If they left the roses too, it's clearly someone who doesn't know they should be yellow. Seriously. Red? Jade always said red is 'a bad omen' because it means danger.

And why are they saying sorry? My stomach goes icy cold. Did this person have something to do with Jade's death? Do they know something that I don't know? I reach into my jeans pocket and dig out my phone, my heart racing like a wasp drunk on Red Bull. I type clumsily into the search bar and predictive text spews up results for *raisins*. I delete some letters before retyping *reasons for post-mortem*. There it is in black and white again. They only do autopsies when deaths are *suspicious, sudden or unnatural*.

A little vomit belches into my mouth as I feel my blood burn like fire. I've been so busy obsessing over the 'sudden' death of Jade, and the 'unnatural' way in which our very first festival ended, that I didn't think about the most important word of all – 'suspicious'.

What if Jade's death was recorded as an open verdict not because it was a tragic accident, nor suicide, but because . . . someone else was involved?

CHAPTER 3

JADE

The airbed was comfy but even with my two pairs of socks, hoodie and sleeping bag, I was shivering in the night. Now the sun is up, I feel like a Christmas turkey roasting in its own juices. My tongue scrapes around the inside of my mouth like sandpaper as I try to swallow. I shuffle forward for the water I put at the end of the bed last night. I prise my eyes apart, but they're blinded by light, so I pat around for the can.

There it is!

I roll over whilst wrestling with the mechanism on the top. I brave opening just one eye again to focus on what I'm doing and sit up to take a sip. My lips have become one big lip in their dryness, forcing me to prise them apart too. Finally I place the metal to my mouth and guzzle.

'Jade,' croaks Lexi. 'Can I have some?' I pass her the can before I drain the whole thing. She's lying face down but somehow manages to drink without moving position at all. 'It's really fuckin' hot in here.'

'Yeah,' I reply flatly as I desperately try to pull my hoodie off. There's a sharp pain running like a halo all the way around my head. Dehydration, I think?

Or is it . . . nah, probably not.

I lean forward and reach for the zip to our tent door in a bid for air. Lexi kneels in her black denim cut-offs and cropped vest, the same outfit she was wearing yesterday, looking the picture of elegance. I, however, resemble a Halloween costume. I've come as a human hotdog that's been run over! My legs are still packed into Dad's old sleeping bag and my vest top is twisted around, squishing my belly. Even though I took my make-up off and moisturised last night, my skin feels crispy.

'Babe, can I borrow your toothbrush? This morning-breath is the worst,' Lexi says. She leans back, arms stretched above her head as far as they can before hitting the top of the tent, and does that super satisfying yawn everyone needs first thing in the morning.

'Sure,' I reply as I head out of Kylie face first, trying hard to kick the sleeping bag off my legs as I go. 'It's in my washbag, at the bottom of the bed.'

The gentle breeze on my face refreshes me immediately. Lex squeezes past me, her Docs on, my toothbrush in hand.

'I'll be back in a min. I might try and find some breakfast too,' she says, heading in the direction of all the action.

'What about the wraps and carrot sticks?' I shout after her. But she runs away comedically, hands over her ears, pretending not to hear.

With Lex gone, I take a look at my phone. There's a message from Mum and I quickly reply.

How was it, lovely? Did you get the tent up before dark?

Yep. We're fine.

Oh good! What about your meds? Don't forget. Love you.

I won't.

If I don't take my meds, but I haven't 'forgotten', is that still a lie?

I head back to Kylie's porch and crack open the carrot sticks and hummus. As I dunk and crunch, I plan which outfit I'm going to wear today in my head. The best thing is probably the green pattern-print mini dress, seeing as it's crazy-hot. I turned it into a mini after buying it as a midi, then made some matching cuffs from the fabric I'd cut off. Mum taught me how to use the sewing machine when I was younger, so I snip and hem a lot. Now they tie perfectly around my wrists to make a co-ord. I'll wear my Western boots and fluff my hair out. With a little wash of brown over my eyelids to bring out the green in my eyes, a few necklaces, and my jade earrings, I'll be set.

After annihilating nearly an entire tub of hummus, I start getting dressed. I'll do my hair and make-up when Lexi gets back. I tug the biodegradable face wipes out from one of Kylie's pockets and run the damp fabric over all the important parts then grab the moisturiser and deodorant. I wrestle myself into pants, cycle shorts (there'll be no up-skirting around here, thanks!), and finally slip the silky mini dress over my shoulders.

I pull on my cuffs and tortoiseshell shades, then head back into the sunshine – just in time to see Lexi striding back towards me, bacon bap in hand.

'Rah!' she shouts. 'Look at you! Not messing around with these lewks, are ya?'

I give her a little spin before pushing down my shades to peer over the top a little.

'How were the bathrooms?' I ask.

'Well, they're not really bathrooms, more shacks with running water, but they were alright – did the job!'

'Oh! Okay . . . Can I have the washbag? I need to sort my hair out.'

'Yeah, here you go.' Lex throws the bag through the sky at me. I panic, desperate to catch it and not make a tit of myself in front of everyone now emerging from their tents. It lands squarely in my arms but as I catch it I trip over the tips of my cowboy boots and fall flat on my face (shoot me now!).

I look up at Lex sheepishly. She tries to suppress her laughter as she helps me up. I dust myself down and unzip the bag, grabbing my spray bottle that's sitting on the top. I press the pump over and over, aiming the mist at my hair to get as much water as possible distributed over my coily strands. I scrunch it in, then reach for some curl cream, unscrewing the lid to dip a finger into the pot. It becomes slippery as I rub it hard between my palms, mixing with the water residue. I push my hands under my hair and upwards, then scrunch the ends, so they get some love too.

Finally, I pull my comb out and place the prongs at my scalp, pulling gently out and up so my shape looks a little less

slept on. I don't really know what I'm doing, to be honest –
that's the trouble with having a bald dad and a white mum.
But Nana always said hydration is everything, so I'm trying.
It's weird feeling lost with something that grows out of your
own head, like a daily reminder that I don't really know who
I am.

Next, I brush my teeth, pouring water from a can over the
brush and smushing a bit of toothpaste into the bristles. After
using all the water in the can, I start brushing. I'm mid froth
when I hear . . .

'Oh! I know you! You're Lexi Flowers from school.'

I spin around, toothbrush in hand, froth flinging from my
mouth and to the grass. It's none other than Cassie Cox and
her band of merry men. Cassie's from home, older than us –
she seemed to appear in Sixth Form totally out of the blue.
We've never said a word to each other. I would die if she spoke
to me in the corridors.

She's amazing – effortlessly cool with this striking energy
that's hard to describe, but you would always know that she'd
entered a room. It's like she brings this stillness and this
powerful vibration all at once. She has rich dark skin that
glistens in the sunshine and a cascade of long, thick braids clad
at intervals with little golden huggers that catch the light.
I've been asking Mum for years if I can have braids, and the
answer's always no. Probably cos she wouldn't know where to
start or where to take me.

Cassie's rocking her signature look: a baggy band T-shirt,
the sleeves rolled so they hug her shoulders, and wide-leg
ripped jeans. She looks as though she literally just got out of

bed and threw on whatever was nearby – and it just so happens that everything nearby was unbelievably cool, so she looks like a goddess from the second she wakes up. Cassie's so free, so at ease with herself, so light. She's also free and light in a very real sense – she's not carrying anything! The boys seem to have all her stuff instead.

They're a ragtag bunch: a lanky one with brown hair and a floppy fringe who's wearing a bucket hat and a T-shirt in Neapolitan ice-cream stripes; a big guy with a shaven head and no shirt, turning more and more pink by the second; and one with perfectly slicked back mousey hair that's giving him a just-got-out-of-the-sea look who's now unzipping his bag and beginning to pass them all drinks. I recognise the crest on the duffle bag – it's from the grammar school down the road from home . . . he must be smart!

I look over to Lexi, who walks over to the group as cool as a cucumber and says, 'Cassie? Hey.'

'Hey, babe,' Cassie replies, giving Lex a brief embrace and kiss on the cheek. If I weren't trying my best to play it cool, my jaw would be entirely on the floor. Do they know each other? 'Who's your mate?' she asks, gesturing in my direction.

'That's just Jade,' Lex replies.

Just Jade? Ouch.

I wave, my toothbrush-free hand bending at the elbow like some weird Lego girl. 'Hey, how're you doing?' I mumble through toothpaste-filled chops, before quickly spitting it out. I wipe the foam from my mouth on the back of my hand – well, on my beautiful cuffs actually. My God, could this be any worse?

26

'We're good,' Cassie says, answering for the group before turning to Lexi. 'Mind if we pitch up next to you?'

'Nah, go for it,' Lex replies, answering for the two of us.

I go to move our sledge to make space, still holding my toothbrush, but somehow manage to trip again – nearly nosediving into the drinks and snacks!

'Hey, I'm Alex . . . You okay?' The cute Neapolitan-ice-cream boy heads over, looking concerned for me.

'Oh, I'm fine, you guys just caught me mid tooth clean.' I giggle, trying desperately to straighten up and sound breezy while knowing I don't.

'D'u want some water?' he asks.

'No, no. I'm fine,' I reply, flashing him the biggest smile I can muster.

'It's just . . .'

'What?'

'You've still got a little bit of . . . foam,' he says, pointing to the side of his mouth.

My hand flies up to mirror his and I look down whilst scrubbing the foam away. I turn to head into the tent. 'Just gonna go and . . .' I tail off, making a beeline for Kylie with my eyes still pointing at the ground. Once inside I pick up the mirror and mouth at myself, 'What the fuck was that?' before grabbing my make-up bag and smearing a bit of BB cream over my face. I brush my brows up, swipe brown shadow over my eyelids and quickly flick some mascara through my lashes. The last thing I do is I shove in some earrings. Now I feel at least a little bit ready to make some new, incredibly cool friends.

Music is playing from the Bluetooth speaker, Lex and Cassie

are deep in conversation about bands, and the others look very serious as they figure out the best way to squeeze their gigantic tent into what looked like a fairly big patch right next to ours. The trouble is, they've brought a six-man thing. It looks like a castle compared to Kylie.

I watch the boys as they're assembling the monstrosity.

It's red. I don't normally like that colour cos, well . . . it's a bad omen. But against the sunshine, it kind of glows orangey, and I wonder if it's actually okay.

Besides, Alex seems kind. He's really patient with the others whilst they fumble around trying to put the tent up. He's literally helping every single one of them and they barely even notice.

I think Sam's a bit of a know-it-all. Except he doesn't know it all. I hear plenty of, 'Yeah, just leave me to it, mate!' as they continue assembling their palace.

Then there's Jonesy, a bit of a #LadLadLad I think. He's not doing much other than cracking terrible jokes, slapping people on the back and destroying can after can of lager. Although there's something in his face that tells me if he wasn't doing this, he'd be crying.

They finally finish constructing their tent and Alex offers to show me around. There are actual rooms in this thing! It has a porch at the front and then, zipped behind their own doors, individual rooms to the back, left and right. Cassie and Alex have separate rooms. Jonesy and Sam are sharing.

As the sun climbs higher in the sky, we zip up our tents and head into the festival, passing gigantic billboards. Flags flapping in the breeze guide us in the right direction – and then we're here. I've never seen anything like it!

There are thousands and thousands of people, just wandering everywhere. Some with rainbow hair, some wearing costumes and some covered in glitter and tattoos. There are people on stilts roaming past, blowing fire from their mouths or posing for photos. The smell of burgers and chips wafts through the air . . . I do love chips!

As Cassie and the boys walk on ahead, I catch a moment with Lexi.

'You never told me Cassie was your bestie!' I say. 'She's amazing,' I add, trying not to show how nervous I am about her being here.

'She's not my bestie! You are.' Lex giggles.

'Did you notice their tent is red?' I mention, trying to sound light-hearted.

'Jade, it's fine,' Lex reassures me.

'So it's not gonna be like the trio again?' I hesitate. 'Because last time . . .'

'No, Jadey, c'mon. Just cos there's three of us girls doesn't mean something bad's gonna happen.' She puts her arm over my shoulder and squeezes me into her. 'Besides, Cassie might not even like you, then you won't need to worry about threes cos I'll have to leave you for her.' She laughs and I cackle right back. 'Listen, I know it's not exactly how we planned it, but maybe we're gonna have even *more* fun than ever?'

'You're right. The energy is amazing. It's gonna be a festival to die for!' I squeal and Lex smiles back with a tiny twinkle in her eye.

CHAPTER 4

LEXI

I've been staring at the note the whole bus ride. *I'm sorry, R.* I've read it a thousand times since I found it yesterday, and even though it's only two words and an initial, it takes me longer to read each go. The way it's written is weird. If it's from a friend who's sad that she's gone or a heartbroken relative, why not just say *I miss you*? It's clearly a confession! Someone went to Jade's grave to apologise for something they did.

I wonder if the cemetery has CCTV cameras. Maybe the caretaker will let me take a look? That way, I could see who left the teddy bear and red roses. If not, maybe I can camp out there for a week, just to see if the person comes back. Ooh, or I can find my GoPro from when I used to skateboard and see if I can somehow attach it to the headstone and record?

I dunno . . . maybe that all sounds crazy.

It's just . . .

I've always believed in fact, not sixth senses, and unless I can *see* something I'm not usually interested in anything supernatural. Still, things haven't felt right since Jade died.

I can't really explain it – it's more of a gut feeling.

Now it's no longer just a hunch cos there's an actual handwritten confession note in my hands. And if it's what I think it is, then that means the people who do the death certificates are wrong.

Perhaps Jade's death isn't so uncertain at all. The more I think about it, I really don't believe it was an accident. Jade absolutely, totally, utterly would've yelled for help. Trust me – I've witnessed how loud she could scream after accidentally walking into a one-centimetre puddle! She didn't even like bath water. We were at a festival. With thousands of other people! Someone would've heard her shout, surely?

And deep down, I just don't feel like she took her own life. Mum told me it's natural to be 'in denial', but it's not that. Jade would've been too worried about leaving the world with bad energy that couldn't be redistributed back into nature for the flowers and animals.

Besides, the only thing that got me through hearing 'teenager's body', 'pronounced dead at scene' and 'deprived of oxygen' roll off the newsreaders' tongues last summer was that they didn't have enough evidence to properly call it suicide.

Which means . . . what if someone really did want Jade dead?

It's wild, I know. Who would want to kill a girl from a sleepy town who lived for harmony and colour-coordinated outfits? I can't imagine anyone wanting to hurt Jade, but it would explain why she left without saying goodbye. Jade wouldn't have just checked out, at least not without a note.

I know because we told each other how we wanted to die.

It might seem morbid, but when you've spoken to the same person every minute, every hour, every day for a decade, you cover every topic *ever* and end up chatting about weird shiz. Jade always said, 'in my sleep', then would laugh at me when I'd say I wanted to die during a skydive – cos at least I'd get to go out on an adrenaline rush before hitting the ground with an almighty splat.

I tear my eyes away from the confession note and look out of the window. I picture myself skydiving without a parachute. If I can't find the answers, maybe I'll just join her?

I stare at the sky, dark thoughts flying through me like rabid bats. Gradually my vision comes back into focus. I didn't even notice it had been raining. There are streaks across the glass from the raindrops. It can only have been a shower as the sun is peeping out from the clouds again and a bright rainbow is shimmering in the distance.

The colours break my thoughts.

I shove the card into my bag then apologise to the bloke in an anorak the size of duvet next to me, who takes forever and a day to move his knees, so I can squeeze past and frantically head down to the lower deck. I always get ready and stand by the doors a few stops early, so that I can count before I get off. But I'm only one stop away!

I start counting as quickly as I possibly can before I even reach downstairs.

Onetwothreefourfivesixseveneightnineteneleventwelve . . .

I'm only at 114 as I spy my bus stop through the glass door. I'm going so fast my brain can barely keep up as the driver hits the brakes. I cling onto the pole to stop myself from hurtling down the aisle as the bus grinds to a halt. I'm still hurrying through my numbers, but I'm not even at 200! The doors squeak open, and I can feel the wind rush through from the street, though I can't get off. Not yet.

I race, race, race through the sequence to get to the end, but the whoosh of the doors closing rushes into my ears. Too late.

I stare out the window as we begin to move again and my bus stop disappears in the distance while we continue further along the road. I feel annoyed and ashamed of myself – but if I get off before the safe number, my mum will die.

Finally, I'm caught up to 341 just before the next stop and I hastily press the bell.

I step out onto the street and look up at the rainbow. I can't help but wonder if it's another sign from Jade. Telling me she's here. To keep looking. The answers are out there . . .

I scurry along from the wrong bus stop so that I'm not late for my appointment while mentally going through all the people I know whose names begin with R. But the problem with only having one friend is that there aren't many people to consider once I've ticked myself off the list. I guess R could be an aunt or uncle, but Jade's dad's sisters live in Jamaica and her mum's an only child like me. By the time I reach the community building, I've got as far as me, Cassie, Jonesy, Alex, Sam. There's no R.

I sit on the sofa in Petra's office. There's a box of tissues on the table beside me for whenever I might cry, a jug of water and plastic cups. A painting of some flowers on the wall behind Petra makes the room feel even more depressing, like it's forcing its zen on me.

'Hi, Lexi, how are you?' Petra asks.

'Okay,' I say, looking down at my phone.

'We spoke last time about perhaps starting the session with our mobiles to one side this week. How does that sit with you?'

'It's on silent,' I reply.

Petra looks at me with a raised brow. 'It's just that it might be a little distracting for us,' she says, softly but firmly.

Petra is pretty. She has ginger hair and a lashing of bright red lipstick on an otherwise make-up-free face. She's wearing a suit with heels that show off her ankles. I think she doesn't know how beautiful she is. She is actually quite distracting to look at.

I started having appointments with her a few weeks ago. She's the third counsellor I've seen. The first one was Hideous, with a capital H. I left feeling worse than when I'd walked in. The guy had a big beard and wore a brown suit, and he didn't even say anything. Nothing! I had to sit in this room with a dude I didn't know while he stared at me and said fuck all. I got told he was a psychoanalyst, and his job was to 'study' me. It was SO gross.

After that, it was the CBT lady, which stands for 'Cognitive Behavioural Therapy'. I wish they'd just call it HAC, for 'Having A Chat'. By making it so clinical it has the exact opposite effect of encouraging me to talk about what's going on inside my head.

I had six sessions with the CBT lady. Six! They think six sessions is enough to get over a dead person. It took me six sessions to even mention Jade's name.

After that, Mum found a therapist by herself cos the doctor

said he'd done all he could for me – but I didn't feel fixed. If anything, I felt crazier.

'What do you think?' Petra chimes again.

'Yeah, I can put my phone away, hold on a sec.' I quickly reach into the front pocket of my bag for the portable charger and plug my mobile into the silver power bar so it can charge while we chat, then rest it on the sofa space beside me.

'Great. Let's start then. Is there anything you'd like to share about the last week?'

'Not sure,' I say, wondering if I should tell Petra about what I found at Jade's grave.

'That's fine – take your time.' She looks at me with so much patience and kindness that it sort of hurts my heart. It reminds me of how Jade looked at me.

'I found something,' I blurt out, diving back into my bag before handing Petra the card with the note.

'What's this?' she asks, a little confused.

'I was gonna ask you the same thing.'

'I'd say it's a condolences card.' Petra turns it in her hand.

'Do you think it could be a confession?' I ask, my thighs jiggling as I bounce my toes.

'A confession? I hadn't interpreted it that way. What makes you say that?'

'It was left at Jade's grave, like someone went there to say sorry.'

Petra scans the card for a final time before handing it back to me. 'It's hard to say. People deal with grief in many ways. We all have a different language for it.'

My shoulders flop to mirror my deflated mood.

Until now, Jade's open verdict had felt like being trapped in a snow globe with the same answers swirling around and around. Yesterday, it seemed like that was changing . . . 'til Petra just rejected my theory.

'Are you okay?' she says, breaking the quiet.

'It just feels like there's more to it.'

'Do you think it could be helpful to talk about what happened to your friend?'

I suddenly feel really claustrophobic, as if everything is closing in around me, as if I'm a snail retreating into its shell. My heart starts beating erratically, like it's screeching at me. I'm not fluent in heart but it sounds like it's saying, 'Get the hell out of here!' I glance over to the charging phone beside me and keep my eyes there to calm myself. We're less than halfway through, but if I stay quiet for as long as possible maybe I won't have to say anything else until our fifty minutes is up.

'Lexi?' Petra prompts me. 'We can go at your own pace; you can say as much or as little as you want. Just whenever you're ready.'

'What if I'll never be ready?' I find myself saying as I twiddle with my amethyst ring.

'That's okay – sometimes we're never ready. Often we do things before we're ready, in the middle of being ready, or after being ready. Progression isn't always linear.'

I try to let that sink in, with my eyes still fixated on the phone.

'Does that make sense?' Petra asks, cutting the silence again.

'Yeah.' I nod. 'It's just hard . . .' I close my eyes and rub my fingers against them, desperate to be invisible. My knees are really jittering now, jerking with toxic energy.

'What's on your mind?' Petra asks. 'It looks like you might be processing something?'

'I, I . . .' I open my eyes to try to stay in control. The nightmares, the shame, the pain – it's too much. I feel so scared cos the lid is threatening to blow off the pressure cooker of my mind and everything that's been locked inside wants to burst out. It's like an angry, inflamed zit that's been swelling beneath the surface and is just about to pop all over the mirror. 'I can't picture her face before she died,' I say. 'All I can see is her lying there, not looking right.'

'You saw her, after it happened? That must've been hard?'

I scrabble around thinking of how to answer, just as the sound of Petra's shoe drops to the floor, echoing through the room. I stare as she takes the other shoe off, the one that's still on her foot. She tucks the pair under her seat, before crossing her legs again barefoot. She looks up and we lock eyes.

'The shoes!' I shout.

'I'm so sorry,' she says. 'I need to return them, they're a terrible fit.'

'No, *Jade's* shoes!' I'm staring at Petra's heels but I'm seeing Jade's boots. *How* have I never thought of the shoes?

'What about her shoes?' Petra asks gently.

'They were by her body.'

'Okay,' she says, waiting for more explanation.

'If it was an accident,' I say, enthusiastic from my revelation, 'Jade's shoes would've been on, wouldn't they? She'd have wandered into the water by mistake – never on purpose, alone. And if it was suicide, her shoes would also be on. She

37

wouldn't have bothered to take them off. You'd just do it quickly, right, in case you changed your mind? But they were off! As if she'd gone for a paddle *with* someone.'

'Ah, I follow now. And have you spoken to anyone else about this?'

'No, I mean, I don't think so. The police questioned us all when they investigated but I was in shock. It was such a blur. It still is. I can't remember what happened that night and it's killing me.'

'Is there anything you *can* remember, no matter how small?'

I shake my head, choosing not to say anything about the amethyst ring.

Petra nods sympathetically. 'And how does that make you feel, not remembering?'

'I dunno, I guess it makes me feel . . . guilty,' I say. The word shoots out of my mouth like a bullet from a pistol, surprising me. I've just explained what has been wordlessly torturing me for the last 341 days. It's like a spiritual awakening, but from the devil.

This freakish pain I've been feeling is not just grief.

I feel guilty.

CHAPTER 5

JADE

Lexi's grip loosens and her sticky palm parts from mine. She crouches down, turns to me and slowly raises one finger to her slightly pouted lips. 'Sshhhh,' she silently mouths. Her knees begin to rise as she pulls her feet high above the yellow-green grass and stalks forward like a cartoon villain. I nod and follow suit.

We tiptoe, at speed, towards the pack. With one eye on my Lexi and another on Cassie and the (Get) Lost Boys, I prepare to ambush. I await Lex's signal, her raised hand holding up three fingers. She begins counting down to two, then one . . . aaannnd strike!

I launch myself into the air, flying like a frog with my knees bent, my arms outstretched and prepared for their landing around Alex's shoulders. Just as my thighs make contact with Alex's hips, a shrill whistle comes from Lexi's mouth.

Loud, purposeful, terrifying.

'Woah!' yells Alex. His can flies from his hand as his arms catapult into the air, nearly knocking me clean out.

'What the fuck?' shouts Jonesy, his fists clenched ready to attack as he spins round to get eyes on the mystery assailants.

'Alright?' Cassie says to us calmly, as though she knew exactly what was coming all along. She pulls Lexi into an affectionate headlock.

'Oh wow!' Sam adds. He looks like he's unsure what the point of all the hustle and bustle is.

I giggle as Alex's hand finds my ribs and he wrestles me off his back, plonking me down right in front of him. Our toes meet, and my hair sweeps past his chin in the breeze. He drops his head to look for the can that was lost in combat. As his lips brush past my nose, I smell the drink on his breath.

His tinny now back in hand, Alex bends at the knees and scoops me into a fireman's carry. He turns to Lexi and I see the grass below rotate a full 90 degrees.

'First rule of an ambush . . . Never. Get. Caught!' Alex belly-laughs as he sprints away, jolting me up and down as he goes.

'Aaahhhhh! A-Aa-a-L-E-ee-e-X. Oh my Goood! Put me dooown!' I squeal with terror and glee, my voice juddering with the movement. The green below me begins to blur and I lose all sense of space and direction. 'My ribs! Ow! Lexi, heeeellllp! Please!' I'm giggling hard now, so much so that I'm weak and achy all over. Oh God, what if I vom all down Alex's back? Or worse, pee down his front?

Finally, Alex whips me around and places me back on the earth, my back pressing into the prickly grass. I cover my face with my hands and wait for the giggles to subside.

When I take my hands away I'm met by Lexi's face peering over me.

'What are you doing down there? C'mon, Jadey. I wanna get a tattoo before we go see Coach Riot.' Lex stretches out a hand to pull me to my feet.

'What? Lex, are you sure?'

'Yes. Get up!' she replies, bouncing on her toes like a kid needing the bathroom.

'Okay, erm, Alex, I'll see you later . . . ?' Now on my feet, I turn to wave at him as I'm dragged in the opposite direction by Lexi's superhuman strength.

'So d'you remember how we always said we'd get matching tattoos when we were older?' Lex asks.

'Course I do,' I reply. Remember? I lived for that dream. I'd draw design upon design when I got home from Lexi's. Then I'd take them back round to hers the next day and she'd tell me all the things that needed to change for her to be happy to wear the tattoo 'for life'.

'Well, we're older! I saw a tent over there doing them, so let's go!'

'What . . . now?'

'Yes, now. We only have an hour before Coach Riot are on and I wanna get a good spot for them. Let's swing by the tattoo place, get inked and then get to the main stage.'

Lex turns to head towards a tent with an A-frame sign outside that says *Needles n Ink*. It's clad in anchors and roses promoting a buy-one-get-one-free offer.

'Lexi, I don't know if this is a good idea.'

'What? Why?'

'Erm, well, it's just . . . I don't have the designs with me and we're staying in a muddy field all weekend and it just . . . I dunno . . . Mum and Dad will kill me if I go back home with a freaking TATTOO!'

'But, Jade! We promised?'

She's right – we heart-hugged on it when we were twelve, in the summer holidays after Year Seven.

'I know and we will, but, Lex, does it have to be right now?' She stares back at me. I'm trying to think fast, quickly scanning our surroundings for an out. 'We could do something else . . .' I trail off. Lex does an exaggerated sad-face pout, looks at the floor and then back up at me with a sigh.

'You're such a goody-two-shoes, Jade! Eurgh. Okay, well, what are we gonna do instead? A piercing?'

'What? No! That's just as permanent,' I reply, panicked.

'I'm joking! Chill.'

'Oh, okay, sorry.'

'Look . . . neon and glitter henna!' Lex's pointing at the opposite side of the very same sign, which is advertising *Glitter n Glam*. 'That could be cool?'

'Yeah, you know I love a bit of glitter!' I say, relieved. 'And neon will look amazing on you.' I take Lex's hand and we run towards our colourful henna dreams.

After we're 'glittered n glammed', we bound out of the tent to inspect our matching designs in the sunshine. Cassie and the Lost Boys are striding towards us.

'Bloody hell, Jade, I didn't think you were a face tattoo kinda girl,' Jonesy pipes up, sounding shocked.

'Well, I'm not exactly,' I reply, 'it's not permanent.' I point to the sign behind us.

'Obviously! Tattoos don't come in green glitter.' Jonesy chuckles affectionately.

I unlock my phone camera to take a look as it catches the light. I feel a little wave of terror wash over me – I know it's temporary, but if it lasts longer than the festival, what will Mum and Dad say?

Lexi didn't want anything too femme, so we opted for two rows of dots on our foreheads that track our eyebrows. Lex agreed to adding a little sprinkle of me with a crescent moon at both sides, sitting just at the temples, to represent the two of us. Mine's in emerald green sparkle to match my eyes; Lexi's is in acid green neon to match her spirit.

As I'm looking at my phone, suddenly she leaps into view on my screen, striking a perfect head tilt and smize. She taps the capture button multiple times, mixing up her poses she goes. My Lexi is such a freaking babe.

'Right then, iiin-fluu-encers.' Cassie's using her best LA accent to take the piss out of our little photoshoot. 'Are we gonna actually watch any bands today or what?'

'Course,' Lex says. 'We were just about to head to Coach Riot – d'you lot wanna join?'

A collective nod ripples through the Lost Boys and Cassie leads the charge towards the main stage. It appears in the distance and before we know it, we meet the crowd that stretches what looks like miles from the front row.

'Wanna get closer to the front?' Alex yells over Coach Riot, who are already onstage. Everyone seems to wait for Cassie's reaction before nodding along with her.

As Alex leads the way, we weave through the sweaty crowd. Somehow he creates space where there is none between the festivalgoers who are packed in like sardines. I squeeze myself carefully past people who tower over me, breathing in as if it'll help me fit.

We form a human chain – Lexi reaching back to grab my hand and me reaching backwards to clutch onto Jonesy's. Soon, we stop in Cassie's 'perfect spot', surrounded by bodies. I guess we're closer to the front – it's hard to tell when all you can see are backs, heads and shoulders. Short girl problems!

We begin to dance a little and Lex starts to sing along as she recognises where we are in the song. Her arms flail like spaghetti in the air, her head tips back and her neck wiggles from side to side like a charmed serpent. Her blonde to pink ombré hair falls backwards and she parts her choppy fringe to reveal her henna.

The songs ends and Jared, the frontman, whispers into the mic, 'Are you ready to play a game?'

'Yeeaahhh!' shout the crowd and the Lost Boys in unison.

'I want you to get down. On the ground. Squat down.' He waits to see if his audience are as dutiful as in the dreams I'm guessing he's had about this moment.

Jared begins to model the move he wants us to replicate by squatting down at the front of the stage and bouncing a little in time with the music.

The heads, backs and shoulders that had previously towered above me begin to fold forward and down, like buildings collapsing in an earthquake. The stage is revealed in all its glory: a black cavern with a gigantic digital banner hung towards the back that's emblazoned with Coach Riot's logo. There are flashing lights that pulse in time with the kick drum, black amps stacked on top of each other, the drum kit set high on a plinth, and microphones everywhere. Dotted around are the four men making all this noise, looking like children on the enormous platform.

'We don't play until Every. Single. One. Of. You. Is. Down!' Jared commands. 'That's it,' he adds, before the few remaining people who are still standing also copy him.

The band start to play. Without vocals the music feels softer, like it's creeping towards me, my anticipation growing as it draws closer.

'Okay, when I say, we're gonna jump,' Jared explains. 'Higher than you've ever jumped before! But only When. I. Say. Can you do that for me, Get Lost?'

'Yeeeaaaahhhhh!' I scream at the top of my lungs with the rest of the crowd. My head is fully tilted back as I squat down. We pulse, like seaweed in the ocean, the thousands of us moving as one.

Lexi's hand grasps mine and we turn to face each other, wild excitement burning behind our eyes. The music speeds up as Jared prepares us for what's about to come.

'Are you ready?' He delivers the words peacefully, like the calm before the storm, and then it comes . . . 'ONE. TWO. THREE. JUUUUMP!'

We explode upwards, drinks flying like Silly String across the dip-dyed sky that looks like Lex's hair – only instead of pink and blonde, it's blue and white. In unison we sing, an extension of the band, at the top of our lungs.

'Oooohhh, we live only for the night, and we won't ever grow up, go home, get lost, ooohhh, ooohhh!'

The lyrics feel more poignant now than ever before. I feel electric, as though I'm vibrating so much my spirit is about to fly straight out of my skin. The entire crowd jumps and screams the words on a loop in perfect unison until the band drops out, leaving just our voices as the backdrop to their sign-off.

'Wow! Get Lost, we love you! Thank you. Until next time!' shouts Jared. Cheers erupt around me, my arms still outstretched skyward. I turn to Lexi with a smile that is now making my cheeks ache.

'That was unreal!' I yell. Lexi, who's all wide eyes and ruffled hair, grabs me around my waist and lifts my feet off the ground whilst jumping up and down.

'Jade! That was INSANE! You loved it too, right?'

'I loved it!' I scream in her ear, surprising myself at my conviction.

CHAPTER 6

LEXI

I fly out of Petra's office, tripping over my feet as I try to make sense of what just happened. I wasn't expecting the word 'guilty' to fall out of my mouth like that, and now I've said it, I can't take it back. Why did I say guilty? Why not sad? Or lonely? Or any other feeling? I wouldn't say guilty for no reason at all, would I? Like, unless . . . I had something to do with what happened.

I don't get it. The dreams. The shopping channel. The rainbow. I so badly wanted them to be signs from Jade, telling me to keeping looking cos more answers are out there. In the universe! Waiting to be discovered. Not because the answers are inside *me*.

But . . . I loved her. Why would I want anything bad to happen to her? I know things were different, when the others came along, but I'd never hurt Jade. I mean, I guess I've said that before, about not wanting to hurt people, but I got careless that time.

I wait for the bus for what feels like an eternity and when it finally arrives, I whizz past the driver. I stand the entire journey home so I'm ready to count in good time. Besides, I have too much energy fizzing inside me to sit still, like those lavender bath bombs Mum uses that sputter in the water. I suddenly feel very sick and I must look as though I'm going to hurl cos the other passengers stay as far away from me as possible. It's like they can see the word tattooed across my forehead, flashing emergency red.

Guilty.

Why did I say that?

What does it mean?

I would give anything to travel back in time. Then I could remember, and none of this would be happening right now. I wouldn't have mushy peas for brains. Tbh, mushy peas is generous. It's more of a soup.

I thought it'd be okay. It was just a few drinks. Okay, maybe more than a few. But everyone was doing it. Cass, Jonesy, Alex and Sam. Even Jade! I just wanted Cassie to like me. And the alcohol made me feel so *free*. For the first time ever, I could forget. Just forget what happened all those years ago, the thing that haunts me every day. But when was the switch – from the moment I remember to the moment I don't? The turning point at which my mind stopped recording memories of that night. All I know is it was fun . . . until it wasn't.

It's not even like it's a blur; it's a blank.

I manage to stumble home in a trance, *GUILTY* earworming its way through my head. The front door swings open. I see a note on the hallway table while my key is still in the lock. I wiggle it free, shut out the street behind me and head over to see Mum's spidery handwriting. Sometimes, I feel Mum writes more words to me than she speaks.

Hi darling. Home late, burgers in fridge. Love you to the moon + stars + back. Xxx

Mum and I get along, but she's hardly ever here. After Dad walked out, I thought I'd see more of her, not less. Cosy nights instead of all the yelling. Dad said he 'fell out of love' with her and it was better to live his truth than a lie. I think he fell out of love with me too cos I never hear from him other than the birthday cards that he sends on the wrong day.

They argued all my life, ever since I can remember. I'd listen over the banisters even though it hurt to hear. I always thought I wanted them to break up so the shouting would stop. But then Dad left and it felt like a magic trick gone wrong, cos I made him vanish by wishing him away and I couldn't bring him back again. Mum sometimes says 'careful what you wish for, it might come true'. She's right . . . cos it's happening again. I've been wishing so hard to remember what happened to Jade and now that I'm starting to get answers, I'm scared because they're not what I want them to be.

After a while, Mum stopped being so sad. She worked her way up from reporter to deputy to editor and now heads up the news desk at a big national paper. There's always some breaking story she has to sort out.

Don't get me wrong, it has its perks.

She's taken me to red carpet premieres and restaurant

openings where we can eat as much as we want. Once we had a free holiday – all she had to do was mention the hotel in an article afterwards. But she's proper chained to the newsroom.

I head upstairs, ignoring Mum's note. I don't feel hungry and anyway, a burger will take too long cos I'll need to count to the safe number before I grill it, and before I use the toaster to warm the bun, and before I put the curly fries in the oven. It's why I eat Pop Tarts without toasting them. Each appliance needs the full count, otherwise I can't use them . . . in case they start a fire.

Once I'm in my room, I pace over to the plug socket. I take my bag off and reach inside for my phone, pulling it free from the portable charger and plugging it into the wall instead to keep it on 100%. That's the way I like it, otherwise the palpitations hit me hard. I watch as the battery bar springs to life again. I sit on the bed, still clutching the handset, my mind pogoing between what I told Petra and what I found at the grave. I need to find out who R is. Which probably means breaking my social media celibacy . . .

Last year, when it happened, everyone was saying all kinds of cray-cray stuff online. At first, it was just a few people from school. They'd gone through their phones to find the one and only photo they'd ever had taken with Jade – from a sports day or play or whatever – as evidence that they really knew her. Then they'd uploaded it with some caption like *Never forget you* or *I can't believe you're gone* as if they hadn't ignored her every day in the corridors.

Soon, other people from our town were posting about Jade and tagging me. I couldn't log on without a zillion notifications from strangers telling me to *#staystrong* when all I wanted was for Death to come and collect me too, saying sorry for forgetting me.

Then it started spreading. Randoms began speculating, saying the open verdict was an injustice to what actually happened. They'd add numbers for mental health organisations or links to similar accidents with conspiracy theories, like that unsolved death at Emperor's Fest in Texas which happened just as a new festival opened a few miles away. Everyone said the Pink Moon organisers did it to get their rivals shut down. My memories of Jade from that final weekend already felt like they had been deleted, and I didn't want them buried in all this. So I quit. Just like that. I signed out of all socials and haven't logged on since.

I felt crazy then, but I feel even crazier now, after so long. My mind is blacker than the soil she's lying in. It's not even a case of wanting to know – I *need* to know.

The randoms are right. I must get justice for Jade.

It's been so long, I can't remember my password. I quickly change it to *imissujade* (I know, not exactly hack-free MI5 security) then I type Jade's name into the search bar, clicking through to see her profile. My heart does a little pirouette as her face appears.

The last photo she posted is of all of us at Get Lost, against the pink and orange sunset that looks like those chewy Fruit Salad sweets. We're a beautiful scruffy mess of unbrushed hair and glitter and grins, with our arms flung in the air or around each other. I look at the caption. Jade has written: *In my happy place.*

Usually, I don't even bother reading captions – I just looked at the pictures when I scrolled. But now, I can't help but think, what does that mean? *In my happy place.* Does that mean she wasn't in her happy place at home? Or when we were alone? What if she never wanted to leave her happy place, so she did the ultimate act to remain at Get Lost?

I start to check her followers and following lists. They're mostly random crystal healers, astrologers and haircare influencers. No R pops out at me other than Rihanna, and I'm pretty sure the note's not from her. Then I spot someone and can't help but click through to their profile . . .

It's Cassie, who I already follow. @CassieCoxCouture now has nearly 56,000 followers. I remember being impressed by her 30k when we followed each other as we sucked ice-pops beside the main stage whilst the sun scorched down at Get Lost.

I'd seen Cassie around school a bunch of times, but unless you're on swim teams or have older siblings, there's an unwritten rule: you don't mix with Sixth Form. She came to Roseville High late, something about her dad's job making them move from LA. We did once have detention together. No one else from my year had been given one that day, but a few Upper Sixth had to stay behind, after staging an animal rights protest (and wanting the cafeteria to stop serving meat) in the middle of a Year 7 choir show, in front of parents and everything. So I got chucked in with them.

I tried to take Jade with me, but the teacher wouldn't let her in. We said bye at the door, and I went towards the back of the room to sit alone. As I was walking, Cassie stopped me from her seat. I looked down at her, not knowing what she was going to say, slightly terrified she was going to embarrass me in front of her boy mates. She pulled me in and swept my hair back from my ear for me, in a way that I can still feel. Then she whispered to me, 'Babes, have you got a spare tampon?' I told her I didn't, but I did have a pad. She told me I was 'a lifesaver'. I opened my bag, and I went to slip it inside hers discreetly, but Cassie took it from my fingers and just got up, strolling to the loos with it openly in her hand, not caring who saw.

After that, she'd give me a smile or wink in the corridor. I'd try to talk to her, but I never knew what to say. Then, when she rocked up at Get Lost, and knew my name(!), I felt special. It's not that I didn't feel special with Jade, but I always felt . . . well . . . like she was more special than me. That somehow her sunnier, rose-tinted outlook on life was something rare and extraordinary, which I should strive for too, and I could never quite match up. With Cass, she had a rawness, a realness, and I felt connected to her.

She's studying fashion and even though I'm not fashiony one bit, her photos look insane. They're all from catwalk shows with hashtags like *#research* and *#luvmylife*. I click on her last post, a photo of Cassie holding a half-made outfit against a semi-naked model. She's captioned it: *Buzzzzing on caffeine – sewing thru the nite to meet deadline!*

Right now, I just want Cassie's life. I hate myself for thinking it, as it would mean wiping out my entire friendship with Jade. But it would be better than feeling this alone.

I scroll down past the ridiculous number of likes Cassie's

had to look at the comments. Most people have left a ton of heart or fire emoijs. Someone has written *OMG, ur life!!! #goals* which makes me feel slightly less daft about feeling the same way. As I keep reading, I notice @AlexDevlinMusic has left a bee emoji, no doubt relating to the *buzzing* in the caption.

I take a breath and click through to Alex's profile. I haven't seen him since the funeral. He was hovering by the cemetery when they were lowering the coffin in. I went over to say hi and he turned the colour of ketchup, saying he was just there to 'say bye'. Then he vanished. I thought it was strange that he didn't stick around, cos if Jade hadn't died at Get Lost I think they'd have become girlfriend and boyfriend, but then I wondered if it might be cos I gave the boys' and Cassie's names to police. They got questioned like me, even though the cops never arrested anyone.

There are hardly any photos of his face. They're all close-ups of album covers with ratings in the captions for his 167 followers. He's tagged his location on each one at Viva la Vinyl, the record store in town. I guess so people will know where to buy them.

I carry on scrolling, spotting a photo of him twiddling some knobs on one of those big switchboard thingies I've seen DJs use. This time he's written: *Studio Day*.

I zoom in to try to check out the band logo on his black T-shirt cos it's not one I instantly recognise. I enlarge the photo further and spy the words *Viva la Vinyl* on it. So he isn't recommending the records in his other posts cos he's been buying them at the store!

I think he works there?

The embroidery is red.

I can't help but wonder if it's a bad omen.

I go back to Alex's grid of photos, planning to go through his followers and following lists to spot anyone whose name begins with R. But my eyes are caught by something . . . I'd spot those silhouettes anywhere!

In amongst his pictures is a video. My belly does a back flip. They're just there. In front of me again. Jonesy, Sam, Cassie dancing. Oh, I want to feel what they feel. Living their best life, touching the sky as they bounce to the house music beat. I watch, mesmerised.

Then suddenly, I see us.

Me and Jade.

This must be . . . the last night at Get Lost?

I don't remember being there, by that water.

Yet we are, waving our arms in the distance as we laugh. We're barely in shot. I can't seem to pause the video but it soon finishes and starts to replay itself automatically.

New memories! Right *here*. In front of me.

I put the volume on my phone up, sharp excitement rocketing through me. But it only makes the tinny sound of the music they're dancing to louder, not mine and Jade's voices. What are we saying to each other? And why am I flapping my arms like that? I have no recollection of being together. I only remember what I saw the next morning.

I zoom in to see if I can lip-read. And that's when I notice. My heart stops in its tracks.

We're not laughing. We're arguing.

I watch the video again, my jaw hanging open in fear. The world closes in around me. I see myself shoulder-barge past Jade, walking off and leaving her alone to cry.

CHAPTER 7

JADE

The sun has now all but vanished and the evening sky is arriving. We're greeted by the outline of a perfect crescent moon, just like the ones on our faces. The cold is beginning to creep in, so our newfound posse heads back to the tents to ditch sunglasses, collect jumpers and, in Jonesy's case, a few cheap beers. As we walk, the sun finally drops entirely. Up ahead, Lexi and I are plunged into a rich blue sky, the Lost Boys and Cassie trailing behind. I hear the rhythmic jangling of keys drawing closer, or it might be change in a pocket. Lexi glances over her shoulder, then turns back to me.

'Oh, lover boy incoming,' she whispers under her breath.

'What?' I reply, about to spin around and look myself. Lexi grabs my arm.

'Don't. Just be cool,' she whispers again.

The jangling is close now, and just like that, Alex appears in my periphery. He walks next to me for a moment, catching his breath, before saying 'hey' through huffs and puffs.

'Hey,' I reply. 'What did you think of Coach Riot?'

'Oh, I thought they were awesome. So cool. The drummer was so in the pocket, you know. Impossible not to dance to. What a groove.'

'Yeaaah,' I reply, having understood almost none of that.

'And that jumping thing Jared did was genius. So smart.'

I nod.

'You really like music, don't you?' I say, looking up at Alex for a second.

'Well, I have to . . . it's my job.' He nods and looks a bit nervous.

'Oh, wow! Are you, like, a musician or something?' I ask.

'Producer,' he replies. 'It's not as glamorous – but without us, no one would ever get to hear all those songs.'

'Cool! So you're pretty special then,' I say, impressed.

'Maybe. Speaking of pretty special . . .' he begins. 'You look amazing in your henna – green really is your colour.'

'Oh, thanks,' I reply, blushing and dipping my head down a little, not quite sure how to respond. The compliment has caught me totally off-guard. I turn to the side and notice Lexi drop back to join the others. She shoots me an eyeroll followed by a playful and carefully timed (so Alex doesn't see) smooch-esque pout.

'So you're into the moon and stars and stuff?' he asks, pointing at my sparkles.

'Erm, kinda. Me and Lex always used to talk about living on the moon when we were little.' I giggle, embarrassed. 'That sounds so lame, doesn't it?'

'No, it doesn't. I'd love to go to space,' he replies. 'Do you know about constellations?'

'Sort of, not much,' I say.

'It's like the order of the stars – the patterns they make up and stuff. It's connected to the zodiac.'

'Oh! Okay. I love star signs! I'm Gemini/Cancer cusp. But I don't really know how to see it in stars or anything.' I turn to look at him instead of my feet for a moment.

'No way!' His face lights up. 'I'm Cancer, too. So, with Gemini being twins . . . you're like three people wrapped into one?'

'Ha!' I laugh. He has no idea.

'You wanna see some constellations tonight? It's a clear sky up there, so there should be a bunch out already.' He looks up, squinting a little.

'Yeah, okay!' Stargazing with a boy . . . isn't this the kind of thing that'd happen in a movie?

We arrive back at the tents, Lex and Cassie arm in arm. They all unzip the doors and start getting ready, Cassie pulling her giant khaki hoodie over her head. She passes a drink to Lex and they look so at ease with each other, like long lost souls finally reuniting.

Alex takes me by the hand and leads me to an uncrowded patch of grass. Oh my God! I think he's into me. Me not Lexi? That's new.

After finding the right spot, he bends down, stretches his legs out in front of him and lies back flat on the ground.

'C'mon!' he instructs, so I follow suit. 'So that one's the Big Dipper, you see?' Alex is pointing up at the sky now, tracing shapes in the air with his hands. My gaze follows his long, gangly arm, trying to spot what he's pointing out. 'It's kinda like a question mark on its side. D'you see it?'

I. Do. Not. See. It.

'Yeah, course! Wow, so cool!' I lie through my teeth, not wanting to spoil the moment.

He reaches out to interlace his fingers through mine with the hand he's not pointing with. Oh wow. Is this really happening?

Over the next few minutes, Alex continues to point out constellations. I manage to spot two or three for real. Every time I do, it's magical, like twinkly little pictures with a hidden meaning.

'How did you learn about all this?' I'm certain it's not standard eighteen-year-old boy knowledge.

'My oldest brother taught me,' Alex says, then pauses for a second. 'We used to go and sit out on the roof of our block of flats at night when I was a kid. He'd point at stuff, and I'd drift off into a dream world. It felt like we had our own little universe together, away from all the drama exploding behind our front door,' he adds, as if he's thinking out loud.

'How many brothers have you got?' I ask.

'Three,' he says, more buoyant now. 'Will, Ben, Matt and then me. I'm the youngest. Will's like thirty. He taught me about stars and got me into music – the old stuff. He used to have his speakers turned up so loud the neighbours would bang on the wall screaming at him to pipe down! Guess that's why Cassie takes the piss – she says my taste is just like her dad's.'

'Lexi says the same about me!' I giggle. 'But I just like music I can dance to. And you can't dance to mumble rap or metal screams!'

He laughs. Wow, it feels great to make him laugh.

'Do you like dancing?' I ask.

'Errrm. I don't not like it. Why?'

'Oh, just figured I might need a buddy to go dancing with at some point. Lexi was talking about Logan's Romance and I don't think that's my thing really.'

He smiles, a proper beaming grin this time.

'Well, we can't have you dancing alone, can we?' he says, rolling his head to the side to look at me. 'I'll go with you . . . and Sam might join us – he loves a dance. That cool?'

'Sure,' I say, disappointed it won't just be the two of us. 'But I wouldn't have had Sam down as a dancer.'

'Yeah, he's a dark horse is our Sam. Oh look.' Alex points skyward again. 'Scorpius.'

I start to feel my body relaxing. Was I holding my shoulders that tight? It's like I'm melting into the grass and into Alex. And just as I feel another wave of calm wash over me, the brightest star in the sky twinkles at me so brightly. Like a wink, just for me.

That must be a sign, right? That she's up there, looking down on me. That she approves. That I'm exactly where I'm supposed to be.

Oh Em, I miss you so much.

I'll find a way to get to you soon, promise.

CHAPTER 8

LEXI

I haven't slept. All I can do is watch the video. *Guilty*. To think I've spent a year not knowing, unable to remember if I even saw Jade the night she died. Now there's proof that we were together. *Guilty*. Actual evidence that something wasn't right. *Guilty*.

Everything inside me feels explosive, like I'm about to be ripped apart.

I'm meant to be finding answers, but all I have is more questions. Like, where did I go when I left Jade? Did she follow me? Did I go back to find her? Did the others notice?

But ultimately: what on earth were we arguing about?

Jade and I never fought. We were yin and yang. We needed the other one to breathe. We just worked together. Her and me.

I lie in bed, the charging cable attaching my phone to the plug socket like an umbilical cord, trying to analyse the video to see if I can make out what I'm saying, but it's so blurry and there doesn't seem to be a way to play it in slow motion. I can't even figure out what direction I walk off in – was it back to the tents or some other place?

Oh. Wait.

LOOK!

There . . .

The corners of my mouth curve up, ever so slightly at the end.

What am I saying? I squint as I watch it again. *Yell? Hell? Tell?*

At school, we were once asked to draw what panic looked like. People doodled knotted squiggly balls and cartoons with thought-bubbles brimming out from their head.

Now, I'd literally draw me lying here right now.

That thing Mum likes to say keeps replaying in my head, 'careful what you wish for'. It's wriggling through my mind, together with the other earworm. *Guilty.* I can't think straight and I feel like I need to count just to shut them up. So I do. All the way to today's safe number – 342.

I climb out of bed, but the earworms in my brain are still squirming around. My heart's beating fast too, it feels like I'm on a waltzer. I don't know what to do! There's no manual for *What to Do If You Might Have Had Something to Do with Your Best Friend's Death.*

I want to take the wish back – the one about wanting the truth. Maybe I don't need answers after all. I'll take the open verdict over this. But . . . how else do I get justice for Jade?

My thoughts are scatty and so is my breathing so I take a gasp, soothing myself with the knowledge that while I might not understand what this video is trying to tell me *now*, I may not have to live with never knowing what happened to her. There *are* answers out there. No matter how ugly they are. And they're right here, hidden in this footage.

I skip the shower and throw some clothes on, then go downstairs. Mum has left for work already but there's a note on the kitchen counter again.

Morning/afternoon. Saw your bedroom light on when I went for a pee at 3am! Get some sleep please. Love you. Xxx

I reach for the cupboards to try to force a Pop Tart down me. I don't toast it. I haven't eaten since yesterday and I just need the energy. I'm still not hungry though. I don't feel anything other than scared. But it's not my normal anxiety, like when I'm waiting for a guy to text back or blagging it in a school presentation. It's more . . . what's the word? Dread.

My own worst enemy is living in between my ears.

Spontaneously telling Petra I feel guilty was bad enough. Now with the video, my whole body feels like radioactive jelly. I want to cry, but I feel too shocked. How can I not remember being in that place, when I'm right there in plain sight? I don't know what I did or said, but if I had to guess who might, it's Alex. He and Jade were tight AF at Get Lost.

I sit on the kitchen stool and find myself googling his shop's opening hours. There's a number. I could dial it now? Ask when Alex is next on shift? I don't have to say who I am.

My finger hits the digits and I wait for it to ring . . . but it's engaged.

I take a bite of Pop Tart and dial again, not expecting anyone to answer, still chomping on the chocolate fudge. But then I hear a voice.

'Hi, Viva la Vinyl. How can I help?'

Omfg! I quickly chew and try to finish my mouthful. It's all stuck in my teeth, and up in my gums, but I manage to swallow the main chunk down as the person speaks again.

'Hello?'

IT'S HIM!

'Uh,' I manage to say, my chest pounding. What is *wrong* with me? I never used to get in such a tizz like this. It's just so surreal to hear Alex after all this time.

I hang up, too panicked to say anything else. I wasn't expecting to speak to him right now. I wasn't prepared! I desperately want to call back and talk to him, but my tongue's paralysed. I finish my breakfast (can you still call it that at 1 p.m.?) while I think. I reach for a second then a third Pop Tart without thinking. There's nothing like procrastination to induce hunger! I get through six before I make my decision.

I need to see him face to face. The phone is harder somehow, without Alex standing in front of me.

I'm gonna go and surprise him . . .

A bell chimes as I open the door. Inside it's pretty dead other than an old guy with an impressive handlebar moustache and a girl with orange hair, orange clothes and orange lipstick, flicking through the albums. Both of them look up at me as I walk in and offer a nod-smile before getting back to browsing. I nod-smile back.

There's not a millimetre of wall on show, all of them plastered in posters promoting band tour dates or new albums. They're all over the ceiling too. There's a giant neon sign that says *RECORDS* above the counter, beside store-branded T-shirts for sale. I've never seen so much vinyl in my life. There are rows and rows and rows of it, organised in alphabetical order of artists and genres like *Funk, Pop, and Soul*. It smells like the past in here.

I head through one of the aisles, counting my steps towards the empty desk. This is new for me. Counting in bed earlier and again now. I only usually need the safe number if there's a risk of death, like kitchen devices exploding or buses crashing. But now I'm doing it cos I'm worried too. Worried about what I did. Worried about what Alex is gonna say. I move slower than a sloth, cos I have to hit the safe number before I reach the desk. It's hard, cos the number's getting higher every day. I hear the shuffle of feet in a back area. The sound gets louder, then I see him.

He's skinnier and scruffier than I remember, and he looks older. He's still 93% floppy fringe though. He's looking down at the stack of records in his arms, placing them by the till before looking up at me.

'How can I hel . . . Woah, Lexi,' Alex says as we lock eyes – but I'm only at 300. 'Lex?' he nudges, as I stare without replying. I missile through the last few numbers, then breathe.

'Hey.' I smile, trying to hide the fact I seem to be morphing into a human calculator.

'It's been a while!' Alex fiddles awkwardly with the slanted pile of records that look ready to topple over any second. 'Hold on,' he says. 'Just going to put something on.'

'Sure, do what you gotta do,' I say, the quiet echoing from the song that's just finished. I watch Alex slip a vinyl out of its sleeve and place it onto the player. As he tinkers with the record needle, I peer over the counter and see two turntables with one of those DJ sliding button boards sandwiched in the middle.

It looks like the one from his photo on social media of '*Studio Day*'.

'So, you after a particular record or want a recommendation?' Alex says, after the album begins to play following a few needle scratches. 'I only do the odd shift here so I'll help if I can, but I don't always know where everything is.'

'I, umm, I'm not here to buy anything,' I reply, cutting straight to the point.

'Oh, okay?'

'It's just, I actually need to speak to you about something.'

He flicks a hand through his fringe. I'm waiting for him to say something, anything, but he just fidgets. Alex never used to be this . . . uncool.

I pull out my phone from my pocket to show him the video from his Insta page – the one I've watched a trillion times since last night. I turn the handset round to face him as it starts to play, and then I watch him watch the footage.

'Do you know what this is?' I ask, trying to read his face.

'Eh?'

'What the arguing's about?'

'I'm not following. We're dancing.'

'In the background. Jade's upset. Why's that?' I point at the video as it plays again.

The girl with the orange hair comes to place a couple of records on the counter, which breaks up our conversation. I look at the name badge on Alex's T-shirt as he tallies up how much she owes. As she reaches into her purse, Alex looks at me and then the shop door as if he's telling me to leave, his face going redder and redder.

That damn colour just keeps following me around.

'Can we do this another time, yeah?' he says after the girl leaves. He reaches for a jumper to throw on, but it's too late. I've already seen his badge that says *Assistant Manager*. That little story about working 'the odd shift' here is a lie.

That post about working in a studio was a bunch of bull too then, I'm guessing.

I can't help but wonder if his whole up-and-coming producer act is fake . . .

What else is he lying about?

'Look. What do you want from me?' Alex says, agitated.

'I need to know what you remember from that night. The night Jade died. I don't think she did it herself. Or that it was an accident. I think she may've been . . .'

'It's just a video, man. I don't know what you want me to tell you?'

'Take it and zoom in,' I say, trying to hand my phone to Alex while jabbing at the screen with my finger. 'Jade was upset, and I think you know why.'

We both look up as the bell chimes again, checking if

someone else walked in. In fact, it's the moustache guy leaving.

'Great, thanks. Lost a customer.'

'I lost my best friend,' I bite. 'If there's anything you know, please just—'

'Know what?' Alex says.

'Why was she upset that night?'

'I don't get what this has to do with me,' he tries deflecting, but he's still talking. 'So what if she was upset at me? It's too late to change anything.'

'Huh?' I say, surprised at the turn he's taken.

'What?' he asks, confused.

'I'm talking about Jade being upset at *me*! Not *you*.'

Alex looks at me as if I've just vomited snails.

'Why would she be upset with you?' I probe.

'That's not what I said.'

'Dude, it is.' A chill stabs me like when I bite into ice cream. 'Please just watch!' I try again to make Alex look as the video replays, but I'm distracted as I notice the battery level's dropped. It gives me butterflies in my brain. I slide my bag off my shoulder to rest on a knee against the front desk while still clutching the mobile and dig one-handed inside for the power bar. My heart is ready to pole vault out my chest.

'Let me look at that,' Alex finally says, taking the phone out of my hand to study the video properly this time. 'Oh.'

'What did you think I was talking about?' I say, still fishing around in my bag.

'Lex, can we chat another time, like maybe when I'm not at work?'

'Please,' I urge, feeling desperate. 'Just tell me what you

know, then I'll go.' Eventually, my fingers wrap around something solid and cylindrical. Got it!

'There's not a lot to tell. We were drunk. I don't really remember,' Alex says.

'Neither do I,' I admit, pulling the power bar out my bag. 'But you thought she was upset at you, not me, and that means something. Why did you think that?'

I yank the phone back from Alex to plug the portable charger in – but nothing happens! Why's nothing happening? I feel heat inside rise. It's hard to control my hands.

Then it dawns on me . . .

No. No. NO!

When I swapped my phone from the power bar to the wall socket yesterday, after I got back from Petra's, I forgot to charge the portable too! I don't like this feeling at all. My chest is tight, and I feel hot – so, so hot – like I'm burning up. My clothes feel tight too. I try not to let it show in my face, even though I'm sure Alex can tell something's not right.

I don't have a choice. If I don't ask him to plug my phone into the socket behind the desk right now, Mum might not make it home alive. My mouth is open, but before the words can come out, something shifts. I don't know if I'm acting weird, or he's embarrassed at being busted over his hotshot 'producer' life, but his posture changes. The look in his eye extinguishes any warmth between us and we're back to being strangers.

'Maybe you should try looking a little closer to home, yeah?' he snarls.

'What's *that* supposed to mean?' I reply, panicked.

'I'm not the one who came back to the tent in ripped clothes that night looking like I'd been in a fight,' he snaps, his eyes piercing through me like a meat skewer, 'you are.'

CHAPTER 9

JADE

After stuffing my face full of burger and chips (deeeeelicious!), Alex and I wander from tent to tent looking for something fun to do. On the hill behind us, a gigantic tower is covered in transparent multicoloured triangles, fixed on one side so they flap in the breeze and reflect the up-lighting at the base of the structure like enormous fish scales.

'Look!' I squeal, spinning around to draw his attention in the right direction.

'What?' Alex replies, confused.

'Over there, on the hill. Look at that amazing rainbow tower!'

'Ha! You love rainbow anything, don't you?'

'What gave you that impression?' I say with a deadpan expression, my eyes looking from side to side like a cartoon. I know full well he saw my clothes taking over the whole of Kylie's floor-bed when I gave him a sneak peek inside mine and Lex's home for the weekend. How else was I gonna have the right clothes for the right mood each day?

'Wanna head up there, kaleidoscope kid?' Alex snickers.

'Kaleidoscope kid? I like that,' I reply, giggling. 'Let's go.'
I grab his hand, like we've been doing this forever, and we race
in the direction of the tower. As we get further up the hill,
I spot a familiar silhouette in the distance. Lexi!

We slow down, exhausted from running. I instinctively let
go of the hand in mine. What's Lexi gonna think? We continue
walking towards her and the others.

'Where you guys running to?' she ask once I'm a little closer.

'The rainbow tower,' I reply, pointing and gasping for air.
I plonk my hands down on my knees both for balance and in
an attempt to relieve the stitch I developed en route.

'Course you were! I was thinking, we could go on the Ferris
wheel actually?' Lexi looks around to gauge interest from
everyone.

'We're good, thanks,' Cassie responds on behalf of the group.

Lexi looks at me and shrugs, giving up on the idea.

Here's my chance to get Lex alone for a little while.

'We could go just the two of us, if you wanna?' I ask,
hopefully.

'Yeah, sounds good,' she replies, as I beam inside . . . She
chose me.

We turn towards the twinkling fairground, making our way
past Cassie and the Lost Boys as we say our goodbyes. But just
as we take our first steps, Lexi buckles suddenly at the knee,
lurches forward and falls flat on her face.

My jaw drops open. 'Oh my God, what happened? Babe, are
you okay?'

'I'm fine,' Lex replies bluntly. She flips herself over on the ground to sit on her bum, legs bent up, arms resting on her knees. She still looks effortlessly cool even whilst gazing up at the group in the dark, mud on her hands, a little on her nose.

'God, I'm sorry!' Sam says, but is he? The others seem to believe him, whilst I'm not so sure. 'I don't know what happened! Did you like, walk over my foot or something?'

My spider senses tell me there's something off about it, but I don't know what. So I laugh awkwardly and put a hand out to help Lexi heave herself off the floor.

'You sure you're okay, babe?' I check.

'I'm fine, I swear.'

We turn to head up the hill. Lex frowns as we trudge upwards holding hands. What do I say to make it better? In the distance behind us, I hear the thud of electronic drums from the dance tents and DJs about to carry the party through to the early hours of the morning. It feels good to be heading away from the chaos for a moment. There's an occasional wave of screams and laughter from groups of people nearby, playing like pre-schoolers in their newfound freedom away from teachers and parents. Lexi squeezes my hand a little tighter.

'Is he a bit weird?' I say softly into the night.

'Who?' Lex asks.

'Sam. I get a weird energy from him. Like not bad, just . . . strange.'

'No, he's fine, Jadey. You got a weird energy from a packet of nuts the other day, babe! And I know this is gonna shock you to your core but I ate them and look at me . . . Still here to tell the tale!' She belly-laughs.

I laugh back. Only Lexi knows me like this.

74

I think sometimes the fact she's not very spiritual keeps me a bit more grounded. Or maybe it just keeps my third eye a little closed off.

Ahead is the big white wheel with delicate yellow-white lights dotted all around the outside and along each spike that feeds into the middle. We arrive, join the queue and realise just how high up this thing is going to take us.

Once we're at the front and a cart swings round to ground level, we clamber in and squish up next to each other. It's cosy, comfy, romantic even! I sit in the space nearest the door and a swingy little gate thing is pushed towards us. We click it into its locked position. Soon, we begin to move slowly forwards and up. Our legs start to dangle in the air as we climb, Lexi's long ones later than mine.

I feel lighter than air as we drift along like feathers, rocking gently back and forth in the breeze. We draw closer to the constellations Alex showed me as the lights down below grow smaller and smaller, making multi-coloured constellations of their own. There's something so freeing about it all, me and my Lex floating through air and time. I feel as though I could say anything up here, where there's no one to judge, no one to be shocked or disappointed. And before I know it, I'm speaking the words I've wanted to say for years.

'Do you ever think about her?' I ask simply.

'Not now, Jade,' she replies, sighing slowly.

'But when? You never want to talk about her, and she was so . . . special! I don't know why but I can feel her here with us,' I reply, doubling down for the first time in a long while.

'What is there left to say? We promised – we said we'd never

75

talk about it again. I let it go earlier, but if it's going to be like this all weekend, I just can't!' she snaps, but I can tell she instantly regrets that. 'Let's just . . . try to enjoy the ride.'

As we float back to earth the energy feels totally different, heavy, oppressive. Not free like before. We don't speak the whole way down. Lexi holds my hand as if to say sorry, but what's she sorry for? For snapping? For shutting me down? Or for having nothing to say about something so . . . big?

After clambering out of our little carriage we head towards the action to try and find the others as we walk in awkward silence.

'Lex,' I cut the tension. She turns to look at me with a 'what now?' expression. 'Let's not let it ruin the whole weekend. You're right, it's in the past. I'll let it go.'

And just like that, she throws her arms around me, squeezing tight as she bends at the knee to line her blue eyes up with my green ones.

'Love you, babe.' She rubs her nose on mine. 'Let's go and have some fun!'

CHAPTER 10

LEXI

I march upstairs, taking two at a time, heading straight to my room. He's lying. He must be. *I'm not the one who came back to the tent in ripped clothes.* Ripped clothes? I've never had a physical fight in my life! Okay, apart from that time in Religious Studies when Maya told Jade she was a 'fucking idiot' for saying she believed that souls are recycled. But that doesn't count. Mr Clayton broke it up before it got bad.

Alex is clearly just deflecting to take the heat off him.

Panting from my sprint, I plug my phone into the wall as quickly as possible then cross the carpet to my wardrobe. Adrenaline buzzes through me as if I'm about to tightrope across Niagara Falls. I reach out and my fingers grip the handle, but my hand doesn't move. I start to count. I don't mean to. I never really mean to. It just sort of happens. In the beginning, it was only occasionally, like before getting in the car with Mum. Now, my brain can't not count. It doesn't listen to me anymore and it just does its own thing. All I know is that it feels wrong when I don't count, and right when I do.

Onetwothreefourfivesixseveneightnine . . . all the way to 342.

The wardrobe door peeps open.

There's a big purple fleece blanket over it for protection, as if it's some kind of rare museum relic that money can't buy. My bag. *The* bag. The one I took to Get Lost. If what Alex is saying has any truth to it, I'll be able to find out for myself right now.

When I first got back from the festival, I was a zombie. Dead on the inside, alive on the outside. I'm still not sure how I've made it from that day to this day. Mum did the unthinkable and took a few days off work to watch me, but I didn't want her to stay at home. I mean, I love that she brought me Cherry Cokes and snacks and didn't complain once that I should eat something more nutritious; I love that she lay in my bed with me one night and fell asleep so we both woke up together; I love that she never once said 'you'll get over this'. But it felt easier to stop being close to her. In case she left me like Jade did. And Dad.

I tried to distance myself by putting the tent from Get Lost up in the garden and sleeping in it. It was only meant to be a night or two, but weeks later I was still there. It made me feel connected to Jade. Though when the weather started turning in September, Mum told me I had to start sleeping in the house again so I wouldn't get sick. I told her that people live in igloos all year around and they're okay. And what about the people that live in the barges on the canal not too far from us? I didn't win that argument, so I had to come inside. I left Kylie up though. She survived autumn, a brutal winter, and now she's living her second summer.

As for the bag, it never got unpacked. I put it in the closet to shield it. I didn't want to clean anything that Jade had touched – it would be like washing her away.

I chuck the blanket to the side and drag the rucksack into the middle of the room. I sit down, legs straddled around it, and see a Post-it note from Mum stuck to the top. She must've written it when I'd just got home from Get Lost. *We'll get through this together. Xxx*

I begin to unbuckle the straps. I pull back the flappy material on top and loosen the toggle. There's a smack of a stench that hits my nostrils as it opens, a cocktail of damp and what smells like . . . lake water?

I fish a hand inside and dig out a pair of black denim cut-offs. They feel crunchy, like the outer seaweed bit on the sushi rolls that Jade liked to eat. They're only in here cos I came home in her PJ bottoms, the flowery ones I was wearing that morning. I didn't remember putting them on, but Jade packed enough clothes for a month's holiday abroad, so I woke up thinking she'd lent them to me when it got cold – until I realised she was gone.

I feel inside the front two pockets. Both are empty. I turn the shorts round to search the back too. There's a rustle as I burrow into the right side, tugging out some scrunched up foil – and a half-eaten cereal bar. Wow, this is hopeless. Alex has got me all worked up for nothing, spouting some rubbish about ripped clothes. I dive into the left butt pocket, and . . .

I feel something.

I clutch at the material, take a breath, then pull it out.

A multicoloured triangle?

I look at it, confused. I turn it over in my hands as the surface shimmers in the sunlight streaming through my window. What the . . . Oh, no, wait . . . I *do* recognise this!

It's from when I climbed the base of that tower, lit up like a big fish. Jonesy gave me a leg-up so I could scale it and grab one of its flags flapping in the breeze. Jade had liked its colours and I wanted to surprise her so she could sew it onto something.

I never got the chance to give it to her.

I stick my hand back into the world's most depressing lucky dip game, my fingers brushing against crisp packets, a squished loo roll, a torch, and . . . something plasticky? I pull my hand back out to see my sunglasses – broken. I don't remember them cracking.

How did they break?

I turn the bag upside down and tip the rest of the contents onto the floor.

I rummage through the things – mainly just mouldy T-shirts speckled with grey fungus. There's nothing here. I give up. Alex is full of crap. I reach for the phone at the wall to message him while accidentally kicking the splayed festival programme that's landed awkwardly by my side. As I do, I see a baby-blue T-shirt underneath.

It doesn't look familiar at first. If it's not black, it usually doesn't find its way into my wardrobe. I turn it round to see the Get Lost logo emblazoned across the front and realise it's the one Cassie bought me from the merch stall when we wandered off alone.

I pick up the T-shirt for a closer look, my other hand dropping my phone to the floor. It's the top I'm wearing in

Alex's video on the final night.

Sure as hell, there's a giant rip across the shoulder.

And worse, it's half soaked in blood.

I flush the toilet to wash the vomit water away. I make the mistake of looking in the mirror and see a face that doesn't even look like mine anymore. My eyes are hollow holes, I'm completely gaunt, and all the colour has drained from my flesh. I look like what would happen if Slenderman and Ghostface from *Scream* had a baby.

Alex was telling the truth.

Maybe I *did* get in a fight with Jade. How else would I have ripped clothes?

Could there really have been a struggle? Am I capable of . . . hurting her?

This is crazy! Surely there'd be a sliver of a memory somewhere inside this useless skull of mine? But I just can't picture it. Then again, I could never picture her dying before being old enough to finish school, and yeah, that happened.

But Jade didn't even know how to throw a punch. Unless . . . she didn't.

And it was all me?

Oh. God.

What have I done? It's like someone just stole the remote and switched my life from the Disney Channel to Sky Horror, playing endless terror 24/7.

Without thinking, I grab the little pink pedal bin that Mum bought to 'jazz up the bathroom' and take it along the corridor to my room. I place it in the middle of the floor. I go to the graveyard of forgotten backpack items, pick up the Get Lost T-shirt and chuck it in the bin. My heart's knocking against my chest like there's a car-crash in my ribcage.

I scout around my desk, sending chewed pencils and my collection of notes from Mum flying. I can't find what I'm looking for. I let out an involuntary yelp that scratches my throat. I feel sweat beading on my upper lip. My breathing is louder than my thoughts. I fly over to my bedside table and peek inside the top drawer. As if by magic, it appears in view beside the white sage incense sticks I had for whenever Jade came over.

I pelt back over to the bin as I count and I'm already sliding the lid away so that I can access the little fuckers inside the box. I grip hold of a bundle and pull them out, striking them altogether against the sandpapery texture. One or two catch alight, their flames triggering the neighbouring ones to spark to life too. Then I throw the matches into the bin.

Nothing seems to happen at first.

I peer over the top for a better look and see the material singe. A teeny hole appears and quadruples in size within a nanosecond. Then the whole thing catches fire, melting and filling the room with smoke. I stand and watch the evidence burn.

CHAPTER 11

JADE

I grab my phone out of Lexi's belt bag. The WhatsApp group chat has been well and truly popping off whilst we were on the wheel. Everyone is telling us where to meet every time they move – until Cassie did the smart thing and sent a live location. We head to the bar to find them buying drinks. They're passed round and sipped, or in Jonesy's case, guzzled. A cold cider is thrust into my hand by Alex. It smells like apples . . . and piss. I smile and politely say thank you but I'm really not sure about drinking this. I look over to Lexi. She's already slurping hers with glee. It is fermented, I guess. Might be like kombucha?

I tentatively take my first sip. Eurgh. Gross!

But I don't want to be ungrateful to Alex and I don't want to give Cassie another reason to think I'm a dud, so . . . I slurp away like the rest of them.

All the bands are done for today, so we head towards the big top, flattening the now dewy grass with our feet. Dance Dance's DJ set blares out of the tent, guiding us in the right direction. As we enter, shapes and faces become hazy in the ever-changing lights.

We meander our clammy bodies through the smog to find a spot, soon pulsing in time with the beat, pressed up against strangers.

Backs touching arms, wrapped in hands, sliding down chests.

Do you know what's crazy about having all your senses so overwhelmed?

It leaves you with no room for thoughts. You're just existing. I don't think my head has ever been this empty. There's nothing but here, nothing but now. This world has replaced the one I always knew, and it feels . . . amazing.

It's like my arms have feathers at the ends of them instead of hands, which float of their own accord towards the sky. They twist around up there, in and out of each other, making shapes that I can't take my eyes off in the smoke.

My head is somehow weightless and incredibly heavy all at the same time (is it the headache I felt creeping in earlier, or the cider?). My neck twists circles in time with the beat as my ribs rock from side to side. Lexi's eyes meet mine and my feather hands float onto her shoulders. Her slender arms are at her side, swinging long and pendulous as she bobs around semi in time to the beat. Her neck is bent forward and her hair falls over her cheeks like curtains protecting her. She tries to hide herself like this a lot when there are people around. I don't know why – she's a force and she could never actually hide – but it's whatever makes her feel good, I guess.

She mouths 'love you' with her head to one side when our

eyes meet. But they soon roll back down to face the ground.

Sometimes, she takes a little sip of her drink and then passes it to me. I pretend to sip along before handing it back. I put mine on the floor when we came in as I'm not sure how I feel about getting drunk, at least not 'til I've spoken to Lexi about it.

The six of us dance and sing as if we've known each other forever. Jonesy stands to my left, hands in fists that pump skyward. His shoulders drop back, looser than before, somehow looking wider as they roll around. His chin is popped into the air, square and protruding, while he confidently mouths the wrong words to the song at the ceiling.

It turns out Sam is an amazing dancer – Alex played it down before. His small frame cuts shapes so free and uninhibited, like his body is communicating. I never knew it was possible for someone to move that many parts of themselves along with their feet all at the same time. I find myself watching, mesmerised. One moment it looks like he's made of water, then suddenly his joints lock out, solid, and he accents every sound in the music with a different part of himself. He looks cool, playful, not so buttoned up . . . fun, even!

I shimmy over towards him, drawn to his dancing, as the room is waltzing all around me. We party close enough to each other to feel like we're in our own little cocoon.

We dance, first moving in unison. Then we battle – he throws out a move, challenging me to one, which I do, better than the last, before I offer him the floor again to try to beat me. He always does.

Jonesy, still fist-pumping the air nearby, spurs us on. Then I feel a hand grip my wrist. My eyes fly down to see who the hand belongs to. Alex.

Someone somewhere in this big top tent placed a pair of thick, black heart-shaped shades onto his face. He pulls me closer to him and for a split second I think he's about to kiss me . . . Instead he takes off his shades and slides them onto my face.

I'm plunged into a heart-shaped kaleidoscope world that hovers on top of reality and moves with the lights. I lift the glasses a little and everything flips backs to normal. Back down and hologram hearts reappear. I pull them up one more time to look Alex in the eye, and I mouth, 'Whaaaaatt!?'

He nods, knowingly, then gestures with exploding hands next to both temples to express just how mind-blowing the shades are.

'You really are a kaleidoscope kid!' he yells in my ear over the music. I giggle back, nodding, pure joy exploding inside me.

'Where's Lexi?' I shout back, suddenly aware she's missing from our group. I notice Cassie isn't here either. Alex turns the corners of his mouth down whilst shrugging.

'Dunno,' he replies.

I grab Alex by the wrist to lead us towards the front, where Dance Dance are smashing their set. Either side of the stage, people are dancing to the crowd on podiums, like they're the main event. I want that feeling! And I should spot them from up there too?

As I drag Alex through the swarm, I explain, 'Let's climb here – we'll be able to see Lexi and Cassie in the crowd then.'

We clamber up onto one of the platforms, smiling at the

group already there who shuffle over to make room for us. The view from here is incredible. I can literally see the heat rising off the crowd below, steam moving upwards and mingling with the smog left by dry ice, drifting over bodies that are sandwiched together and pulsing like a gigantic jellyfish. Before I know it, I'm dancing again, my feather hands floating, as if being pushed by the steam towards the ceiling. My eyes follow them to watch the green lasers dance above in new heart formations. The peak of the tent is far above us. Even stood up here above everybody else, I feel so small. A tiny mouse in this gigantic house of fun.

A tap on my leg jolts me out of my dance-dream. I lean forward to swipe at the hand, now clamped around my ankle, peering down to see a blonde-pink girl raver shimmering with sweat as if it's a fashion accessory. Lexi!

'Are you coming down anytime soon?' she yells.

'Soon, I've only been here a minute.'

'More like thirty! Come on, we're going to the bar!' Beside Lex, Cassie smiles up at me too. Maybe she doesn't think I'm a square after all.

Alex jumps down first, stepping back a little and gesturing for me to leap so he can catch me. I pause for a second, shaking my head at him. He nods back assuredly. So I soar as delicately as I can towards his chest, wrapping my legs around him as I make contact. He stumbles backwards on impact and spins me around, lowering me to the floor.

'Bar?' Cassie yells to us, pointing to the back of the tent. I see Lexi nod in my peripheral vision, but now I know she's safe I can barely take my eyes off Alex. He shakes his head at Cassie.

'We'll be there in a bit,' he shouts at her over my head and the music, wrapping his arms over my shoulders.

I feel myself drifting towards him, my feet pushing up onto their tippiest toes, so my face draws closer to his. And then, we're kissing.

His lips are on my lips! This is not a drill.

I'm in a festival tent, in the middle of a kaleidoscope dream, kissing!

Alex gently moves his hand from my shoulders to my neck and tickles it a little as his lips press more firmly on mine. He pulls away and we both smile, joy flooding our faces. He takes the shades off my face so he can look deep into my eyes.

I have never, and I mean absolutely never ever felt anything quite like this.

CHAPTER 12

LEXI

I've opened all the windows to air out the house and used a couple of white sage incense sticks to try to get rid of the fumes. I don't know why I didn't light them sooner; they remind me so much of Jade it's been like having her here in the room with me.

I spent most of the afternoon hoping Mum wouldn't come back too soon and smell the smoke. Now, I don't care if she busts me, I just wish she was here.

I called a bunch of times but she's not answering. I'm downstairs now, my phone plugged into the hallway socket beside the lamp, waiting for her. I twitch the curtains and look out onto the empty driveway. I should be used to Mum's lateness, but this is next level. There's a pain in my chest that's tightening like when I twist the Coke cap back on a bottle.

It's Saturday. Mum was only meant to be going into the newsroom for a few hours this morning to help with some royal event. But it's 5.01 p.m. She should be back by now.

My breathing is funny again, short and wispy like I've run a

400m sprint. But I'm just standing here not moving. It's as though all my breath is in my throat and if I inhale I'll use it all up. I'm trying to do the maths – the time it took me to get home from Viva la Vinyl, my phone would've dipped below 100% for about twenty-seven minutes.

Is that enough to kill Mum?

Now it's 5.30 p.m.

She *really* should be home.

I pace around the room restlessly, counting my steps as I go. But by the time I reach 342, she's still not home . . . so I find myself doing it again. If you shook me I'd make a sound like a baby's rattle – only instead of beads clattering around it would be numbers. I keep telling my mind that it's stupid, and that counting won't bring Mum back, but I keep going, too worried that I'll have blood on my hands – again – if I stop. I can't tempt karma. So I keep counting.

I used to feel in control when I counted . . . but now it's like the counting controls me.

A magic ping pierces the air and I lose my place in my latest number sequence. It's okay though cos the sound is more satisfying than being in the front row at a Coach Riot gig. I grab my handset to see the notification, a surge of excitement rocketing through me. I can relax. It's all good. Mum's okay. My counting saved her. I look at the phone to read the text.

It's not from Mum.

It's from Cassie?

I open the text, my fidgety fingers making the slippery mobile feel like it's made of jam. It starts with *Hi Everyone!!* It hasn't even been sent to me on purpose? Well, sort of, not really. It's another of Cassie's group messages which she's sent to her entire contacts list – with details of her end-of-year fashion show that she's named *The Cass-hion Show*.

Urgh.

And how is it 6 p.m. already?

I call Mum for the umpteenth time. She's still not picking up.

I repeat my step sequence. Onetwothreefourfivesixseven eight . . . all the way to the safe number – 342. It's the only way to keep Mum alive, cos each number of days Jade has been gone cancels out the number of days that Mum might die and get taken from me too.

I count and pace so many times, the carpet burns against my soles.

Where is she?

IT'S NEARLY 7 P.M.

I close my eyes and try miserably to take deep breaths instead of the prickly short ones, like hedgehog spikes. I keep them shut as I count again and manage about ten seconds of wheezing before I hear the sound of a car pulling into the cul-de-sac.

I peer through the window and watch in relief at Mum's blue Audi appearing into view. She glides into the driveway with a satisfying crunch of the handbrake. The invisible hands choking me loosen their grip around my windpipe and I can breathe again.

I shimmy the curtains back into place and rush to greet Mum at the door, opening it whilst she's still walking over from the car.

'Hi! You beat me to it,' she says, jangling the keys in her hand.

'You're late.' It spills out of me, my heartbeat jittery.

'Am I?' She looks at an invisible watch on her wrist, pretending to check the time.

'Your note said a "few hours",' I reply, trying to hide my upset.

'Oh, honey, you know what the newsroom is like,' she says, shutting the front door behind her. She takes off her shoes before untying her sandy blonde hair from its ponytail.

'You could've called.' I hate myself for sounding so needy.

'But . . . I'm always late.' She chuckles as if she's just told a joke. When I don't laugh with her, she adds, 'I don't understand, darling. What are you worried about?'

All of a sudden it feels like everything I've been holding in for the last year comes flooding to the surface. I'm embarrassed and ashamed as the *guilty* earworm tumbles through my mind along with all my numbers. At first, it's just a little sound and Mum thinks I'm laughing with her and she titters again. But my dry hiccup turns into cries and the fear I've been squashing down rushes out of me like an evil spirit. I begin to sob, like, really sob, bobbing up and down with each cry. Tears stream down my face and snot bubbles out of my nose. I feel naked even though I'm fully clothed.

'Lexi, sweetie.' Mum puts her arms around me and ushers us through to the living room. We plop down onto the sofa together as one. 'What's going on?'

'I thought something had happened,' I confess.

'To me?'

'Yes,' I say, through the snivelling.

'Okay.' Mum takes a big breath as she wipes away the wet strands of hair sticking to my cheek. 'Why did you think that?'

'You didn't pick up your phone.'

'I was working, Lex. Then driving – it was just traffic. Nothing to worry about.'

'But I thought . . .' I trail off, not sure how much I actually want to admit.

'Go on?'

'That you were dead.'

'Dead? Oh, Lexi. No, darling. I'm right here.' She flops me forward into her lap and strokes my arm. 'Why, baby?'

'I don't know,' I say, truthfully.

Mum sighs. 'I'm worried about you. You've had five sessions. More if we count Daniel and Elizabeth.' She's talking about my breadcrumb trail of therapists. 'Isn't Petra helping?'

'Not sure,' I reply, feeling self-conscious that I should be 'recovered' by now.

'I'm concerned things don't seem to be getting better,' she says.

'It'll never get better,' I mumble into her skirt. I find myself starting to count the numbers of polka dots on the fabric . . .

Suddenly, I'm being nudged.

'Darling?' It's Mum.

'Huh?' I say, as I land on the 342nd polka dot.

'I said we can't change what happened, but we can move on.'

Her words are like scissors to my heart, as if she's making one of those paper snowflakes from it, shredding it apart to leave something full of holes. I jerk up and fly off the sofa as I half-cry, half-squawk, 'I don't want to "move on".'

'Lexi, don't be like this,' Mum says. 'I'm on your side . . .' She's still talking as I cross the room and disappear through the sliding doors to the garden.

I march to Kylie and crawl inside where it's safe. There are a few empty Hula Hoops packets from when I last came here and a lip balm I spent ages looking for in the house.

I lie back against the hard ground, resting my head on the pillow I left in here. I want to talk to Mum, but what do I say? *Oh hey, there's a T-shirt with Jade's blood on it upstairs and a video of me making her cry. So, yeah, that open verdict may not be so accurate after all.*

I can't say anything in case she tries to make me go to the police, and I'd have to tell them I burned it. What if they re-open the case, and Alex knows more than he's letting on? What if there are *other* things that he remembers?

I know I said this is all about justice for Jade, and it is, but I didn't think getting justice for her would mean *this.* What if I . . .

Oh, I can't even. I just want the world to stop so I can get off.

I want to take my brain out too and get a new one that remembers everything or one that remembers nothing, cos right now being piggy-in-the-middle is making me feel INSANE. The only reason I have any sanity left at all is that confession note.

It is the one thing stopping me from thinking I somehow killed Jade.

But I didn't write it, so who did?

Maybe there's a reason they call it 'going mad'. You don't just become mad overnight. There's a whole journey as you wander off Path Normal and venture into Mad Land. That's what my brain feels like now. On that journey, strapped to the trolley, and I can't unshackle myself.

I hit the tent wall in rage, feeling the fabric wobble. I hit it again out of frustration, then a third time. As I do, something bounces out of nowhere and onto my foot. I jolt up to see what it is and pick up what I've just discovered.

Here, in my hands, is a little metallic rectangle.

I turn it over and see two rows of round pills neatly packaged inside.

I flip it back round to look at the black writing on the wrapping. *Lamotrigine*.

They're Jade's. The ones we thought she 'lost' that weekend.

CHAPTER 13

JADE

'Truth is the boring part,' slurs Jonesy, the self-appointed authority on Truth or Dare.

We're heading away from the big top, towards 'home'. Sweaty, achy, exhausted, some of us more drunk than others, some of us floating on more of a cloud than others.

'If you say so, Jones,' Cassie replies. 'That must mean you're up first then! I dare you to—' She pauses briefly, concocting the perfect instruction.

I gasp in shock as a cascade of cold water hits me. I snatch my breath, feeling like I'm being submerged. Wait, is it water? Wow, did Cassie just dare Jonesy to dunk me? Cold liquid splashes over my hair, thick streams of it racing down my back and dripping onto my face, in my eyes and all over my clothes. I splutter and cough, desperate for air. It feels like I'm drowning. What's happening?

It finally stops and the hairs on my arms stand up in the breeze we were all so grateful for when we left the big top. There's a wave of gasps and giggles from other Get Lost-ers walking home in the same direction as us. Some of them go so far as to point and laugh; others look over to me with pity in their eyes.

'What the FUCK was that?' It's Lexi, all but squaring up to Sam. Her eyes look wild, but he just seems to laugh back.

'Oh, shit! I just tripped, then next thing . . . I'm so sorry, Jade,' he says through stifled laughter. But is he? Maybe. His apologies always just sound fake.

I look down to let the liquid drip off my hair as quickly as possible and hide how embarrassed I feel. It's only then that I see the empty plastic pint rolling by my feet and realise it was an entire drink that flew over me.

Lexi tries to push soggy, drooping curls away from my eyes.

'It's okay,' I say, not wanting to make a scene. I tip my head back and try to shake my hair playfully, copying the move of the influencers I follow. I manage to hit Sam with droplets of booze that catapult from my tendrils.

'See! She's fine,' he quips, as he jumps back trying to avoid my fire. 'You owe me a pint now though.' He laughs at his own joke.

I wanna cry, but fake laugh instead, giving the others a green light to release the chuckles they've all been holding in.

'As long as you're okay?' Lexi replies.

I nod silently while smiling, but she knows when I'm faking. She pulls me by my hand away from the group as they continue walking behind.

'Don't worry, I've got you.' Cassie comes running to catch

us up, pushes my hair out of my face and asks if I have a bobble.

I don't.

'How come?' I say, intrigued.

'Cos what you need to do now is be super gentle with it whilst it's wet, rinse it as much as you can back at camp, then do a clarifying wash on it. D'you have your clarifying shampoo with you?'

'Err, I, I don't know what that means,' I reply, embarrassed. 'I have shampoo, but I don't know if it's . . . clarifcating or not.'

'You mixed girls and your hair! You have no idea what to do with it, do you?'

'Not really, no,' I mumble, looking down at my feet. I'm grateful for the help, mortified that I need it. I've spent hours scrolling Insta, I even managed to find influencers with hair that looks just like mine, but when I try what they tell me, it never turns out right. Now Mum's banned me from buying any more products 'til I've used the ones I've got.

'Right, well, we'll check when we get back, but you can't walk all the way to the tents like that,' Cassie says, reaching down to her boots and tugging at her laces. 'This'll have to do for now.' She whips the lace out of the eyelets of one boot. 'I barely tie them anyway, so it's fine. Right, scoop your hair up in your hands.' I do as I'm told. 'Gently. Gently!' she says, firmly. 'I'll tie this around.'

'Are you sure?' I ask, wondering if that's entirely wise.

'I mean, unless Lexi has a decent hair tie?'

Lex offers her wrist up for inspection.

'Nope, too thin,' says Cassie. 'That'll tangle up in your curls, babe. Trust me, the lace is better.'

After wringing my hair out, I lean forward with it in a bundle between both hands. The curls aren't just wet, they're sticky! What even was Sam's drink? I see Cassie's laceless boot appear on the floor in front of me as she begins to tie her lace gently around my hair.

'Thanks,' I say when she's done.

'It's okay. Now come on, before you freeze.'

We head towards our camp spot, spying the moon as we go.

'Alex knows all about the moon and stars,' I say, sort of thinking out loud.

'He does?' Cassie asks. 'He's never said anything about that to us.' She raises her eyebrow.

'Oh yeah, he knows about all the constellations and even what cycle the moon is in! It was pretty obvious I didn't know anything about it, but I told him that me and you promised each other we'd live on the moon one day, Lex.'

She turns to face me. 'You told him that?' I nod. 'And he still kissed you? Wow,' Lexi teases.

'Lex!' I squeal.

I'm too self-conscious to talk about Alex in front of Cassie. And my teeth are chattering uncontrollably now. 'Race you back to our tents,' I say, and take off at a sprint towards the campsite.

When we eventually arrive back, laughing and stumbling, there's no sign of the others.

Cassie yawns. 'I'm calling it a night,' she says, heading into her tent. 'See you in the morning.'

Cassie is really cool and she was super sweet to help me with my hair, but I'm secretly glad to have Lexi to myself again. Just like old times.

We try to unzip our own tent quietly but it's very difficult in the dark. I stumble over the ropes that stick out from the tent to hold it into the ground, much to Lexi's amusement.

'Sssshhh!' I 'whisper' far too loudly.

'Here,' Lexi says in an equally loud whisper whilst fumbling around in her pockets. 'Use the torch on my phone.' She whips it out and shines the light almost directly in my eyes.

'Ooooow!' I whisper-scream.

'Ooops! Sorry,' she says, pointing the light to the floor immediately.

'Okay, that's good. Keep shining it there.' I reach for the little metal zip tags and finally am able to open Kylie's door with a less than quiet *zzzzZZZZ* sound.

I reach for the torch inside that's dangling from the centre of the tent, swapping it for Lexi's phone torch as her battery is dying. I click it on and see our oh-so-inviting bed. We stumble in and I fumble for a towel to squeeze out the rest of the moisture from my hair. I guess I'll show Cassie my shampoo in the morning.

Lexi points the torch in my direction to help me find my towel. As she does, she creates a perfectly circular 'sun' on the wall of our tent.

'Oh my God, Jade, your shadow! It looks so cool,' she whisper-screams in glee. 'Hey, remember when we used to make shadow puppets at sleepovers?'

'Of course,' I say, revelling in the fact that she's reminiscing.

'And we'd rate them out of ten.' I flutter my hands in front of the torch. 'What's this?'

'Butterfly!' she replies. 'That's a seven. What else you got?'

'Errrrm, a crocodile,' I reply, snapping the croc into position and moving his mouth up and down as though he's on the hunt for dinner.

'Awesome! That's a nine. Anything else?'

'Of course!' I know this one is going to be my pièce de résistance. 'This little guy.' I draw my hands up to the torch slowly, so he creeps into view on the tent canvas. I position him perfectly at the bottom of the big round light, and then let out a loud wolf howl. 'AHHHHWOOOOOOO!'

'JAADE!' Lex says. 'That's a blatant ten! Can I have a go?'

'Course. So, you put your fingers like this,' I say, demonstrating, 'and then just hold them up to the torch. Here, I'll hold that.'

We shuffle round to find our new positions and Lexi moves her fingers to get it right. Into view snaps a perfect-looking werewolf. She lets out an impressive howl. Then we hear an answering howl from Cassie's tent next door! The two of us erupt in cheers as we hear Cassie fall into laughter.

There's another howl from a few tents away. We poke our head out of the door and see a shadow puppet from Cassie's tent as the rest of the howls are ringing out.

'Oh!' I giggle nervously. Our campmates are doing it too.

Lexi howls back and before we know it there's another tent, and another, and another, howling. Goosebumps appear on my arms, even though I'm not cold anymore. What felt fun and friendly seconds ago suddenly feels dangerous. I'm surrounded by wolves . . . strange, terrifying wolves, creeping nearer.

Lexi is one of them too.

I shiver, fighting off the feeling of dread.

But will I be able to fight the wolves off if I need to?

CHAPTER 14

LEXI

I run back into the house, my bare feet squelching across the damp grass. Eventually, I reach the sliding doors and hurtle into the living room. I fly past Mum on the sofa, slipping on the rug as I go and pinging my arms out for balance as if surfing on one leg. She goes to speak but I'm already gone, disappearing into the hall.

I reach for my phone where I left it charging while Mum was still out and pull it free from the cable. My mind is racing like a wolf chasing prey.

I can't believe I had them all this time!

But . . . when did Jade's pills vanish from her washbag and reappear in my side of the tent? I'm trying to think, but my brain's spidering off in different directions to connect the dots. What day did Jade realise they were missing? Did someone take them – on purpose?

'Careful, Lex!' Mum's voice shoots through the open doorway as she sips her favourite red wine. 'I'm thinking of taking some time off work. How about spending a few days together?'

'Sure!' I reply, not really listening as I leg it upstairs. The carpet burn from earlier stings against my soles. It's like Jade's energy is pulsing through me, pushing me to discover the truth. She wants to tell me something. Through these pills! I found them for a reason.

I open my door and am greeted by the smell of white sage and burnt T-shirt. It hits me like a brick to the face. What if Jade is trying to reach me because she knows I had something to do with what happened that night? Maybe the pills and T-shirt relate to each other. Did I *hide* them to stop her from taking them?

I flop onto the bed and begin to type into my phone. My fingers have their own heartbeat as I write *Lim* into the search bar then realise I have no idea how to spell Jade's meds. I shake my arm so that the packet slides down the inside of my jumper. I hid the pills there before I ran inside, so Mum wouldn't see. They peep out the bottom of my cuff and I pull them so hard, the metal foil cuts my skin. I check the spelling, then type again. *Lamotrigine.* Then I add *what happens if you stop taking.* I'm so jumpy I can't stay still. I bounce up and pace my bedroom, counting my steps as the results fill my screen.

People stopping lamotrigine experience withdrawal symptoms including: Headache. Moodiness. Hostility.

Oh Jade, what did I do?

There's more too.

Dizziness. Seizures. Hallucinations.

Then it gets worse . . .

My heart plummets out of my chest and I swear I hear a sound as it hits the floor.

Suicidal ideation.

I click the link and my eyes glaze over the information. I can't believe what I'm seeing. It's painful to read.

Suicidal ideation refers to thoughts of harming or killing yourself.

I reach for the pillow on my bed, squash it hard against my face, then I roar.

'I swear, I don't know how they got there,' I say; I'm brushing the leaves away from the marble tenderly as if I'm sweeping them away from Jade's hair.

'I'd never have taken them from you,' I add, swigging the last of my Cherry Coke and closing my eyes from the sun beating down as I tilt my head back.

'Even as a joke.' I'm rambling now, while reaching into my rucksack for the incense sticks from my room. I take one out of the packet to light it.

'I know how it looks, but it's not what you think.' I use my empty soda can as a holder and place the white sage in it, soon watching the smoke spiral away.

'I'm tripping balls, Jadey! Ever since I saw that video, I've been pooping my pants that there's more to what happened than I can remember. Now I've got your pills, I don't know what to think. You said you needed them to function. Sooo . . . why do I have them?

'I know you probably hate me right now, and I get how it looks. I'd hate me too if I were you, but I just . . . I can't remember anything.' I trail off.

'Maybe I need to hunt down that psychic whatsaname – Sarah? Sue? – from Get Lost. Cos even though I don't believe in crystal ball stuff, I'm running out of options!

'Apart from that thing Alex said, when I was at Viva la Vinyl. "So what if she was upset at me? It's too late to change anything." What d'you think that means? I'm thinking you were mad at him! Like, maybe you guys fought too, after we argued, and it tipped you over the edge . . . I've just been so freaked, thinking I did something. I should have gone back to ask why he said that. Cos, what if it was *him* who did something, not *me*?'

I've got used to these one-sided conversations. For months, I was delusion-free. I accepted Jade couldn't hear, and I was never going to get a reply. Lately, it feels like she wants to answer. Like, she needs me to be her voice. Or . . . maybe I'm just losing it?

'I promise, Jadey,' I continue, repositioning myself to get comfy. 'It's made me even more determined to find out what happ . . .'

Suddenly, there's a crackle and I hear footsteps behind me.

I swivel my head round, but whoever it is turns to walk away, but not before I catch a glimpse of his face.

Perfectly slicked back gelled hair. Pale skin. Thin as a rake. Kind of cute if you like that preppy, head-boy vibe.

'Sam?'

What is *he* doing here?

He freezes and is forced to spin so we're face-to-face.

'Lexi! Hi,' he says with a forced friendliness.

'You . . . I . . .' I stumble over my words. 'Didn't you realise it was me?'

'Eh?' Sam takes a pouch out of his jeans and a thumb's worth of tobacco. His spindly fingers start rolling it into a cigarette. He holds the half-rollie with his right hand while reaching into another pocket with his left to bring out a piece of paper. He rips off the corner with his teeth then makes a one-handed roach. He goes to put the paper back in his pocket, but it drops to the floor and he kicks it away.

'You were about to walk away,' I say.

'Ohh, that,' he interrupts with a smile as he lights his roll-up. 'I just didn't want to disturb you, if you were saying sorry, or anything like that.'

'"Saying sorry"?' I quiz, immediately thinking of the note I found. I stand up and edge away from him. *I'm sorry, R.*

'Yeah, y'know, saying sorry to someone that they're gone,' he says.

'It's a weird thing to say, is all.' I'm starting to wonder if it was a letter R after all. Could I have mistaken an S for an R?

'Is it?' Sam replies, looking at me with eyes that I wish I could read.

'You wrote it, didn't you?' I blurt out, unplanned.

'Wrote what?'

'The guilty note!' I say, loudly.

'The what?' He steps towards me, but I jump back.

Think, Lex. Think. I'm trying to picture the note. The lines of the R. Could it have been the letter S? There really wasn't much curl on it though. Or maybe a squiggly X? Like, he could've signed a kiss beneath the confession, not his own initial. *I'm sorry, X.*

'You're R!'

'What?' he says, now puffing on his cigarette.

'Or X!' I say, proud of myself for cracking the code.

'Lex, you're not making any sense.'

'You left the bear!' I feel scared and brave at the same time, like I could take on the world. 'What have you brought *this* time?' I say, accusingly. He's not going to get away with this!

'I have no idea what you're talking about.' Sam's eyes are wild now.

'What did you do to her? Did you hide the pills? Plant them in Kylie?'

'It's you that needs a chill pill, mate,' Sam says.

'Tell me the truth.' My voice is wobbly.

'I'm done.' He turns, making his way back along the footpath.

'Stay,' I beg. 'I need to know!'

'Need to know *what*?'

'Why you did it!'

'Dude! Listen to yourself. You're just as crazy as she was!' Sam circles his finger at the side of his head to gesture that I'm speaking nonsense. Then he turns and walks away, muttering to himself, as if *I'm* the unreasonable one when he's been caught in the act!

I've seen on TV shows that when someone commits a crime, they often like to return to the scene and watch the police try to figure it all out. It's like they get off on the cops not being able to solve it when who they need to catch is literally standing right there.

What if it's the same with Sam? He's coming back to

the grave to rub it in Jade's face that she's never coming back. Meanwhile he's wandering around totally free because no one has a clue that he had anything to do with her death. I know though.

He wrote that note!

But . . . why?

Why would Sam hate Jade that much to hurt her?

In the shows I watch, there's usually *always* a motive.

I scurry my things together, leaving the white sage to burn, and I go after him. But the slippery snake is quick and I have to count to keep myself alive so the space between us widens. I race through my numbers as I run, speeding to today's safe number while trying to keep my balance on the uneven ground above the bodies beneath me. It's hard to do both cos my brain thinks I'm counting my steps, but I'm not. My mind's going faster than my feet.

Counting used to be fun, like when Jade and I would play hide and seek or see who could fit the most marshmallows in their mouth at once. Now it's exhausting. By the time I hit 343, I'm safe – but Sam's disappeared out of sight. I wonder if he might be hiding behind a tombstone or if he found the way out already. I stand on the spot and peer around the place, but it's just me, silence and the souls.

I'm riled up and wondering what direction to take, as something grazes my leg. I bat it away with my shoe, ready to keep charging after Sam, but this leaf is persistent. It flaps against my shin like it's dancing. I gaze down to shoo it away and see it's no leaf at all.

It's a piece of paper.

I bend down to pick it up and as I reach the grass with my fingertips, I see Coach Riot's logo! Only the *Co* is missing from the top corner, so it reads *ach Riot*.

I stare at the dates and venues magicking into view.

Sam tore his roach from the corner of a flyer!

A flyer for Coach Riot's latest tour.

And they're playing in town on Thursday.

CHAPTER 15

JADE

'Jade,' croaks Lexi. 'Y'okay? It's boiling again, isn't it?'

'Yeah,' I reply flatly, desperately trying to pull my hoodie off. 'Did I bang my head last night? It really hurts.'

'No, babe. You just drank cider. I reckon this might be your first hangover.'

But I didn't really drink the cider, I pretended. Maybe I'm dehydrated, but would that make me dizzy?

My hair feels simultaneously crusty and fluffy from the dunking it received last night, and the make-up I didn't feel the need to remove because of my impromptu 'shower' from Sam is making my face itch. I poke my head out of Kylie's front door hoping the sun and the breeze will feel as restorative as yesterday.

'Aw'ight, Jade,' comes Jonesy's voice, far too loudly for my liking, as I fling the tent flap up. I squint in the daylight to see him tying an inflatable cow to a pole on his tent. 'Meet Monty! Got him after my breakfast pint. He's gonna make it a helluva lot easier to find the tents than last night.'

'Hey, Monty.' I wave. 'D'you find anywhere good for brekkie?' I ask Jonesy. He seems remarkably sprightly. Right on cue, the tent flap falls down to hit me in the face.

'Eatin's cheatin'! You gotta learn the rules to this game – it's not for amateurs,' he replies, matter-of-factly. He makes his way over to me and lifts the tent flap again whilst he talks me through the ins and outs of managing my 'hangover'. I'm oscillating between listening and trying to fight the dizzy.

With my eyes closed to stop the sun beaming into them, I'm met with a vision of mottled orange. Suddenly, I feel something brush against my lips. I open my eyes to see Lexi holding a Hobnob biscuit to my mouth with a smile.

'Thanks,' I mumble. 'Will it make me throw up?'

'Don't think so – too dry. Start on these and then we'll move on to a fry-up,' she says. I retch a little at that thought, hoping for more of a rainbow fruit bowl with chia seeds, before stuffing the Hobnob into my mouth.

I undo my hair from Cassie's shoelace and hear voices near our tent. Our howl-friends are waking up too. There's a faint sound of music in the distance. A few metres away, Cassie's lying on her back with hands placed behind her head, braids spread out on the ground as she sun-worships, but there's no sign of Alex or Sam.

'How you guys feeling?' Cassie asks without opening her eyes.

'Horrid!' I announce for both of us.

'Nah, I'm ready for round two,' Lexi says, meandering over to Cass to sit next to her.

I turn back into the tent in search of a face wipe. I drop a hydrating tablet into a can of water and down it in the hope it'll shake this seasick feeling. Out of nowhere, Mum's voice jumps into my head. 'Don't forget your tablets, sweetie,' starts to swirl around with the dizziness, followed by a shooting pain that feels like it flies from my right ear to my left eye. Ow! Maybe I should take one just in case it'll stop this pain.

I hunt around on Kylie's floor for my washbag.

'What are you doing in there, Jadey?' Lexi yells from her spot next to Cassie.

'Nothing!' I shout back, not yet ready to bring my real life crashing into this fantasy weekend. I unzip the washbag and rifle through my colourful skincare products in search of the silver strip of tablets. Nothing. *Think, Jadey. Where did you show Mum they were?*

I emerge again to lie in the sun with the others, hoping they'll distract me enough to push down the panic rising in my belly. Is this withdrawal? What was I thinking?

But soon I decide it's best that me, my crispy hair and my washbag head to the showers. I might feel better after that, be able to look for the pills properly and fix my hair before Alex sees me looking like . . . well, this!

When I arrive, the shower queue is loooong. Get Lost-ers line up one behind the other, all sharing the same stance, drooping like sunflowers without enough water on a hot day. Their eyes look empty, and their arms hang heavy as they clutch at towels and bottles of 3-in-1 shampoo. It feels as though I've walked into some sort of zombie apocalypse.

As I edge closer to the front, I notice the cubicles look exactly like Portaloos. I spy Sam and Alex queuing ahead. They don't seem to have a change of clothes. In fact, they don't even seem to have towels! The only thing I can see from here is Sam clutching his tub of hair gel. If I wasn't so intent on hiding I'd have bounded over to say hi and push in with them, but I think I'd die if Alex sees me right now.

I edge sideways to hide a little better behind the guy in front of me. I can make out a few things Alex and Sam are saying . . . about Bitcoin, I think? Sam's talking about 'alt coins – they're the future of finance, man'. Is he telling Alex to invest?

'You trust me, right?' Sam questions.

'Yeah but . . . I don't trust *it* – like what is it? It's not actual money, so what's the point?'

'No no no. I mean, yeah you should trust me about coins, but I mean generally, you trust me?'

'Course I do,' Alex replies.

'Well, then listen to me, buddy . . . don't get too close to Jade.'

WHAT?

'What?' Alex sounds as surprised as my thoughts. 'What are you talking about?'

'You can't trust her. Or her mate.'

'But she's basically the most genuine person I've ever met.'

'I know she seems that way,' Sam says, 'but I'm telling you, dude, there's stuff you don't know about her.'

'Right, but you do?' Alex replies, sceptical.

'Well, yeah.'

'How?'

'I just do, that's what I mean – I just need you to trust me.'

'Or you could just tell me what you're talking about? Cos

she seems pretty cool to me. She's kind, she's fun. What's the problem?'

He's sticking up for me. He's defending me to his friend. But also, what is Sam's problem? He doesn't know me!

I'm trying to think . . . if there's something me and Lex might've done. Could Sam be annoyed that I led Alex away from dancing last night? I didn't mean to – it just sort of happened. Or cos Cassie came to my side instead of his after he spilt the drink? Maybe he's aligned with energies too . . . Y'know, our auras are constantly in flux, moving with light or sound, and I think Sam's might just be clashing with mine instead of them harmonising together.

The queue's moving quickly and they're at the front now.

'I'll tell you everything when the time's right, you just need to trust me,' Sam's saying.

'I'll trust you when Jade gives me a reason to doubt her.' Alex shrugs as he heads into his shower cubicle.

Now I just have to pray I get to dive inside mine before they come out again. It'll be nearly impossible to hide if I'm still here when they reappear.

Luckily, within a minute, I'm heading into a humid plastic box. There's a drain on the floor, a shower head hanging from the ceiling, and big drips of condensation gathered all around that sound like raindrops as they hit the floor. Okay, so anything you take in here is going to get soaked – I guess that's why everyone else only brought one or two things!

I do my best to focus on my positive vibes not Sam's neggy ones as I drape my clothes for today on the back of the door, hoping they won't get too wet. I went with a lilac ensemble to make my green henna pop, as they're opposite each other on the colour wheel. It's a no-brainer really! I hang up my linen shirt dress and loop the violet fringed suede waistcoat over too – I'm in love with this thing. Then I wrap my matching Lycra cycle shorts over the top, along with a tan and gold paisley headscarf.

I take all the hair stuff I need out of my washbag before balancing it on the hook, then carry the tubs and bottles a few steps forward, placing them on the floor in the shower section of the cabin. I strip off and douse my hair in water, trying to comb it through and detangle my curls. It's even harder than normal because of the sticky. I squirt the non-clarifying shampoo into my hand and massage it over my scalp. I wish the water felt like it was actually helping me get clean. Instead, I feel like I'm getting sweatier by the second in this plastic greenhouse.

I rinse out the shampoo, comb again and slather leave-in-conditioner onto my hair. I quickly wash my body, before I jump out of the shower to pat myself 'dry'. I moisturise everywhere too. If I had one wish, I would be one of those people who can jump in and out of the shower in five minutes and just throw clothes on straight away, safe in the knowledge that their skin won't flake and crack and crisp up within the next hour. Lexi is one of those people – the 'low maintenance girl' we're all told we should be.

My head still hurts, and the dizziness is starting to make me feel like I'm off balance if I move it at all. Maybe the heat's making it worse?

The moisturiser begins to slip off almost as soon as I've put it on. I reach for the washbag again and rummage inside, half expecting my little strip of pills to appear after a good shake. They don't. Nothing. I shove my hand right down to the bottom and swirl it around inside . . . Still nothing. Okay, so now I'm freaking out.

There's a thud at the door, making me jump, followed by a disgruntled, 'Hurry up, mate! I wanna see some bands today.' Wondering where the pills are, I wrestle myself into my now damp outfit, tip my head back to get all the hair moving in the right direction, and tie the headscarf over the front of my sopping curls. I fall out of the shower feeling more gross than when I went in. Great.

I head back towards our tent slowly, trying to keep my balance. I watch my feet the whole way, wracking my brain to remember where I put the pills. My heart's thumping now, and I'm sweating even more from the panic rising from my feet. My hands shake and my thoughts race. Where are my meds? What the fuck am I going to do?

'There you are – missed you!' Lexi hollers as I arrive back in view of our tent. 'How was your shower?'

'They're awful,' I reply. 'Lex, can I speak to you in the tent for a minute?'

'Yeah, in a min – I'm just tryna nail this trick Jonesy showed me.'

'No, I need you now, it's important,' I insist, walking directly to Kylie without waiting for her to agree.

'What's going on?' Lex asks as she ducks to get through our door.

'I can't find my meds,' I reply. 'They were in the washbag and now they're not.'

117

'Oh,' she responds, now lying casually on the airbed. 'That sucks.' She really doesn't understand the importance.

'No, it doesn't just suck, Lex. It's a really massive problem.'

'Okay. Then what shall we do?'

'Well, did you see them when you borrowed my bag yesterday?'

'No, babe. I didn't see much, just dug my hand in for the toothbrush and stuff. Lucky I didn't accidentally put shampoo in my mouth to be honest.' She laughs.

'But they were in there before we left to get here, Lex. I checked and Mum checked, so they can't have just disappeared?' I'm shouting now. Not that I mean to, but I'm angry at her for not getting it and I'm angry at me for being so stupid. I thought I would just start to feel more like myself going a few days without them. But this pain is agony – the shooting pains keep coming and I don't know what's going to happen if I don't start taking my pills.

'Hey.' It's Alex, poking his head around the tent door. 'Y'know, super-thin layers of fabric don't do much to trap sound, right?' He smiles awkwardly. I know he's just trying to keep things light.

'Of course I know that, Alex,' I snap, before storming out of the tent to get some space.

Moments later, I find a quiet space on the edge of the Blue Zone campsite we're in and sit on the grass with my head between my knees trying to count to ten. I feel a hand arriving gently on my back, rubbing softly. I feel my rage dial down just enough to turn into some other emotion – one that brings streaming tears and sobs along with it.

'I'm sorry, that was a stupid thing to say,' the voice of the owner's hand offers. I don't want to lift my head from my knees to reveal my tear-stained face, but I know it's Alex. He sits down next to me and wraps one of his lanky arms over my shoulders.

'It's okay,' he continues. 'Whatever it is, we can fix it.'

'No, we can't. I need my tablets!' I shout through snatched breaths that creep up on me out of nowhere.

'Well, Lexi's looking around the tent as we speak, and I have paracetamol and Rennies and stuff like that. I'm sure between all of us, we'll have pretty much anything you need – you just have to ask.'

'You won't have this,' I reply.

'Try me,' he insists.

'Lamotrigine?' I ask, almost hopeful that maybe I'm not alone. Maybe he's going to tell me he needs the same thing to be normal too.

'Well, no. I've never heard of that but the others might?' he offers, sweetly.

'I don't wanna tell the others, Alex. It's not a painkiller, it's . . . more complicated than that.'

'Okay,' he replies, squeezing my shoulder a little.

'It's to keep my brain level. It used to get a bit funny up there before I had them,' I say, trying to hold back some of the awful details about just how nuts I really am.

'What d'you mean, "level"?' he asks, confused.

'Just like, even. Straight. Normal.'

'I'm not sure I'm following,' he says.

I've run out of ways to hide my secret and part of me doesn't even want to anymore, so I begin to reel it all off . . .

'It's bipolar, Alex.' I turn to look him in the eye for the first time. Trying to gauge his expression.

'Okay, so, what, like you have voices in your head?' he asks.

'No, it's not like that . . . well, sometimes it is, but mostly, I just get really down, and my brain tells me I just shouldn't be here anymore, and I can't wake up or get out of bed or make a cup of tea or eat, and I'm freezing cold, and my head just won't stop hurting.' The floodgates have opened and he's staring but I can't tell what he thinks.

I've only told him half the story – I don't know if he's ready for the rest. But I've started now, so I may as well finish.

'Other times, I'm so ridiculously happy and I can do five billion things at once and I'm boiling hot and I don't need sleep at all, but I see things and I don't know if they're in my mind or not and, yeah . . . I do hear things and it's the same, like no one else can hear them and it feels like I'm on another planet, a better planet than everybody else, and it's technicolour and everything moves at the speed of a shooting star.'

I drop my head back to focus on the floor again.

'Well, that part sounds kinda fun,' he replies.

'Yeah it is. Until it isn't!' I continue. 'Because before I know it, I'm doing things that I would never normally do. I get snappy and mean with people. I do things that hurt them, and I do things that hurt me. And I don't want to be like that but it's like I can't stop. And the thing is, since I've had my meds I haven't been like that and I never want to feel any of that stuff again, but I forgot to take them yesterday,' I lie, 'and I can't find them this morning, and now my head is pounding and I'm dizzy and I feel like I might be sick. I'm afraid of what's gonna happen without them.'

I turn to look at Alex again and he stares back, saying nothing.

I'm trying to read his expression but it's impossible. Is that because of my tear-clouded vision or because he's deadpan through shock? He pulls his legs up underneath himself, about to stand up. So, this is when he walks away? I brace myself for how much that's going to hurt. But then he turns to me and takes my hand, pulling me to my feet at the same time as him. He flings his arms around my body and holds me in the tightest, most comforting hug I've ever felt. I cry with relief into his chest.

Maybe he doesn't care that I'm crazy?

CHAPTER 16

LEXI

I spent forever yesterday trying to find Sam on social media after I got back from the cemetery. I got a headache being online that long. Turns out Mum's right and looking at a screen all day *is* bad for your eyes. Although she does the exact same thing.

Anyways, it was all for nothing. I failed to find him after trawling through Cassie's, Jonesy's and Alex's followers and following lists. Sam doesn't have an account.

Or . . . he's blocked me?

The sun streams through the curtains I didn't close last night as I roll over in bed and reach for my phone. Now that I've slept on it – if you can call sleepless social media stalking 'sleep' – I have a new idea. But first, I need WhatsApp. I'll call Sam. Then I can finish what we started at the grave. I just need him to admit he wrote the note.

I dive into the app with my phone battery bar glowing green. It's attached to the charging cable like the string that Jade and I tied to yoghurt pots to make walkie-talkies. Just like that string, this cable is my link to her. I start scrolling through my chats to find the group we were all in together last summer. It doesn't take long as the app's not exactly poppin' with conversations right now, other than my messages with Mum. I guess it's cos I don't have friends anymore.

Cassie is group admin. She called it *Get Lost Rave Heads* and added a bunch of fire and dancing girl emojis. The icon picture is bare-chested Jonesy wearing a broken fairy wing and what looks like a Burger King crown by one of the stages.

I feel a lump in my throat the size of the world, remembering how happy I was at Get Lost. Before it all went wrong.

I do the only thing I know how to do these days – I start to count. It's just to keep us safe, cos the fact Sam avoided me like that at the grave makes me nervous. I think he's keeping secrets from me.

Why run away unless you have something to hide?

It's hard to know for sure but the questions and numbers swirling through my mind are warning me not to trust him. It's not like when Mum used to watch the lottery number balls tumble around in a machine, hopeful that the numbers we played would be picked. These numbers are loud and bossy. They get angry if I don't listen – cos bad things will happen.

I hit 344 then click into the *Rave Heads* group, anxious but excited that I'm getting closer to finding him, only to be slapped on the cheek by a little notification. *Sam left*.

Hmm . . .

I come out of the group to start a new chat, just with him. It felt safer to banter with the others chipping in though I don't have a choice. But as I'm typing his name into the app, my heart sinks. There's no photo beside it. Just a blank icon of a white silhouette against a grey background, which means he's changed numbers or blocked me on here too!

FFS.

What do I do now?

Maybe I can ask one of the others for Sam's number. Only, that might not work if they warn him I'm getting in touch. If he's already avoiding me, it'll only make things harder.

I need to do this another way.

On my own.

I flop my phone beside me on the mattress and lie back on the bed as I try to think. But all I can see is Sam: his face, his eyes, his pity . . . his flyer!

Could Sam be going to see them? I'm pretty sure he was the only one apart from me at Get Lost who knew the lyrics to 'Perfect October', and it hadn't even been released yet.

I think I might just have a plan.

I leap out of bed, with morning breath that could knock out a horse. It's hot already even though it's early so I don't bother with a top, racing out of my room in a bra and PJ shorts, throwing myself downstairs to make my plan come to life.

Relief floods through me as I see Mum lounging in her summer dressing gown in the living room. It's Monday, but she's home today as she ended up working the weekend for the royal wedding. I run over then settle beside her, giving her a massive squeeze.

'What do you want?' she asks, warmly.

'What makes you think I want something?' I say, teasing.

'Because you're not this affectionate unless you want something.'

'Mum!' I reply in faux offence, pulling away from the hug.

'So?' She smiles, waiting for me to drop the bombshell.

'I need to use your bank card,' I confess.

'Ahh, the truth is out. And what for?'

'A ticket,' I add, sheepishly, convinced she won't let me go when I give her the full story. Or worse, she'll want to come with!

'A ticket?' She reaches for her coffee and takes a glug.

'For a gig. It's one of my favourite bands!' I say, hoping and praying Sam will be going too.

'Coach Riot?'

'How do you know about Coach Riot?' I laugh.

'I know more than you think I do, Lexi.' Mum ruffles my hair like she did when I was little and God it feels good. Even though we live in the same house, I really miss her. Things haven't been the same since her promotion. I know I'm guilty of pushing her away too.

'It's just, they're extra special, cos we saw them at Get Lost.'

'I understand, darling. When is it?'

'Thursday.'

'And where?'

'The Forum.'

'Okay,' she says with her thinking-face on, 'and who would you go with?'

'Cassie.' I surprise myself at how easily I lie.

'I thought you lost touch?'

'She messaged me! She invited me.'

'Oh, that's great. I'm really pleased. It's good for the soul to keep busy.'

'Soo, is that a yes?' I paint on my biggest grin and please-Mum eyes.

'Go on, then. My wallet's in my handbag – bring it here and we'll do it together.'

I jump off the sofa and head to the coat rack in the hall, rifling through Mum's stuff until I find her purse.

I turn back and slide against the hard wood on the heels of my socks towards Mum, buzzing with energy. I thought it'd be hard convincing her, though she's in such a good mood. She's acting like I've just offered to hoover the living room!

I sit beside Mum again as she opens her laptop to start searching for the Coach Riot ticket page. I snuggle against her to show my appreciation and she wraps an arm around me while typing with her spare hand. I feel a warmth in my belly and like my heart might not have turned to stone after all.

We're both fizzing with excitement as the Coach Riot website loads. She clicks through, while telling me how proud she is of me for taking these steps to have fun again. Together, we find the *Live Shows* tab to buy a ticket. We feed off each other's hype while pointing at the screen and wiggling the mousepad over to the right spot.

There's a list of venues where they're playing that mirror what I saw on the flyer Sam dropped at Jade's grave. Our fingers flitter and my eyes try to keep up, darting down to Thursday's date.

I crash down from Cloud Nine with an almighty thwack when I see the words:

The Forum – Sold Out.

'What am I going to do?' I ask. It was the perfect plan – or so I thought. My eyes are wet and there's a tight feeling in my throat like I've eaten a dish scourer.

'I don't know, Lex.' Mum looks just as deflated as I do. She stares at the laptop, as if it holds the answers. 'Maybe we can google ticket agencies?'

'Yeah!' I say, as a little surge of hope soars through me. 'Let's try that.'

We search and we search and we search, taking loo trips and breaks for making breakfast, then again for lunch, but no one has any tickets left. It's pointless! None of the agencies, no one on social media and nothing on eBay.

By the time dinner rolls around, we agree to put the computer away. Mum offers to get us Chinese takeaway to cheer us up. She reaches into her wallet to find some change to tip the delivery person, and I'm struck like lightning with an Einstein moment.

'Mum! I've got a new idea!' I announce.

'You do?'

'I'll just need to borrow some cash.'

My nerves have been knotted like barbed wire all week waiting for tonight. What if Sam doesn't show up? Or what if he does, but denies writing the confession note again?

Either way, it's better than sitting at home wondering. So I'm here!

I turn the corner and see C O A C H R I O T illuminated on the dome of the venue, boasting to passers-by who's playing tonight. I feel a rush just looking at it. There's a line snaking around the building, filled with people desperate to be first in and up against the barrier when the band come on. Some are standing drinking, others sitting on the pavement eating MaccyD's. The latecomers get eyerolls for pushing in with friends saving their spots.

I don't even have to hunt for the touts. As soon as I near the queue, they're all hustling, shouting, 'Buying 'n' selling, buying 'n' selling,' in between sucks on their ciggies. They're wearing beanies and puffer jackets even though it's 20 degrees outside. I want to ask if their tickets are legit but I feel I might get a broken nose just questioning it.

I approach the youngest, friendliest looking one to ask how much the tickets are. He quotes me £80 – double the original price. I try to barter but he begins to walk away so I hastily hand over the wad of notes Mum gave me that's meant for food and a taxi home, not just the ticket. My fingers wrap themselves around my prize as I pray it's not a fake.

I join the back of the queue which now loops round to the alleyway behind the venue. The whiff of the giant black bins here makes me gag. A random girl in front tells me she likes my hair before turning back round to her mates. As I wait in the queue I keep my eyes peeled, hoping to spot Sam.

After what feels like forever, the swarm in front of me starts to slowly move forwards. Chatter and laughter fill the air, everyone looking slightly mad with excitement. It's contagious. I can't help but feel a little ripple of giddiness that I'm back seeing live music, even if Jade isn't by my side.

As I get to the front, I hold my breath as if I'm about to

deep-sea dive without an oxygen tank, and hand over my ticket. The security guard, who's about 10ft tall, looks down at me like I'm a Borrower. He takes the ticket and spends an eternity trying to scan the QR code. He raises it into the air to examine, like cashiers do when you hand over a bank note.

He's taking his job VERY seriously.

Huffing and puffing, he fiddles with the scanner, clicking a button on it left and right, and grumbles something about batteries. Finally, something lights up, and he shines it on the ticket. He's examining it so intensely you'd think I'd just smuggled him diamonds.

My heart's spinning like a revolving door.

What if I've been sold a dud? I'll be right back at square one!

Eventually, he completes his task, and we lock eyes.

'Go on in, love,' he declares. I want to hug him. And the tout who sold it. I thank the guard enthusiastically, but he's already turning to the person behind me.

I move along in the queue to where you swap tickets for wristbands at the booth and start to feel a little high. The drone of the warm-up band from the stage melts into the foyer. It feels *good* to be around music again.

I find a place to stand then whip out my phone. There's a flurry of messages from Mum saying how happy she is that I'm 'being proactive' and enjoying myself again. I reply quickly before heading over to Cassie's Insta instead, scrolling through her last few photos and checking her stories. A wave of disappointment floods me as I just see her usual posts.

I've been checking for days, convinced one of them would drop a hint that they're going to be here. If Cassie had a ticket for tonight, there is no way she'd be keeping it to herself. She shares everything. If she's having a bubble bath, click. If she's eating sourdough with avocado for brunch, click. If she's getting dolled up for Coach Riot, click click click.

The venue is getting busy and more chaotic as people continue to arrive. Their voices are loud to compete with the music that's bouncing off the walls. The lights are low, and I can't see well, especially as I'm surrounded by bodies that are crowded in like sardines.

I jump out of Cassie's account and take a detour to the @JonesysBalls profile. It's a shrine to nothing but rugby. I look for clues, but his last post was shared ten days ago. I go to check his stories even though his photo icon isn't illuminated – there's nothing to see.

My last hope is Alex.

I leave Jonesy's account and notice my phone battery's dropped from 100% – dipping into double digits. It dawns on me that my handset has become separated from my power bar that was charging it on the bus. Panic rises through my chest, then into my head. It's already in my cheeks, making them burn like someone's rubbed chillies all over them.

I dig into my pockets; they're empty! I unzip the belt bag around my waist that's holding my keys and my wall charger, but the portable one is nowhere to be seen. It must've come dislodged and fallen out my pocket when I got up from my seat on the bus?

The palpitations are firing up in full force. It's not like before I sit exams or after I drink coffee. They're faster and louder and scarier. It feels like I'm having a heart attack.

I start to stalk around for a socket, but struggle. I move through the crowds, looking down at the sea of feet to hunt for a power point on the wall.

'Move along!' A bald security guard ushers me along as he tries to control the throng.

'Excuse me?' I say, over the racket, but he can't hear. 'Excuse me!' I try again.

'Toilets are that way,' he says, pointing.

'No, I need to charge my phone!' I hold up my handset.

'Upstairs!' he shouts, then whizzes off to help a drunk girl who's just fallen over.

I head for the balcony lobby that overlooks the main foyer. I'll get a better view of people as they arrive up there. I move as quickly as I can through the crowd and spy a socket on the wall by the bar. I squeeze past the bodies all flocking round trying to get served. I bend down to reach through legs and take the charger from my belt bag to plug in.

It's all cables and feet and noise as I go to look at Alex's account while turning around into position to lean against the wall. At the same time, I realise I've completely lost my view of the downstairs foyer and I'm too far back to look down!

There's nowhere to wedge the phone, and I don't have a hoodie to hide it beneath, so I've no choice but to leave it leaning against the wall while I go to the balcony railing. I try to train one eye on the crowds still arriving and another on my phone, to check no one pinches it. But it's hard to focus with my chest closing as if I've shoe-laced my ribs.

I'm also desperate for the loo now. But I can't lose this chance. I make a mental vow to Jade that I'll stick it out a bit longer. Though it feels like the crazier the venue gets, the more my breath is being squeezed out of me. I do *not* feel right.

As I'm trying to figure out what to do next, it happens. Out of nowhere, I hear his signature cackle. It sounds like an in-joke you desperately want to be in on. I look down and my eyes scan the foyer, trying to locate what my ears can hear.

Holy crap, it's him.

My plan worked.

'Sam,' I shout, but he doesn't hear. 'Sam!' I try again. This time he looks around left and right, then behind him. 'UP HERE!' I yell, before he eventually cranes his neck skyward.

I wave manically. 'Sam!' Our eyes meet. I'm still waving, but . . . he's not reacting. I lose his gaze. Now, he's nudging Alex beside him. There's no sign of Jonesy or Cass. The two Lost Boys start talking and I can't lip-read, or even attempt to listen from here. They're moving again now towards the stairs and . . . 'HEY!' I shout but they're out of view, disappearing under the balcony towards the main auditorium.

Wait, did I just get ghosted IRL?

'Sam! Hey!' I leg it from the balcony and head downstairs, my feet on the third stair before I remember my phone. I try to get back to the wall as quickly as I can, though no one lets me past – they all think I'm pushing in to buy a drink. The venue is bursting at the seams now and it's like wading through treacle.

I finally reach my mobile. It's not 100% yet. I grab it anyway then dash back to the stairs, but as I do, my leg bends funny. I stumble. My phone slips and drops to the ground. I immediately pick it up, clamping my fingers around it as I see I've cracked the screen. I stand, ready to finish bombing down the stairs, but something pulls me back down so that I touch the manky carpet again. My brain's ordering me to do it again . . . and again. I don't have time so I tell it to be quiet but it's saying I have to, otherwise it might not just be the screen that gets cracked – my skull might too. I touch the carpet for a third time then a fourth . . . I stay down there until I've touched it 347 times.

Then I'm safe. I fly down and towards the door to the auditorium.

'WRISTBAND,' snarls a female security guard in a neon yellow jacket.

I show her the plastic band I was given, panting from my gallop as my heart booms like thunderclaps.

'THIS IS STANDING,' she yelps, over the hubbub.

'Huh? Can you let me through please – I've lost my friends—'

'YOUR BAND IS FOR SEATED. THIS IS STANDING,' she shouts, pointing upstairs.

I look down at the wristband that says *Seated Only* in red letters. The words grin smugly at me like Eric the school prefect does each time he busts me for skiving class.

R.E.D.

Like the roses. Like Alex's vinyl store logo. Like their tent.

I should have known this would be a bad idea.

Argh. I was too busy getting excited that the tout had tickets left to check which section it was in. I swear the seated tickets are cheaper too. Which means I've been doubly ripped off!

'Please!' I beg.

'I DON'T MAKE THE RULES,' she growls back.

I slink away feeling utterly worthless. But I'm not giving up that easily. I loop around the staircase leaving Mardy-Pants to bark her orders at someone else. I watch as couples kiss their way past and best friends giggle through the threshold, waiting until there's a rush of people all trying to get in at once so I can seize my moment.

I count again, then prepare to go . . .

NOW.

There's a group of girls all wearing heavy eyeliner (even more than me) and self-made shirts spray-painted with Coach Riot lyrics. I get as close as I can then shimmy my way into their pack, turning my head down towards my phone to conceal my face.

We're starting to get through. The security guard is struggling to keep up with all the arms thrust in her direction and now she's the one getting flustered.

This is it.

Sam, you'd better be ready.

Without warning, there's an arm blocking my chest.

'OI! I'VE ALREADY TOLD YOU!' the security guard bellows.

'You don't understand.'

'NO! YOU DON'T UNDERSTAND. IT'S UPSTAIRS OR I THROW YOU OUT.'

'FINE!' I snap back, beaten, before trudging upstairs in a mega grump.

Sitting at a gig sounds weirder than it actually is. As soon as the lights go down for Coach Riot to come on, everyone in the seating area is on their feet. There's an unmistakable scuzzy guitar sound and suddenly Jared appears in view, lit up by a spotlight. There's a huge roar from fans and I find myself swept along.

He's tiny from up here in the seats but as the music bursts from the stage, it still feels like we're all part of something. Like I'm part of something again.

It feels so good and so wrong. All the tension that's been corseting around me starts to unravel like ribbons. I throw my head back and surrender. I'm singing, remembering every lyric as if tattooed on my brain. My arms are in the air, my feet are stomping the ground, and I'm doing something I haven't done in a very, very long time – having fun.

Soon, I'm shouting. The words spill out drenched in relief and guilt. My heart is full. FULL? I never thought I'd feel this again. It feels naughty, like I shouldn't be here without her. It's so freeing. I don't need permission. I'm in no one's shadow. I can shine on my own.

'Oooohhh, we live only for the night . . .' I belt out. I try to time-travel to Get Lost. I want to go back but my mind stays in the present, as if it doesn't want me to remember.

' . . . and we won't ever grow up . . .' I force my eyes closed and keep singing.

' . . . go home, get lost . . .' The more I sing, the more I can see her face.

' . . . ooohhh, ooohhh . . .' I think I can hear her voice too.

She's touching the new amethyst ring on my finger. I'm half in the present watching Coach Riot here, half in the past watching them there. Here. There. Here. There. The scent of her sweet perfume tickles its way up my nose. She smells like Skittles. She looks at me and says, *Y'know, when we're not together, there'll always be a piece of me with you.*

I try to remember more, clinging to the edge of the memory as if dangling from a cliff by my fingernails. But I'm slingshot back into the moment as Jared and the band finish their song, greeted by a demented cheer and a shower of plastic pint cups thrown into the air. Beer rains down on the people below.

It's only now, standing here, that I realise loneliness doesn't just happen at 3 a.m. It can happen at 3 p.m. or 6 p.m. or 9 p.m. in a festival full of people.

At the time, I thought Jade was talking about leaving me to hang out with Alex. *When we're not together* . . . Now, I think she might have been talking about leaving me for good . . . *there'll always be a piece of me with you.*

CHAPTER 17

JADE

Alex's arms squeeze me in tight. With my ear pressed into his chest I can hear his heartbeat. It's soothing. My breathing slows a little, my shoulders drop again. It's like his calm and kindness is sucking all the bad feelings out of my body. I feel him kiss the top of my head before he pulls back and bends down so his eyes line up with mine.

'We're gonna figure it out, okay. Let me do some googling.'

He taps around on his phone, patiently waiting for the 4G that's flooded by thousands of people trying to use the same network.

'Okay,' Alex says after reading a page, 'it looks like if it's only a day or two without them, you'll probably be fine. You're not really supposed to just stop – it's best to, like, taper off them if you were gonna do that. So you might have some headaches and stuff, but then it'll settle down. It's only if you leave it too long that things might get a bit, well, scary.'

I nod, trying to give Alex my calmest face. How long is too long? I count in my head . . . It's been five days since I stopped.

'You can take some paracetamol to help with the headaches and it says to drink lots of water.'

'Okay.'

'And then when you get home, you just need to take a tablet as soon as possible but make sure it's . . .' he trails off to read the rest, 'twelve hours before the next one.'

'So I'm gonna be fine then?' I ask, hoping for reassurance to all the worries in my head.

'You're gonna be fine! And listen, Lex will probably find them in the tent anyway.'

'Yeah, okay – she will, won't she?'

'Hey, d'you wanna take a detour?' he asks, peering down to look in my eyes, interrupting my thoughts.

'A detour to . . . ?'

'I dunno yet. Maybe we should just take a minute before we hang with the others.' He looks at me, cheekily, out of the corner of his eye.

'Okay, sure!' I reply, relieved. I was starting to feel a bit embarrassed about having to face them all even though I know I will sooner or later.

We find a place to grab breakfast – bacon bap for him, falafel wrap for me. We meander through vintage clothes stalls, trying on hats and faux fur coats. We pose for one another, sussing out each other's style. Turns out Alex looks like a runway model in almost everything he puts on, but clearly has no idea of this. My favourite is the lemon-yellow bucket hat teamed with tan grandpa trousers he's holding against his body on the hanger.

'GET THEM!' I yell gleefully as he looks at the price

tag dangling around the hanger.

'Nah, think the boys'd tear me apart if I rock up in these.' Alex dips his head a little. Is he . . . shy?

As I spin around to find something for me, I'm drawn to a brightly coloured wooden caravan just opposite the pop-up store we're in. It's beautiful! Sunflower yellow with intricate paintings all over it in lilac, teal and terracotta. There's a stack of steps leading to the porch, with an arch draped in floaty fabric blowing gently in the breeze. Something tells me that all the answers I'm searching for lie inside it – if Alex is as amazing as I think he is; if Emily really has something to say from the other side. I race over without a word.

'Jade, what are you . . . ?' And then he sees it. 'Oh, right, course. You wanna hang out in the massive rainbow caravan.' Alex laughs as he wrestles his arms out of a boxy, indigo shacket and jogs over to join me.

'It's not just a rainbow caravan, silly!' I say. 'It's Psychic Sally's rainbow caravan!' I point to the sign.

'Oh! So, you wanna talk to someone in the spirit world?' Alex looks at me with one eyebrow raised.

'Well, I dunno, maybe? Or we might be able to find out which one of us is gonna make millions!' He stares blankly at me. 'Are you scared?' I tease. 'Anyone would think you've got something to hide.' I giggle, heading up the steps and through the archway.

There's a soft voice welcoming me into the dimly lit cave.

'Come in, my child,' it utters smoothly. 'What brings you to my door today?'

'Thought you'd already know, to be honest, Sally!' I laugh at my own joke. Sally does not.

'A common misconception,' she replies. 'Come, sit. All will be explained.'

It's not quite as fun as I thought it would be in here. The air is stuffy, with barely any sunlight creeping in, and it smells like Sally only lights incense to cover up the smell of her vape. I shuffle forward to sit on the chair in front of her desk, which is covered in all kinds of trinkets. Crystals like I have, a bundle of sage and a perfectly domed frosted ball resting on fake marble. She says nothing, just glares at me, as though waiting for something.

'I was thinking about a tarot card reading,' I offer to break the silence. 'And I don't know if you do this kind of thing, but, I'd like to make contact with my friend. She's on the other side.' I look into her eyes with purpose, hoping she knows what I mean.

'Good. Yes. Tarot is an excellent way to understand the path you are on. With understanding, we can evolve.'

'Right! Okay. And the other thing?'

'We can try. Do you have anything that belonged to your friend with you?'

'Oh, no, I didn't know . . .'

'Okay,' Sally interrupts, 'well, this isn't the ideal setting and that would have helped, but we can try anyway. Let's see what the cards have to say first. What would you like me to focus on: friends, love, career?'

'Oh, just sort of all of it, I guess . . . And, erm, if Emily has forgiven us.'

Sally reaches for a stack of cards. They're gigantic, much bigger than the playing cards we take on family holidays, and covered in beautiful, swirling patterns in all of my favourite colours. She looks meaningfully into my eyes, then passes me the deck and asks me to shuffle them. As I do, she explains, 'We're going to look into your past, your present and your future. Please cut the deck of cards into three.'

I do as I'm told, placing the three piles in front of us both. She instructs me to turn over the card on top of each pile, so they face upwards.

Even though a trio of images appears, my eyes zone in on just one – the black card with a skeleton holding something that looks like an axe and the word *DEATH* on it. Even though it's sweltering in the caravan, I feel a chill run down my spine.

'Interesting. These three cards are all named cards, which means this is a very strong reading. Although, that's quite unsurprising, Jade. You have a very strong energy.' Wait, did I even tell her my name? 'Your cards are the Fool, the Magician and Death.'

Why is Sally so calm about death being in my cards?

She continues, 'I wonder, were there moments in your past when you were too trusting?'

Maybe, I don't know, but I nod at her anyway, feeling uncomfortable. She can clearly see into my soul and knows everything about me.

I'm beginning to sweat and panic.

'Now, I don't want you to worry,' she says, 'the Death card doesn't always mean death in a physical sense – it can symbolise the end of something or a new beginning. I sense that now you are finding your place, you are excited for new connections and experiences. There will be a big change for you soon.'

'What kind of big change?' I question, nervously.

'You have no reason to fear, Jade. You will recognise it when it comes, my dear.'

'Okay, well, do you know when it will happen?'

Sally continues looking deeply at the cards. 'It's all about the relationship the cards have to each other, Jade. The Magician symbolises the manifestation of desires, so this change may even be starting now. It seems this is about trust – a shift in your ability to trust which enables you to manifest what you really want. I feel that it has something to do with water as well. Does that mean anything to you?'

Water? I hate water. Bad things happen in water, even when it looks calm. It's so powerful. Why would I have a new beginning with water?

Suddenly, there are footsteps behind me.

I leap out of my skin as a hand lands on my shoulder.

'Woah, Jade! You're jumpy. It's only me.' I turn around to find myself staring up at Alex's face. 'I just thought you'd been in here a while.' He turns to Sally, who looks pretty pissed off at the interruption. 'How's it going?'

'I was just explaining that Jade's cards are very strong,' she replies, flatly. 'But interruptions may well affect the accuracy of this reading.'

'Right. Well, I'll just be outside when you're ready then.' Alex knows when he's not welcome. He squeezes my shoulder then turns to walk out.

'Wait!' I shout, a little louder than I'd planned, still staring Sally in the eye. I spin round and jump out of my chair. 'I think I'm done, I'll come with you.' I turn hurriedly back to Sally. 'Thaaanks!' I say, voice shaking. I accidentally knock the pile of cards over as I go, chasing Alex back to the safety of the sunshine.

As I reach the fabric-laden archway, I notice a few cards that I knocked over have followed me. The High Priestess and the Lovers lie face up on the floor and one is stuck to my shoe. As I peel it away I instantly recognise it from just moments before: the Death card.

I throw it back towards Sally. It flies like a Frisbee in her direction before turning, as though captured by a breeze, to head back towards me.

I race out of the door and fly down the steps, bashing straight into Alex.

'You okay?' he asks.

'I think so,' I reply. But it's a lie. 'The Death card followed me.' I look to him for reassurance.

'What d'you mean, it "followed" you?'

'I mean, when I ran out, it came with me – it stuck to me!'

'Well, did she explain what that means?'

'No, I ran out before she could tell me. She did say we were looking at past, present and future.'

'Okay, I don't really get what any of that means?'

'Which one do you think the card relates to?' I ask.

'Eeerrrm, I dunno,' Alex replies, shrugging a little.

'Because it felt like she could see into my soul and . . . what if she knows about things like that?'

'Things like what?'

'Like . . . if I'm gonna die! Or if someone you know has

died,' I whisper, looking left and right to make sure no one is listening in.

'Isn't that kind of why you went in there?' he asks.

'Yeah, maybe. I don't know!' Perhaps I didn't think this through properly. 'I guess, but I just didn't think it would be so scary.'

'Okay, well, if she can see into the future, it's not a big surprise that she'd see death, is it? We're all gonna die eventually, right?' he reassures me.

'I hadn't thought about it like that.'

'And I doubt you have anything to worry about when it comes to the past, do you?' He chuckles now.

'I guess not,' I reply, trying to chuckle too.

'You don't, do you, Jade?' he quizzes.

Maybe I wasn't very convincing.

'Well, no, not really,' I try again.

'What do you mean, not really?' He's looking nervous now and he clenches his jaw. 'Did you lose someone? Like, your nan or something?'

'I did lose one, yeah. They weren't that old.' He looks at me, saying nothing but pressing for more with his eyes. 'They were really young actually. It was when I was little – when we were little.'

Why does this happen around him? I can't stop my mouth from saying almost everything in my head. But I have to stop this time. I can't tell him the one thing that I'm certain will send him running. We were just starting to feel close.

Alex stares back at me, a frown crossing his brow for a second. 'Oh, I'm sorry. That sounds horrible.' Why. Is. He. So. Nice?

'Yeah, it was. And I know any kind of death is horrible, but no one saw it coming and we were so young, and it was just . . .' I stop myself.

'You can tell me what happened, y'know. You've got a lot to deal with already – you don't wanna have this swirling round your head too.'

'I know, but . . .'

'A problem shared and all that. Sometimes, just saying things out loud makes them feel easier.'

'Well, it's just that, I could tell that Sally knew, like she saw all the bad stuff from before. She saw me, like inside me – all the good, but all the bad too.'

'Okay, but, Jade, we all have some bad. You're no worse than anybody else.'

'You don't know that,' I reply, matter-of-factly. 'You don't know me yet, Alex. I know deep down I'm a good person but that doesn't mean I've always done good things.'

'But that's just like anyone, Jade.'

'No, it's not. Everyone hasn't . . .'

'Hasn't what? Is this about when you said earlier, that sometimes you hurt people?'

'No, nothing like that. When I'm sick, I'd never hurt anyone, just maybe their feelings. But when I was little, a horrible thing happened. With me and Lexi . . . she was playing, at least I think she was, then someone, well, not just someone . . . someone we knew, they . . . well, Alex, they died.'

CHAPTER 18

LEXI

I wake up to a special kind of back ache. I roll over but the new position is just as painful. After I got home, on a night bus that took a millennium and smelt of kebab, I came to sleep in Kylie. I thought that as I'm struggling to make sense of anything maybe she could trigger some journey back in time to remember what happened. I feel like I'm having to put a jigsaw puzzle together without seeing the picture on the front of the box.

I think back to seeing Sam and Alex. I can't believe the shitbags avoided me. If they thought that was a clever move, then they're not as smart as I thought. They sure as hell look guilty to me if they're not even willing to come over and say hi in a venue full of people.

Could they . . . be in it together?

It would explain why they're both acting so shifty with me.

What if something happened between Jade and Alex? He lost it then killed her, but needed Sam to help him cover his tracks? That's why Sam left the sorry note! Or I was right before, and Sam's the ringleader? He really didn't seem to like us very much at the festival. Alex stepped in to help Sam and now he's in too deep to admit the truth. But then, why did Alex point the finger at me at the vinyl shop? Was he just trying to throw me off their scent?

There's still one small problem though.

I can't explain *my* T-shirt with *her* blood on it.

UNLESS . . . one of them planted it in my bag?

Whatever happened, I'm getting closer. I can *feel* it. I finally get what Jade meant when she talked about following your intuition. And judging from their reaction at The Forum, they know I'm onto them too. Otherwise, why run away like that? I get that my chats with them at the record store and Jade's grave didn't exactly go well, but not enough for them to blank me.

Last night, I left my seat during the encore and waited in the foyer for them while everyone poured out of the venue. I was there until a security guard told me to leave when I was literally the last person in the building, aside from the people working there. That can only mean one thing: the boys left before Coach Riot finished their set to avoid me again.

I wriggle up and push the sleeping bag down towards my knees. The half-moon on my wrist flashes into view. Urgh. It's a constant reminder I'm a terrible friend. I touch it with a fingertip, softly at first, then I rub it angrily. I wish it could disappear!

All I do is make the skin redder.

Red. Red. Red.

Everywhere.

I reach for my phone so I can go online to see if Alex has posted anything. I'm thinking if he uploaded any photos or stories from the gig, he might've tagged Sam then I'll easily be able to find his social media account. My fingers wrap around the handset as I pull the cracked screen towards me, only to see the state it's in – far, far away from 100%!

Everything inside me triggers into action. The phone wobbles as my trembling fingers struggle to keep still and my palpitations begin beating like I've just had a gallon of Monster energy drink pumped into my veins. How could I let the battery get this bad?

Bad things happen when it's below 100%.

I scramble out the sleeping bag fully, then lurch forward to unzip Kylie. I tug so quick that the zip gets stuck. Every last atom of air is sucked out of my lungs.

Panic. Is. RiiisSSIINGGG.

Breathe, Lex. Breathe.

I've forgotten how!

I fiddle the zip back into position then yank again. If I don't charge this now and Mum dies, it will be my fault. This time it works and I manage to open the door. The breeze swoops in to dislodge the sweaty air inside as I rush out and abandon the tent, the moist grass making my socks soggy. I reach the sliding doors – gasping for breath as if I have asthma – and scurry through the living room into the kitchen towards the table. I emptied my pockets here last night before eating cold shepherd's pie as it was late and I was too tired after the gig to count before using the microwave to heat the food up.

I can see the wristband, my eyeliner, some chewing gum . . . My heartbeat is speeding like a heist getaway car. I bend down to peek under the table. I look on the counter by the kettle. I know it's not in my room as I didn't go upstairs last night so I wouldn't wake Mum.

Wheezing, I run into the hallway and look in my DMs in case I dumped it in a shoe, even wiggling them about and turning each boot upside down just to be sure. I head back to the kitchen and open the everything-drawer to rifle for a spare, though there's nothing but Sellotape, old bills and dried superglue bottles that aren't super or gluey anymore.

I pick up the landline, palms shaking so much it makes me dizzy just to look at them, and dial Mum's mobile. Only, I don't know her number!

I've never needed to.

It just lives in my phone. And I can't use it right now or I'll kill more battery.

I take the landline and race up to my room to open my laptop. I type Mum's name and the newspaper into Google, though no direct phone number appears. I have no choice but to dial the generic one for the paper. It rings for an eternity. I'm pacing and counting, pacing and counting, as I finally get through to switchboard and they connect me to her line.

'Hello, news desk,' Mum *finally* answers.

'Where is it?' I reply.

'Lex, is that you?' she says, confused. 'How was last night?'

'Mum, where did you put it?'

'Put what, darling?'

'My charger!'

'Charger?'

'I left it on the kitchen table!'

'Oh. Wait.' I can hear her rustling through her things. 'That was yours? Ah, yes. It's here. Silly me. I've got one stuck in the office wall and one in my bag.'

'I need it,' I say.

'Well, I'll bring it home with me later.'

'But I need it *now!*' I beg.

'You'll just have to wait—'

I hang up and I scream until my throat is raw.

'Are you okay?' Petra asks. I'm sure she can sense I am not in fact okay.

'Not sure.' I shrug, staring down at my mobile. 'Can I borrow your charger?'

'Sure, if mine fits yours. Hand it over – there's a socket right here.' She waves her short but manicured green fingernails at me. They look like shiny M&Ms.

'Thank you.' I hand her the phone feeling jittery, praying that she doesn't look at it and see my crazy staring back at her. It takes all of a nanosecond before she does, then I watch as her brain catches up with what her eyes are seeing.

'The battery is on 94%,' Petra states, although it sounds like a question.

I don't say anything.

'You know it's fully charged?' she says.

'It's not,' I mutter under my breath.

'Hmm?'

'It's not fully charged,' I repeat.

'Very nearly, no?' She looks at me with her head tilted to one side, beckoning me to say more even though I'm pretty sure she's figured it all out.

'Pleeease, can you charge it?' I find myself begging in frustration.

'Do you want to talk about it?'

'No.'

'It might be helpful?'

I shake my head.

'That's okay. Perhaps I can offer a few thoughts of my own?' Petra uncrosses her cropped pinstripe-trousered legs and sits back in her armchair.

'Sure, whatever,' I say, the heat under my skin burning and spreading like wildfire. She still hasn't plugged in the charger.

'I'm noticing, not just from today but some of our other sessions, that maybe there's a need to focus on your phone in some way. Does that sound fair?'

I wriggle in my seat.

'Every so often we do things to distract ourselves from what's going on in our lives. It feels like the distractions help in the short-term, so that we don't have to feel our feelings, although—'

'I don't want to feel my feelings,' I butt in.

'Sometimes, neither do I,' says Petra. 'It's just when we bury our feelings, and our emotions get pushed down, we tend to create more trauma instead of healing.'

'I . . . I don't know what to say.' I squirm.

'You don't have to say anything.' She pauses. 'How about if we leave emotions aside and instead I ask you to name one thing you feel when you're with your phone?'

Silence balloons around us. I want to tell Petra so badly, but I know how mental it sounds. It's not normal that when my phone isn't fully charged it feels like the wind is being crushed out my lungs, that when it's charging it feels like I'm being resuscitated, and only when it reaches 100% I can breathe again.

'Safe,' I eventually say, '. . . but only when it's fully charged.'

Petra smiles. 'It's really good that you've identified that. And what about when you're without your phone – what then?'

'I don't know,' I say, flustered.

'Okay, that's fine. Often when we say, "I don't know", it's not that we don't know but that we're not ready to know yet.'

'Can I get it back?' I ask. I've realised that no matter how nice she is, Petra is not going to indulge me by plugging my phone in. She looks at me hesitantly but hands it over. I keep it on airplane mode, turn the brightness way down to save battery, then pocket it.

'Thank you,' she says, acknowledging I've put my armour away. Now I sit exposed.

'Do you believe in psychics?' I say, changing the subject. Right now, thinking of justice for Jade is the only thing keeping me together.

I know how much she believed in 'the other side' and that people 'with a gift' can help the living connect with the dead. I was never a believer before, but . . . the dreams, her pills, the shopping channel, the rainbow – maybe they *are* signs. If I find a psychic who can chat to spirits, they might help. Cos what if Jade really *can* reveal what happened.

'Well . . .' Petra takes a moment to think about her answer. It tells me everything I need to know. 'I'm not sure if it's a case of believing, but I know they help some people.'

'I was thinking of maybe going to see one.'

'Okay.' Petra nods. 'What might you want to ask?'

'I dunno,' I say, honestly. 'To try to find out what happened.'

'That condolences card you showed me,' Petra says. I sense she's trying to lead us away from the spirit world and back into the land of the living.

'The confession?' I correct her.

'Mmhmm.' Petra doesn't argue. 'From the card, it sounds like other people who knew her are struggling too. Do you speak to any other friends who were with you at the festival?'

'I'm trying,' I say, 'what makes you ask that?'

'It's always good to have more than one person to chat to. I just wonder who else you are speaking to outside these walls.'

'It's only ever been me and Jade.'

'What about any other acquaintances, even if they weren't best friends?'

'There was this one other girl at school for a bit—' I say, boomeranging down memory lane.

'Could you reach out to her?'

'Not really, no.'

'I guess that's why I'm asking: now Jade's gone, who do you talk to?'

'I like talking to you,' I say, candidly.

'I like talking to you, too.' Petra smiles.

Silence swells again. I'm kind of in love with Petra. I wish she could be my friend.

'Do you think it's worth persevering with your festival friends?' Petra says, and it's clear even away from this room me and her can never be proper mates.

'It's just, I don't think Alex and Sam like me much,' I offer up. 'And Cassie ignores my texts! I guess I could try Jonesy. See what he says?'

'Sounds good. You never know, he might help you find what you're looking for.'

CHAPTER 19

JADE

'Lex!?' I jump out of my skin for the second time in minutes as she pops into my vision beside Psychic Sally's caravan.

'Alright?' she asks.

'Erm, well, I just saw Psychic Sally. It was a bit scary, Lex.'

'That kind of thing is always gonna be scary, Jade.'

'No, Lexi . . . the Death card followed me all the way out of the door!' I whisper. 'Like, all the way! I had to grab it and throw it back. Death stuck to me! What d'you think that means?' I ask. She must be thinking about Emily too, right?

'I dunno what it means. What does any of that stuff mean? They make it all up. Don't get yourself spun out over it.' Is she trying to be reassuring, or dismissing me?

I look back at her, hoping for more; it doesn't come. Well, not about *that* anyway.

'I searched all over for your meds, but I couldn't see them anywhere. You'll be okay without them though, right?' It sounds as if she doesn't really want an answer other than 'yes'.

'Oh yeah, I think I'm gonna be fine.' I beam at Lex, trying to convince myself more than anyone else.

Cassie, Jonesy and Sam arrive at the caravan too. I turn to Alex, hoping he's okay, but he won't look back at me. Is half the story worse than the whole one? Now he probably thinks I'm crazy and dangerous. And just when I thought it couldn't get worse, it does . . .

'Oh hey, wanna see what we just had done?' Cassie bounds over. 'Tattoos! We just thought, "Fuck it!" Didn't we, Lex?'

Wait . . . Lexi had a tattoo with Cassie?

No. We talked about it. She said she was gonna wait.

We all gather in a circle as Cassie stretches her arm out, at waist height, into the middle of the group. She turns her wrist over, so the inside points upwards. Inked into the middle of it is a detailed half-moon.

'Oh wow!' I respond, as enthusiastically as I possibly can. Cassie nods, reaching out her other hand to wrap it around Lexi's forearm. She pulls it over towards her own so they're side by side. Cassie spins Lexi's skinny little wrist around, into the same position as hers, and right there in the centre of it is the other half of Cassie's moon. My eyes fly up to look at Lex's expression. She smiles but I can see she's masking panic behind her eyes. She knew that was gonna hurt me, didn't she? Why did she do it?

It's taking most of Eva Skowl's set to make it through the crowd and we're missing all her good songs. As we push through, multiple people grab at my hair, even though it's mostly covered by my bandana. By the third time, I feel rage bubble up from my feet. I can't control it anymore. I stop in my tracks, spin around and before I know it, I'm asking.

'What was that for!?' I say, more blunt than I'd ever imagined I could be.

'I just wanted to know if it was a wig,' a random guy replies idiotically.

'And do you know now!?' I snap back, rolling my eyes and turning to walk away, the anger becoming nerves. My mind races; was I out of line? Maybe I should have just carried on, not made a fuss, he was probably just drunk, probably didn't mean it.

'What was that?' Alex asks, surprised, looking back at me as though he's trying to figure out a riddle while still leading us all forward. I flounder, searching for an explanation.

'That was racism,' Cassie interjects from behind me, 'and it was a badass challenging it.' I turn and she flashes me a reassuring look.

I guess I did the right thing then, so why do I feel so weird still? I can't stop my thoughts racing or the shaking in my legs. What if that guy comes for me? What about the cards that followed me out of the caravan? Could they be a warning?

We finally make it and my chest is pressed up against the metal barrier, right in front of the stage. Security guards look over the top of me, eyeing the Get Lost-ers living their best lives in the sun. Alex's arms are either side of me now, his hands wrapped around the top of the barriers to prop him up. His body acts as a human shield, protecting me from the crowd behind – or maybe it's protecting them from me? Eva's mesmerising, sort of witch-like, draped in layers of cream floaty fabric, like the ones that hang from Sally's caravan.

Eva's midriff is exposed as she struts and stamps around the stage, clutching her microphone with two hands. Her straight jet-black hair with neon yellow highlights parts just enough to show her eyes as she sings, which seem to flash neon yellow too. She gestures skyward like an angel. I gaze up – the oranges and pinks are beautiful as the sun sinks lower in the sky. White patterns against the blue sky aren't quite clouds – they're sort of dancing lines that look like they're forever swirling.

Eva turns her back on the crowd as if she's about to be pulled up into a vortex that will catapult her into the sky where she belongs. Her band leave the stage and her digital backdrop switches to reveal Kreep's logo, the band coming up next.

The crowd around us disperses, and Sam and Cassie head off to the bar even though it feels like we only just found a good spot. I decide to seize my moment now that Lexi is alone as Alex chats to Jonesy nearby. I reach over to grab her face in my hands, turning her head round so that she has no choice but to focus on me.

'Ha! You okay, babes?' she asks, surprised by my hand around her chops.

'Yeah, I'm great,' I reply, falsely. 'We're not alright though, are we? You're pissed at me about something. What is it?'

'What?' she asks. Is that faux confusion? 'Oh, Cassie asked if we want wine. I said yeah, thought we could get on it while

Kreep play?' Classic change the subject tactic. It's not gonna be that easy I'm afraid.

'Cool. So, you didn't get that tattoo with Cassie cos you're mad at me?'

'What? Jade, a tattoo for being mad at someone? That doesn't make any sense,' she replies. 'Anyway, why would I be mad at you?'

We're interrupted by a wave of cheers erupting around us as Kreep walk out to play their first track. Soon, we're getting crushed against the barrier as everyone behind us surges forward. The drummer's sticks click four times and we're smothered in a cushion of guitars, synths, drums and bass that rumbles my chest. All the noise and chaos outside fills me up inside, igniting something I haven't felt for years. A buzz. A tingle. Oh, I've missed that tingle. This is what I didn't wanna miss out on because of those stupid pills . . . I don't need them, do I? My headache's nearly gone now anyway.

I turn around to look at the crowd. I can't see further than a few rows back, but I know there are thousands of people around me, thousands of faces. Probably some of them the Fool, some Magicians and probably some Death cards too. But . . . you can't live in fear, can you? Try to catch me, Death – I bet you can't. I'm much smarter than you think.

I spot Cassie weaving back through the crowd with Sam, trying desperately not to spill the drinks as they go. The sun is going down, the sky's like a painting and the stage lights fill me with excitement. Drinks are passed around, Lexi unscrews the top from a plastic wine bottle, and as she takes the first sip – well, glug – she bounces around to the beat of 'Tonight' from Kreep's last album.

I dance with Lexi and feel the acidic burn of wine trickling down my throat. It tastes grim, worse than the cider, but I don't want to feel left out.

'Jade! Come here,' Jonesy yells. 'Can you see?'

'Not really, but that's okay!' I scream back. I'm concentrating hard on my dancing, feeling the music racing through my body, amplifying the buzz.

'Nah! Come here.' He's tapping his shoulders. 'I'll lift you up!'

'Oh my God, awesome!' I shout back.

He squats down, and Lexi gives me a boost, making a little stirrup out of her hands.

Once I've successfully plonked my bum on his shoulders and my legs flop onto his muscular chest, Lexi passes me the wine bottle. I take a sip just as Jonesy draws himself up to full standing height and my teeth take a bash.

I am on top of the world now. Literally, head and shoulders above everybody else. The sky is in touching distance and my arms spring up of their own accord, trying to reach the purple-blue.

As if it wasn't already perfect, mine and Lex's favourite song starts to play. I scream every word of 'Parties' at the top of my lungs as though I'm forcing all those fizzy feelings out of me. I stare into the frontman's eyes. I'm willing Trent to notice me – it's probably only a matter of time. And it happens! I hear him say: 'Wow! You know every word!'

And now he's looking right back at me. We share an electric connection.

'Woah, you sang the whole song word perfectly!' Trent adds, the cluster of tattoos around his eyes and cheekbones framing his smile.

The crowd cheers for me, and my face pops up on the huge screens either side of the stage for the thousands of people behind me to see.

'I love you!' I scream at Trent, waving my arms in the air as fellow festivalgoers whoop and laugh at my delight.

'And give it up for whoever's shoulders you're sitting on! You guys are coming backstage later!' Trent turns to the side of the stage for a second and says something away from the mic. When he comes back to address the crowd again, he adds, 'Marty will come and get you after the show.'

I look down at Lexi. Her eyes are wide as she stares back up at me. 'What the fuuuuuuckk!?' she mouths, as the next song begins. I dance on Jonesy's shoulders, singing at the sky in pure unadulterated bliss.

My cheeks start to tingle, from the wine, I think.

Everything looks hazy, the lights starting to blur into each other. My head is light and heavy all at the same time and I feel a bit dizzy again, like this morning. Jonesy must be getting tired cos he bends down to place me gently back to earth. As Kreep head towards the end of their set, all I can think about is what backstage is gonna be like.

'Marty will be here soon. Don't go anywhere,' one of the security guards shouts over to us, holding his hand to his earpiece. So we wait as the throng of people head to the bar or their tents or to DJs and the field becomes ever emptier.

'Purple girl and friends?' comes a voice from the left. I spin around and see a middle-aged man with curly salt and pepper hair who's still wearing sunglasses, like *he's* the rock star. 'Mike will help you over the barrier and then I'll take you to meet the guys.'

After climbing the barriers and stumbling a little, we all wait to be instructed. The sunglasses man walks over.

'Hi, I'm Marty, Kreep's tour manager. Come on, the guys can't wait to meet you.'

'Sure,' I reply, as the others try to look cool even though they're already stanning.

'Yeah, they love to meet real fans.' He scrabbles in his pockets for something and pulls out a tangle of fabric and plastic. 'We'll head back there, get you all some drinks, and then bring the lads out to meet you. Purple girl, sorry, what's your name?'

'Jade,' I reply.

'So, Jade . . . and was it your shoulders she was on?' He gestures towards Jonesy.

'Yeah, I'm Ryan.'

'Ryan?' I laugh at how formal he's being. 'He's Jonesy.'

'Right, nice, well . . .' He hands me the lanyard tangle. 'Put these on, then.' We hang the fabric chains around our necks. The dangling card displays the letters *AAA* in bold.

'Access All Areas,' Marty says, with a wry smile. 'This is where the real festival's at. Everyone follow me.'

We follow in a line along the length of the stage. It's so high when you're stood this close, it towers over my head. It even towers over Alex's. Eventually, we reach the dark green panels that keep fans away from the celebs. Marty bangs on a secret door disguised in the panelling which pops open and he shows his pass to the security guard, ducking to walk through to the other side.

I turn to Lex. She smiles as I show my pass to the security guard just like Marty did. I go to step through, but the guard stops me.

'Can't bring your drink back here,' she says, matter-of-factly.

'Oh! Okay!' I say, flustered.

'Don't worry, we'll get you a drink this side,' Marty offers, and I pass the wine bottle to the guard. Only then am I allowed through to the other side. The others obviously finished their bottles ages ago, so they walk right in.

And just like that, we're in a whole new festival world.

There's a tiki bar . . . without a queue! Deckchairs and inflatable palm trees are laid out on what looks like an unspoilt tropical beach. There's a stage with DJs playing. Everyone walking around is. So. Well. Dressed. They don't look like they've slept in tents or had to shower in a sweat box this morning. Their tattoos are real like Lex's and Cassie's, not henna like mine. There are hardly any wellies in sight – just gladiator sandals and heeled wedges!

'Let me just go tell the boys you're here.' Marty heads off towards some Portacabins in the distance. I stare at Jonesy, who stares right back at me.

'Jade, this is fucking nuts! Who's got battery on their phone? No one's gonna believe this happened if we don't get evidence.' I fumble around in the pocket of my cycle shorts while Jonesy's still talking. 'Look, there's a bar over here. Let's get drinks.'

'Oh, I don't . . .'

'Jade, I'm gonna need you to stop being such a buzzkill.' Jonesy laughs. 'We're at a festival; we're backstage. We're here to have fun, so just have a bloody drink, will you?'

I eyeroll at him. 'Alrriiight, but you're gonna have to help me find something I actually like the taste of!'

'Now that I can do,' Jones replies, clapping his hands together excitedly.

We head over to the bar and the others follow us. Jonesy orders a lager and a cider, some white wine, some Prosecco, something called a snakebite, and lots of sambuca.

'Woah, Jonesy . . . isn't that a bit much?' I ask.

'You said you weren't gonna be a square, Jade.'

'It's just that . . . no judgement, but how can you drink all that?'

'I'm not gonna drink all that . . . *we're* gonna drink all that.' He winks at me. 'Welcome to your crash course in booze!' He throws his head back and belly laughs.

When the bartender comes back over to deliver the final drinks of the order, Jonesy whips out his bank card ready to tap it against a contactless machine, but is met by a flat-raised hand and a head shake.

'It's a free bar back here, mate,' the barman replies. Jonesy's eyes pop open wide as though he's just been told he's entered heaven. He orders a couple more pints for good measure as Cass, Sam, Lexi and Alex get in on the action too by ordering a few extras.

There's an all-black figure in the distance walking towards me, surrounded by others in a flying V formation.

Jonesy grabs me. 'Oh my days, Jade! It's happening.'

'Yeah, it is!' I reply.

As he gets closer to us, Trent throws his arms wide like we're long-lost friends and he's saying, 'Ah man, I've missed you guys.' What he actually says is, 'D'you guys enjoy the show?'

'It was awesome,' I say.

'Yeah, it was an awesome show!' repeats Jonesy.

'Glad you think so.' Trent turns to his bandmates as they order drinks. 'Make mine a whiskey, Dave.'

Dave? Cute name for a mega star.

Dave soon saunters over, handing the whiskey to Trent, then runs that same hand through his blond hair before a smile crosses his elfin features. His locks tumble forward again almost immediately, like silk, landing perfectly in line with his chiselled cheekbones that frame his face. Jonesy carries on the chat, which is handy, because I can't seem to stop my mind from racing. Sally's tarot cards jump into view, each one flapping in the breeze that I don't only feel on my skin but see their card design in my mind's eye too.

Lex's hands cup my face, and when her hands are gone her piercing eyes stare into mine. She says hi to the band, cool as a cucumber, then checks back in with me. 'C'mon, Jadey, let's go to the bathroom. Back in a bit, guys.'

She turns to me once no one's around and waves the lanyard around her neck now. 'Can. You. Believe. This?' she asks.

'Absolutely, 100% I can, yeah!' I laugh. 'I was looking at Trent, and I told him, "We're where the party's at."' I press my lanyard against hers.

'You "told" him?'

'Yeah, with my eyes and my thoughts. Like, connection is powerful, Lexi. I knew I could get him to see us. I just had to get the cosmos to make the connection.'

'Okay,' she replies, looking a little sceptical.

But it's okay if she doesn't get it, cos she's got me, and I get it, and things are starting to happen. So eventually she'll believe it.

We make our way up the steps to the fanciest Portaloos I've ever seen. The surfaces are gleaming white and brightly lit, which makes it almost impossible to see anything, like when you open your curtains in the morning and are blinded by the daylight. I squint one eye at a time, trying to get accustomed. There's a scented candle burning next to the sink that smells like Mum's day-long Saturday relax-a-thons.

We instinctively head into one cubicle together, even though there are three available, and take it in turns to pee. 'Hurgh!' retches Lexi. The blue liquid inside the toilet bowl overpowers any scent from the candle, the chemicals racing up our noses to make us heave.

As we fling the door open again, we're greeted by our reflections in the mirrors that fill the wall behind the sinks.

'Wow! We look really bad!' I gasp.

'I thought it might be bad. But not *this* bad,' Lex says.

There are panda eyes, flyaway hairs that somehow look both ratty and voluminous, and sallow skin lurking beneath patches of glitter. My lips look even crispier than they feel, and my bandana has slipped backwards so my curls poke out both at the front and back.

'Oh no!' I giggle. 'I thought this looked really chic!' I flap my arms in a bid to grab the back of the bandana and pull it off my head. I begin waving the scarf around, trying to refold it, but it's much more slippery now it's not cloaked in humidity like it was this morning. I catch my reflection. She's behaving like a butterfly caught on a gust of wind in summertime, unable to figure out which direction she's flying in. It dawns on me how ridiculous I look, and I double over in fits of laughter. Lex immediately does the same.

'Okay, now don't tell anyone,' Lexi says in hushed tones whilst she unzips the top of her black, studded belt bag. 'I've got something for you.' She pulls out a small packet.

'Something for me?' I reply.

'Yes.'

'What is it?'

'Well, that's what I'm trying to tell you. It's a secret – you can't tell anyone.'

'I won't,' I respond, flatly. But will I? Accidentally? Like I've told Alex everything else?

'I know the boys think "eating's cheating",' Lex continues, 'but I had a feeling you might need a little something to keep you going, so . . .'

The foil wrapping to an oat Valley Crunch bar glistens like a gem in the light.

'Oh, I LOVE YOU!' I yell. 'But I'm not hungry.'

'You're not? That's not like you,' she replies.

'Yeah, I guess. It's cool – you have it, babe.'

Lex unwraps the bar and snaps it into bite-sized chunks. She chews quickly at first but I can tell that as her mouth becomes drier, chewing becomes increasingly difficult.

'Wait. You need water,' I say. I reach for the tap and cup my hands underneath the flow. She leans forward to place her lips to the puddle of water I'm now holding. Lex slurps for a second but that doesn't work too well so she begins to lap the water up with her tongue. It's a surprisingly effective way of drinking.

'You alright, Jade?' comes a voice from outside. It's Alex, stood at the bottom of the steps looking in. How long has he been there?

'Haven't you heard of privacy!?' Lexi teases. 'The gents are that way,' she instructs, pointing to the right. She turns to me as he heads dutifully in the other direction. 'Okay, let's clean ourselves up and get back to the others.'

I dig around in my bra for my lip balm and smear it over my lips. I rub a bit under my eyes too and then smudge the panda-ness out into some sort of winged liner. I hit the tap again and rub water through the back of my hair – Nan always said hydration is key – then place the now perfectly folded headscarf in a triangle on top of my head, passing two of the points under my curls to tie them in a knot. Finally, I pull out my afro comb from the pocket of my cycle shorts and fluff the underside.

'Okay!' I turn to Lexi, who's taking the exact opposite approach – applying more eyeliner and creating more hair volume at the root by shaking it upside-down. She flips herself back up the right way again and teases strands between her fingers. Perfectly dishevelled. 'We look great . . . let's go!'

Lex turns, giving me a little wink. She spins on her heel to head back down the steps.

I follow, my head spiralling about all the characters we're about to meet. There's bound to be a Fool here, Death, a

Magician. 'Do your worst, cards – you're no match for me!'

'What are you talking about?' asks Lexi at the bottom of the steps.

Oh, I said it out loud.

'Nothing,' I reply. But really I'm planning how I'll fight them all off when the time's right.

CHAPTER 20

LEXI

I'm trying on my new dress. Jade picked it, saying yellow will suit me and I should 'ditch black today'. I'm not really a dress kinda girl but I told her I'd try it, to make her happy cos it's her birthday and she's having a party. Outside in the garden, there's a bouncy castle. She's turning 17 but all the balloons and unicorn cake say *Happy 8th Birthday*.

The dress is on, and Jade zips me up. She takes me by the hand and leads me over to the full-length mirror. I'm excited to check out my look . . . but something weird happens in the reflection – my daffodil-yellow dress turns red.

I hear a scream.

'BAD OMEN!'

It's Jade.

Suddenly, it's not only the dress that's changing colour.

I watch in horror as my skin turns blue. Not blue like a blueberry, or blue like a summer sky, but a faded blue like jeans that have been washed too many times.

We're both screaming now.

Jade is pawing at my face, trying frantically to pull the blue skin off to reveal my real skin beneath. Her hands are like claws and her nails dig in. She manages to peel back the top layer to expose my peach flesh, though within seconds, the skin is blue again!

Each time my real skin reappears, the blue flesh grows back. It hurts as Jade keeps scraping and scratching, doing the same thing on repeat. As she's mauling me, I feel a rustle and my eyelids fly open. The sensation on my cheek is actually a Post-it note on my pillow – not Jade's fingers.

I take a giant sigh of relief that the bad dream is over.

My brain!

What is going on in there?

I wait a minute for my psycho heart palpitations and trembling body to chill, then pick up the paper that Mum must've left if she got home late while I was sleeping.

Sorry, honey – charger on beanbag. I've booked hols next week!!
Xxx

Instantly, I leap up from under the covers and pounce over to the beanbag where the charger glistens like a shooting star. Now I've got it back, I can use my phone again.

I can't help but feel like an idiot after nearly confessing to Petra. I know she's there to help me but saying these things aloud makes me sound bananas. I don't care what anyone says about mental health and that it's okay to not be okay. The truth is no one wants to be around crazy. No one knows what to say to me anymore and I don't know how to be around people either. And all the rubbish quotes like *This too shall pass*. Urgh!

It WON'T pass.

Jade is *never* coming back.

I plug the handset in and feel my soul twitch back to life in tandem with the mobile resurrecting from its slow death. Then I click onto socials and search @JonesysBalls.

Jonesy's face lights up my screen. Or rather, his muddy thighs and calves – all his pictures are mid-run with a rugby ball or in huddles with arms around teammates. There are a few photos with shiny medals or him lifting a trophy, and one of the lads all in suits at a posh charity event. There are still no new posts since I last looked when I was at The Forum.

I stare at his profile a little longer so I can read his bio.

Act like a gent. Play like a beast. @ScorpionScrummers prop forward.

I press the Insta account he's linking to. A rush of images appears – more players in flight as they're captured spreadeagled in the air or sliding across the grass. The last post was uploaded just minutes ago with *GAME DAY* printed across it and details of the match below. I scan it quicker than my eyes will let me, having to go back to re-read what I've seen. It's a home match this afternoon and it's showing the Scorpion Scrummers' grounds are right by the Heath! I can walk it from my house.

I try to make myself look presentable, given I've not showered or brushed my hair since Coach Riot. I just don't really see the point of looking nice anymore. Who would I be doing it for, anyways? Myself when I catch my reflection in the mirror? Mum, so she can look at her daughter without wondering if she's going to have a mental breakdown?

After I look less like the possessed doll from *Chucky* and a little more like me, I head out. It takes less than thirty minutes to reach the Heath. I wish I'd come here sooner. It might've saved me a trip to the vinyl store. Jonesy might even know why Sam is being so shady with me.

I walk along the grass, feeling an anxious buzz at the prospect of seeing Jonesy again. I follow the grunts and whistles to find the boys playing on the field. I edge a little closer, counting my steps, but it's hard to see who's who with all of them either running around or clustered together. A bunch of them are wearing headgear which is obscuring their faces even more.

Nope. Can't see him!

My belly somersaults – I don't even know if he's playing today.

I keep hunting for Jonesy in amongst the pack, scanning the players for his face or to try to recognise his body. It's harder than I thought it'd be, without his festival uniform of glitter and neon so easily visible. Instead I'm faced with grubby shorts, long socks and boots.

I head over to the gaggle of girlfriends, parents and younger siblings who watch from the side of the pitch and try to mingle. I ache when I hear their conversations: planning what takeaways they're ordering later, what colour their gel nails are, and what reality shows are on tonight. It all sounds so ordinary and I can tell they don't realise how lucky they are as they chat over their Pringles. All smiles and giggles and not-dead friends. I want to tell them, 'Please don't ever take normal for granted. You'll miss it when it's gone.'

I distract myself by continuing to skim my gaze across the

pitch, praying he's out there and I'm not the world's worst detective.

There are legs, arms and bums everywhere.

I try to focus from the right side of the field and work my way left, desperately attempting to keep up with the players as they move out of alignment with my eyes. The sound of cheering erupts around me and shrieks of, 'Go Scorpions!' pierce my eardrums.

I think someone just scored?

The players celebrate, all slapping one another on the back to show their masculinity. They walk to the centre of the pitch before the game continues. And this is when I see . . . There's no mistaking . . . the shoulders, the shaven head, the grin.

I've just found Jonesy.

I'm caught up in the excitement of it all, clapping and whooping along with everyone. Only, the others are applauding the score and I'm celebrating the fact there's a connection to Jade and our final weekend right in front of my eyes. I mimic their chants and hope that if anyone's looking at me, they'll think I know the rules – which I very much don't.

As the game winds down, it's hard not to feel giddy from the carnival vibes here. I've gotta stay focused though, so I do my best to sneak away from the families in case Jonesy's mum or dad happen to be close. I need to get him alone.

I wait for the players to start piling off the pitch, giving each other one-armed hugs. Jonesy chatters with some of them then breaks away as he ties his shoelace. He jogs across the grass solo, and I seize my opportunity.

'Hey!' I say, hands open as if to show him there are no

concealed weapons.

'What the . . . hi! I would hug you, but I stink.' Jonesy laughs.

'Sorry, I should've said I was coming.' I smile, hoping he won't be too mad.

'Ooooooooh,' jeer a group of lads with mud-smeared faces as they stroll past, eyeing me up. Jonesy smirks and takes a play jab in the ribs from one of them.

'How come you're here?' Jonesy says to me.

'Oi, oi, who's getting drinks in after showers?' a voice bellows from behind me.

'It's Harrison's turn!' another shouts, practically into my ear as he passes.

'Harrison, your round, mate!' a third guy roars, high-fiving Jonesy as he goes.

'And a juice for Jonesy!' someone else yells before they all howl with laughter.

'Juice?' I can't help but ask. To say Jonesy drank like a whale at Get Lost would be the understatement of the century. 'Is that code for triple tequila?'

He shakes his head and I can see his mood shifting. 'It's what it sounds like.'

'No booze? Just doesn't seem very . . . you?'

'I've not caned it for a while,' he says, looking small despite his huge build and bulky muscles bulging below the sleeves of his rugby shirt. 'Just prefer not to.'

'But you were the life and soul of the party?'

'You think I don't know that?' he bites, unexpectedly.

'Sorry, I just . . .'

'You think I like being the "boring one" now?'

'I meant it in a nice way.'

'Well, that Jonesy you knew then is not who I am now.'

'Ookaaay,' I say, surprised at the direction this is going. I had wanted to talk to him about Sam and Alex, but now I want to ask about Jade cos it's kinda strange and feels like no coincidence that he's just decided to stop drinking *after* she died.

He seems so . . . uncomfy!

And guarded? Like he's hiding something.

'Soo,' I add, 'who were you then and who are you now?'

'Are you here to interview me?' he says, clearly irritated.

'Well, no, but—'

'But what?' Jonesy pushes.

'Just, when I last saw you at Get Lost, you seemed fine. You got us drinks with your ID. I guess I'm curious what happened to make you not fine. To make you go sober?'

'Last summer, it just really messed with my head.'

'Makes two of us.'

'Sorry.' He softens a little. 'I should've called. I just didn't know what to say.'

'It's fine,' I fib, batting a bumblebee away. 'We're here now . . . When you say it messed with your head—'

'Lex, can we leave it?'

'But it's important.'

'Important for you, maybe.'

'Important for Jade!' I retaliate.

'Okay yeah.' He hesitates, looking over my shoulder. I guess he's checking his teammates are still in the changing room and out of earshot. 'But dwelling on the past won't bring her back.'

'Jesus, Jones.'

'What?'

'You *have* changed. You sound like Sam.'

Suddenly, his hand grips my forearm. He pushes it towards my chest so that my fingers hit against my shoulder, then he looks at my elbow.

'What are you doing?!' I ask, equally confused and surprised.

'See that?'

'What?'

'There.' He points at a scar on my outer forearm where it meets the elbow joint. 'Remember how you got that?'

How does he know about this? I remember the scab taking an age to heal last summer though I never knew why or how it got there in the first place.

'That right there,' Jonesy adds, 'is where I had to pull the glass out.'

'The glass?'

'On the Saturday night – you had a giant shard sticking out of you.'

'Aa . . . aaa . . . at . . . Get Lost?' I stammer.

'Yes, Get Lost, where else?'

'I . . . I did?'

'And given we weren't allowed glass at the campsite, only in the backstage area, then . . .' Jonesy trails off, shrugging.

'What are you saying?'

'I don't know.'

'Yeah, you do.'

'Well, don't you think it's strange how the last time I saw

Jade, she's swigging from a glass bottle, then you somehow end up cut and bloodied . . . and she ends up dead?'

'What are you saying?' I repeat, nervously, just as some lads return from the showers. One of them drapes an arm over Jonesy, then thrusts a bag into his chest.

'Look, we'll do this another time, yeah?' Jonesy says, fishing a T-shirt out of the bag and whipping his rugby shirt off to change into his regular clothes. 'We can meet up.'

'Now is good,' I plead.

'Don't mind us!' a voice comes from the boy-huddle, prompting a wave of chuckles.

'It'll be better away from here,' he says, trying to sound cheery again. He's pulling his T-shirt down to cover his belly and already walking in the other direction.

I give him a *REALLY?* look. 'But this is urgent,' I shout after him.

The lads titter again, and I hear whispers of 'urgent!' as they mock me.

'I promise I'll message later today,' Jonesy says, trying to zip his bag closed as he gets sucked into a cyclone of 'who's that?' ribbing.

I stand like a loner as everyone vanishes, that feeling I had at Coach Riot rushing back. WTF just came out of his mouth – a 'giant shard' sticking out of me?

I bend my arm again to look down near my elbow and examine the bumpy white scar that's several centimetres long. How the hell did it get there?

I feel sick. Soon the numbers fill my head. My mind's noisy, telling me that counting is the only way to stay safe. From

Jonesy? From myself? I don't have a choice. So I count. All the way to today's number. It's not as good as a hug from Jade, but it comforts me.

I finally hit 349 and just when I think it's okay, I'm going again. Onetwothreefour . . . My brain's making me start over for luck and the numbers fly, fly, fly through my mind as I wish, wish, wish that Jade was here. I don't know who to trust or where to run, so I wait helplessly, watching the boys get smaller and smaller as they cross the field.

Just as they're about to disappear, I spy Jonesy's rugby shirt fall on the grass.

'Hey,' I holler, but no one turns around. 'Hey! You dropped something,' I try again, but the boys are on the edge of the Heath where it meets the street, heading to the pub.

I jog over to the shirt and bend down to pick it up, ready to run after them. As I do, something catches my eye. There's a scrawl of black marker pen on the label inside. I guess it's needed in a changing room where everyone has identical kits.

I look down to read it and my stomach knots like a pretzel.

I've been so dumb!

How could I forget Jonesy has a first name?

Suddenly, everything clicks into place.

The name. The freaking name!

It says Ryan Jones.

Ryan.

R.

CHAPTER 21

JADE

We head back to Kreep and the Lost Boys, and Lexi gets chatting to Trent. Dave walks towards me, saying, 'Jonesy asked me to hold onto this for you. His name is Jonesy, right?'

'Oh yeah, that's him, thanks!' I reply and take a sip of whatever's in the cup I'm now holding.

'So you enjoyed the show then?'

'Yeah, it was amazing! I've never seen you guys live before. It was, like, pure energy flying off the stage. So cool.'

'Oh, you think so?' he says, modestly.

'Yeah!' I reassure him.

'I was just saying to Trent in the dressing room that you guys gave us so much love tonight. Especially you – it was amazing to look out and see you singing every word.' He smiles before pushing his hair back again.

'Ha! Why thank you.' I give my hair a little flick to demonstrate I'm feeling myself. 'Mum and Dad don't appreciate my energy at all!'

He laughs back.

'Okay, right, I'm just gonna ask. It'll be super weird if I don't . . .' I say.

'Okay?' He waits, confused, nervous, I think.

'What d'you play? In the band, I mean? I probably sound like an idiot, but mostly I've just seen Trent and then today I was kinda in my own little world dancing and stuff. I just don't know who's who.' I give him a comedy grimace as though I find it awkward when really I don't.

'Haha! Yeah, no one ever recognises the rest of us, but that's just proof we've got the perfect frontman. I don't want anyone to know me anyway – it's a bit of a ball ache being Trent. He can't really go anywhere anymore. I get to wander around the supermarket with a hangover and no one bats an eyelid.'

'Riiight!'

'I play drums, so if you were too busy partying to watch me it means I was doing my job right.' He looks genuinely pleased, his navy-blue eyes twinkling with delight. 'D'you dance a lot? You looked like you knew what you were doing, even on that guy's shoulders.'

'Yeah! My whole family loves to dance – we have parties a lot. We'll turn the music up, my dad will get on the decks like he used to back in the day and we'll boogie all night. It makes me feel properly happy. Y'know, just . . . free.'

'That's so cool.'

'What, the partying parents or the freedom?'

'Err, both!' he replies. 'We're DJ-ing this afterparty in a bit – you should come.'

'Oh cool! In one of the tents? We saw Dance Dance's set last night in the big top.'

'Nice! No, this is more of an afterparty for the bands. It's over by the lake.'

'Oh, yeah . . . the lake is back here, isn't it?' I say, remembering the map from our arrival. We've been edging closer to it all day, but I don't feel scared like normal. I'm stronger today than normal, I can feel it. Like my bones are unbreakable, and my muscles are full of the kind of electricity that lets me know I'm growing. Another pulse of it races from my feet to my head. I'm ready for you, Lake!

'Yeah,' he replies.

Just as Dave is about to tell me more, I feel an arm fall over my shoulder, and I'm pulled into Alex's body whilst he plants a kiss on the top of my head.

'Don't hog the band, Jade!' he says, putting out a hand for Dave to shake. 'I'm Alex.'

'Dave,' says Dave. 'I was just telling Jade how we're gonna play a DJ set over by the lake in a bit. You guys should come.'

'Oh, sweet – yeah, we can swing by for a bit, I guess,' Alex replies, coolly.

'If you're not feeling it, Jade can just come along with her friend – no pressure, man.' A tense energy replaces the easy flow that was there before. Alex isn't replying, he's just staring at Dave. Dave is just staring back. Ew, this is gross.

'Yeah, speaking of . . . I'm gonna go and find Lexi actually,' I announce, turning quickly to escape the tension.

Lex, Cassie, Jonesy and Sam are standing together when I arrive, with Trent holding court. Something about the trials and tribulations of travelling so much. I'm guessing Cassie can relate.

'Oh, shit!' Trent pulls his phone out of his trouser pocket to check the time. 'We need to get to the lake for our DJ set. You guys have to come.' He turns his tattooed face to Lexi, his expression saying, '*you* have to come', before heading towards the band to rally them.

'So we're really gonna do this then?' Lex asks, looking over to me. 'You okay with that?'

'Yeah, I'm fine! It's a once in a lifetime thing, isn't it? And y'know, what's the water gonna do to me anyway? Being here backstage, it's like I know I'm more powerful than I thought – like, I made this happen, against the odds. I can handle a little lake, Lex.'

'Okay, cool.' But Lex looks a little confused.

We make our way through the woods that surround the festival site. The moon is full and crisp white, making it surprisingly easy to see where we're going as we weave our way through pine trees that are beautiful and majestic and so, so tall.

The band are up ahead with their team, Marty leading the way. Alex, Sam and Jonesy are behind them, with Lexi a little way back, followed by Cassie and me. Her energy is different now. Softer. Or maybe mine is just stronger?

'Hair looks good!' she compliments. 'Your own handiwork?'

'Thanks!' I beam. 'Guess I just needed someone to show me.'

'It's easy when you know how,' Cassie replies. 'Why don't you know?' she questions.

'Well . . .' I feel awkward about the confession I'm about to make. 'My mum can't show me. Her hair's different.' I look towards my feet.

'Okay, but you must know someone black who can help?'

'Not really, just my dad but he's clueless. I have aunties, but we don't see them much.'

'Classic,' Cassie says.

'What d'you mean?' I ask, feeling hurt, or annoyed – maybe both. She doesn't know me.

'It's just how it always goes – that's why you don't know about your hair. I bet you don't know the food where your dad's from, or the culture. You're not connected to it. It's not uncommon.'

'I guess, but it's no big deal,' I retort, feeling exposed and like I'd rather talk about anything else.

'But it is. Culturally you're connected to your whiteness, aren't you? And the reason you're not connected to your blackness is cos you've chosen to disconnect from it, or your dad did years ago or whatever. I mean, I know you think it's better that way. Makes sense, white people have an easier time of it, so maybe you just wanna be seen as being close to that or something, but no one's ever actually gonna see you as white. You know that, right? It just doesn't work like that. And thinking it's not a big deal is . . . I dunno, sad. It's like you're connected to a culture that doesn't really want you. And your blackness is beautiful, and the cultures we have are beautiful, so why hide from yours? You're missing out.'

'WOW! Tell me what you really think, Cassie,' I joke, trying to make light of the whole thing. I don't know how else to reply.

Besides, she doesn't know me at all.

But . . . how can she see all the knots I tie myself in? She's figured me out when I can't even figure myself out. I've always felt awkward around black people – like, I know one day they'll rumble me. Now Cassie has. She hasn't replied, waiting for something more than a joke I guess.

'I know I'm missing out,' I say. 'I hate that I don't understand and that I don't feel like I fit anywhere. You're wrong about one thing though – it's not that I don't want to connect. I wish I felt safe in my skin, in my hair, in both cultures, but how? I'm used to not fitting in in a white world, cos you're right, no one will ever see me as white and I don't want them to, I don't think. But people do see me as black and not knowing or understanding the thing that everyone sees first – it's . . . embarrassing!'

Woah, I've never said any of that before to myself, never mind anyone else.

Cassie stops walking to look at me for a second, so I stop too. 'Well, I can't do it for you, but you're gonna have to figure it out. It'll eat you up if you don't. And the longer you leave it, the worse it'll get.' She shrugs and then takes me by the wrist. 'Come on.'

We walk in the same direction as the others. They're now faint outlines ahead of us. I start to feel the energy of water; I'm excited by it for the first time in my life. A beam of moonlight cuts brightly through a clearing up ahead and . . . wow! It. Is. Magical. Its power flows into me. I think about what Cassie said and I don't feel angry, I feel energised. Like I'm finally on the cusp of figuring out who I really am.

We're greeted by a perfectly round lake that matches the deep blue colour of the sky. It's hugged tightly by ferns and reeds that creep up onto the rocky bank. The moon sits squarely in the middle of the picture, its reflection dancing in the water's ripples.

We join the others on a pier that holds a sound system and DJ decks, stretching into the middle of the water. There are people jumping off it, diving, bombing even. It's like a festival all of its own. Some are dancing in the moonlight, others just swim around aimlessly, and there are loads of them on the banks smiling and drinking.

Trent turns to us. 'We're gonna go get ready – see you in the lake in a bit!' he says, disappearing. Alex and Jonesy whip off their tops and hurtle towards the water, shedding their trousers as they go. They cannonball off the pier, making an almighty splash as they hit the water.

'C'mon, Jade, let me grab you a drink.' Dave takes my hand calmly and walks me over to the mini bar.

'I'll be back in a minute,' I tell Lex, Cassie and Sam but I'm not sure they hear me.

After Dave has located the band's rider, he mixes some alcohol with a can of Coke – his drink of choice, apparently – then shows me over to the decks.

'So your dad used to DJ?' he asks.

'Yeah, he and his brother used to do it for their mates' house parties in the 90s.'

'Has he ever taught you?'

'He tried when I was younger, but I was more into being on the dance floor.'

'I reckon you'd be a natural – you obviously understand groove to be able to dance like you do. Wanna try?'

'Course I do!' I say, firmly.

'Awesome, you're gonna smash it.' He moves to stand behind me as I square up to the mixing desk full of sliding and spinning things. He moves one of the headphones onto my right ear and explains everything into my left one.

'So, right now, what you can hear in the cans –' he taps at the headphone – 'is coming off this deck.' He points to a mini whirling platform on my right. 'And what everyone can hear out front is coming from this one.' He points to the left spinner.

'Okay,' I reply, semi-understanding.

'And if you wanna change it so that people hear this one on the right, you just slide this.' His arms sneak through mine as he reaches for the slider. 'So the way to make a good mix is to pick a track that has the same BPM. See the numbers here that say BPM after them?'

'Yep,' I reply. As I wonder what the letters stand for, I revel in the fact that the drummer from Kreep seems to be giving me a DJ lesson!

'So, to start, just choose ones that match. Listen to your headphone with one ear and see how it fits with what's playing out front, then either go across slowly so they're both playing at the same time or jump between them by switching it quickly. Like this.' He demonstrates with a few tracks himself. Dave never misses a beat, and the crowd are lost in the music as he turns to me and says: 'You ready to give it a go?'

'Uh-huh!' I nod, the energy of tonight pulsing through me.

'Okay, it's gonna be fun,' he says, handing me the headphones back.

I begin to listen, scrolling through song options looking for the BPM, but it's hard to read the little orange lights. I look out at the crowd, my heart starting to leap out of my chest. Are they ready for what I'm about to serve up?

I focus back in on the lights that spell out the track names, scrolling until I find a nice groove, letting it play along in the headphones. I feel the beat moving through my body and I use the pulsing motion of my ribs to help me sense when to switch the slider.

It's as though I see the tracks in my mind's eye and the perfect moment for them to collide up ahead. I close my eyes and watch the moment as it moves towards me from the distance. The closer it gets, the faster it races until we unite, and my fingers flick the slider abruptly to the other side. I hear the drop and as my eyes fly open, one of my hands swings into the air of its own accord, punching at the sky in time with the beat. My stance is mirrored back to me by the crowd, who cheer loudly at the change of track. Dave picks me up around my middle, pogoing so I bounce up and down to the beat.

'Whaaaat?' he yells into my ear. 'That. Was. So. Goooood!'

'Wasn't it!?' I scream into his ear over the music.

'It was huge. Look at the crowd!' he says, returning my feet to the ground. As I look out, I see Alex. He's now out of the water. I wave, but he doesn't wave back. I scan around for Lexi. She's locked in conversation with Cassie. Did she even notice that it's me playing the tunes?

'Did you like it?' Dave interrupts my thoughts.

'Yeah, it's a rush. I was so focused and then when I changed the track it felt like an explosion!'

'I knew you'd be a natural! Better keep 'em coming before

Trent kicks you off – you're gonna be a tough act to follow. Just lemme know if you wanna swap.'

I play a few more tracks before the drink Dave poured me kicks in, and I feel rushy. After I hand the decks back to him, I race around the lake to Lexi and the others.

'How the fuck did you know how to do that?' asks Jonesy. He's standing clothes-less in just his pants and shivering in complete disbelief at what I just did.

'It was amazing! I never knew I could do it, but Dave showed me, and I just thought like, "Don't fuck this up!" He was a good teacher.'

'Yeah, we saw that,' Alex says, sounding annoyed.

'He thought it would be fun, and it was!' I say, but Alex doesn't reply. 'Right, who's coming in?'

'Me.' It's Jonesy.

'Me too,' adds Cassie.

'Sure,' says Alex, softening again.

'Yeah, go on then,' Sam chimes in.

'You sure?' Lexi whispers.

'Yeah, I told you – what's the water gonna do to me? I've got it.'

'Okay then,' she replies, but I know she's still sceptical.

I feel a strange mix of excitement (the kind that makes my insides vibrate) and power as I instruct them all to join hands. We run and leap into the water like lemmings off a cliff.

CHAPTER 22

LEXI

I can smell the sunscreen lingering on my skin, entwined with the smoke from the rollie Sam just smoked. There's an electricity in the air as night falls, the sky scribbled with pink zigzags of sunset. We've all looped fingers to stay connected as we float through the air to jump in the lake. I feel alive, the magic of Get Lost fizzing in my bones. My invisible wings extend like an eagle. We're drifting to the stars. I feel Jade's hand clasp mine. I look to the left to catch her eye, then there's a squeeze on my right hand. I turn away from Jade and see a blue girl. The blue girl holds tight and I can't let go. I panic and look back at Jade, but *my* voice comes out of *her* mouth: 'I know what you did. But ssh! Remember we can never tell.'

With that, my eyes flash open. I'm back in my room.

Seriously. Another nightmare? Every day I wake up feeling like my heart's being shocked back to life by those paddles I've seen on hospital dramas.

Today, the mattress under me is drenched from sweat too.

Sleep used to be the only time I could catch a break. Now,

the night terrors are getting worse the closer I get to figuring out what happened. All the chaos from my head that exists when I'm awake writhes its way into my dreams – there's no escape. Thoughts of Sam and Alex and Jonesy twist and turn in my head, along with all the numbers. Honestly, I don't know who or what to believe anymore.

One thing I am certain of though . . .

They're clearly ALL in on it together.

I'm just not sure *how* or *why* they did it?

I feel like a total sucker for trusting Jonesy. Even he admitted he was a different person at Get Lost compared to now. Does that mean he did something so horrible he forced himself to change? He obviously left the sorry note at the grave cos he's full of guilt.

Then there's Sam. Fine, I got it wrong that he wrote the confession, but he's the one who avoided me like I was going to infect him with a deadly virus at the Coach Riot gig.

And his minion, Alex. I know he saw me at The Forum too and chose to disappear into the crowd like the sneaky weasel he is. He lied to Jade about being a producer, lied on social media about working in a studio, and lied straight to my face about doing the 'odd shift' in the store when actually he's Assistant Manager. Then there's the argument with Jade that he let slip but doesn't have the guts to tell me why they were fighting.

Who the hell were we hanging around with last summer?

Did they *really* stumble across us by accident when they were looking for a place to pitch their tent? Or did they seek us out? I saw a documentary once about serial killers that said they have a vision of what their 'ideal victim' will look like. Then they go out and find them, like a director casting their own imagination. It said that even if murders seem random at first, they very, very rarely are. It's all planned. A sick, twisted fantasy.

What if we were their ideal victims?

It makes me shaky thinking about it. Why were we so trusting? Cos they're from our town? Cos they're near our age? Cos they were with Cassie? If three old blokes came over and looked like stereotypical murderers, with teardrop or 666 tattoos, we'd have run a mile. But just cos Jade thought Alex was fit, we assumed they were okay?

Shows you the power of a cute face.

Everything I thought I knew about them has evaporated. It was all lies. Just cos we spent a magical weekend together doesn't mean I *ever* knew them. Who knows what they're capable of – and if they're capable of hurting Jade, are they capable of hurting me?

But . . . the scar.

I push my racing thoughts right down into my belly and into the pit of darkness within my mind – where the bloody T-shirt and the argument caught on camera live.

How would Jonesy know it was there?

No. Just NO. I wouldn't hurt her . . . I couldn't.

It wasn't there before that weekend.

I'd remember if I put my hands on her!

Really? Why was the amethyst ring by her body then?

I sit up in bed and reach for the water on my bedside table, then tip it over me. I let out a gasp as it hits my hair and slides coolly down my skin. I'm already wet from waking up in a sweat, but I need to wash the dreams away to try to wake up from this nightmare.

Right now, it feels like there are only two people left who can help – Cassie, or a psychic who can talk to Jade on the other side.

But it's Cassie who knows those boys inside out.

I place the glass clumsily on the bedside table and it wobbles back into place, then I reach for my phone. I'm going to message her right now and ask to meet. It makes me nervous just thinking about it. What if she can remember everything that really happened?

Stuff about . . . me.

But I'm done not knowing. It's exhausting. Mentally and physically. I'm on a merry-go-round that won't stop turning. Whoever hurt Jade needs to pay for what they did.

Only, what do I say to Cassie now?

She's not so hot on the *send* button.

I need to think carefully cos I don't want her to ignore me like how she usually does, even when I text on Christmas Day. She replied in March to say, *Soz! Missed this msg! x*

That was it!

Maybe I should pretend it's my birthday and I want to invite her round here? Or that I need some advice about getting into a fashion college? Then again, if she's going to protect her Lost Boys, can anything I do even sway her to open up anyways?

Eurgh. I'm overthinking this.

I go into my message thread with Cassie, feeling indecisive about what to type . . . perhaps . . . something like . . . *Hey! Do you want to meet for –*

OH!

No way!

She's already messaged! Of course. There's a WhatsApp RIGHT HERE that she sent to me (and everyone else in her contacts list) about her looming *Cass-hion Show*. Did it drop the day Mum was late? I can't remember – I wasn't in a good place then.

I read the message with extreme precision as if I'm balancing on top of a cheerleading pyramid. I don't want to get the times, dates or venue wrong. My fingers tap at lightning speed as I jump into Google Maps, put in the postcode and realise I can get a train there.

Cassie, I'm coming for you.

Today's finally here! I'm antsy and anxious and a little bit scared – but excited too. Cassie's going to have answers, I just know it. I'm super prepared and have two charged power bars that I got from Amazon after losing my old one on the bus to the Coach Riot gig.

I reach the venue where people swirl and flap around outside. If clothes could talk, the ones they're wearing would be shrieking. One boy looks like he's arrived in a wedding dress, there's a girl with antlers on her head, and an androgynous person in a tartan suit.

Some in the crowd are holding clipboards and look mega serious as they talk through headsets. It's all a bit extra. I thought it'd be at some college that'd be dead easy to gatecrash, but it looks like Cass has hired this out – and booked her own security team! It's a giant brick building with *The Old Brewery* embellished across the top near the roof, above boarded-up windows.

As I approach the doorway, I start to worry that I don't have a ticket. There's a queue of people waiting to go in, all buzzing around like they're waiting to be papped on a red carpet. *Red*. Only Cassie could make a university fashion show feel like the Oscars. Some are in equally bold and bizarre clothes as those with the clipboards, looking like fellow students on Cassie's course, others are in blouses or suit trousers. I guess they're friends and family.

I hang back as far as possible, while still able to hear the guys in headsets. Some people are being let inside now. They're not showing tickets and they don't look fancy; they're just wearing jeans and T-shirts, most of them with their hair tied up in messy buns.

I tiptoe closer, pretending to look at my cracked phone as I continue to eavesdrop.

'You're late! The models are getting ready in there,' a girl with a crew cut says. She ushers a pretty brunette through the doorway before opening her cigarette pack.

If Mum and Dad were here, I'd hug them. Hard. And say thank you for having sex one random day to mix genes and conceive me! I always hated being tall at school, especially when I shot up in Year Six to be taller than the boys. It was mortifying. The teacher would proudly tell everyone I was the 'tallest girl in the school', while I wanted to shrink and be petite so that I could be cast as Ariel in *The Little Mermaid*. I'd get called giant, Avatar, beanpole, lamppost, Eiffel Tower. I hated giraffe the most.

Right now, being model-tall is my ticket to getting in that building.

I quickly tie my hair into a bun like the other girls. My belly cartwheels and I do my best to saunter to the door as if I'm meant to be here.

'I'm so sorry I'm late,' I say, 'major traffic on the bus.'

'Name?' The girl sucks on her skinny menthol.

'I'm . . . Cassie's cousin,' I blurt out.

She stares at her clipboard, blowing smoke out. Gawd. Why didn't I just say Chloe? Or Olivia? Anything other than Cassie's cousin! My cheeks burn. Our parents *clearly* aren't related.

'Umm.' She's still looking at the list of names.

'Her step-cousin!' I say, trying to tidy up my mess.

'Yeah, okay.' The girl takes me by surprise as she shepherds me through the doorway.

I scurry into the huge space. The ceiling is sky high – if Jade were here, she'd be testing its echo. She'd probably say it had a 'paranormal energy' too.

I'm in awe, gawking at the stained-glass windows, derelict spiral staircase and pillars that look to be holding the building up. I pass more clipboard people and hear one shout at another, 'We're out of sequins! Find some or get your arse to a stationery shop!' I drop my head and follow the other models, hoping I blend in enough.

I'm expecting someone with a guest list to confront me any minute now and tell me I need to leave, but I manage to reach a door with *Dressing Room* etched on it.

I try to take a deep breath, though it comes out shallow, so

I count to the safe number – 356. It gives me the courage to place my hands on the door and push.

I disappear into Narnia.

Turns out there's a shit ton of hairspray in Narnia. I quickly inhale a truckload of the stuff. It chokes its way down my throat as bodies weave around me, half-dressed in silver futuristic outfits. I've never seen so many nipples! There are elbow nudges as people compete for mirror space, and queues by the make-up artist and hairstylist who seem to be doing all the models in turn. It's more Hackney than Hollywood in here.

I see a spare costume hanging on the rail and in a moment of genius – or madness – grab it. Now that I'm here, I can't risk being thrown out. I need to hear what Cass knows. And I know that she'll know cos those boys are like brothers to her.

God . . . what if she's in on it too?

I distract myself by looking at the silver shoulder pads on the hanger I'm holding, wondering how to get this bodysuit on without stripping naked first.

My heart stops.

I hear that sweet sound of her voice.

'No babes, do it like this.' I spin and spy Cassie crouching to help a model lace her ballet slippers. Soon, she's up again, commanding, 'We need tights! Suzie's are laddered.' She swaggers through the girls, staying chill amongst the chaos as people compete for her attention. She hasn't clocked me yet though she's heading right in my direction.

I panic. Is she going to be livid that I've trespassed? I must look like a total fangirl. I'm literally standing here holding one of her designs, having lied my way in. What if she just walked into *my* space, uninvited, and appeared in front of me? It's pretty stalkerish, isn't it?

'LEXI? You're . . . HERE?'

Is that happy shock or angry shock?

Cassie leans forward to land an air-kiss on each cheek, and all my fear dissolves.

'I, yeah, I mean, I wanted to support the show,' I fib.

'Babes, soz! It's carnage.' She takes me by the hand. 'Come chat while I finish my face.' As she leads us to the make-up artist, the models shimmy out of the way to make space for us. Two girls sitting in the only available stools jump up to free them. 'How's tricks, gurl?' Cassie continues as the artist begins to stick diamanté gems across her forehead.

'Okay, y'know, been better.'

She nods fiercely. 'Of course, of course. We should hang.' She's clearly forgotten about the messages I sent last December trying to do exactly that. The make-up artist holds Cassie's chin gently to steady her, as Cassie mouths 'Sorry!' for moving. I'm relieved Cass is so relaxed around me; it makes me feel good – like she has nothing to hide.

'You look well,' she says, even though I hand-on-heart do not.

'Listen, Cass. Can I ask you something, about the boys?'

'The boys?'

Is she playing dumb already? How can she *not* know who I'm talking about?

'Yeah,' I say. 'Sam, Jonesy and Alex.'

'Sure, babes. What've they done this time?' She laughs, offering me a gem from the make-up artist's kit to glue on my face. I take it out of politeness and end up placing it below my left eye like a tear.

'Are they . . . trustworthy?' I stumble, knowing I need to keep her on side.

'Huh? Yeah, yeah. Why?' Cassie replies, before adding, 'Looks gorge!' and raises a finger towards the gem I'm now randomly wearing.

'It's just . . . I think there's something weird about what happened to Jade. I don't think her death was an accident.'

'Oh?' she says.

'Jonesy left a note at her grave saying sorry . . . Did he say anything to you about it?'

Cassie shakes her head, her braids jostling. 'Her grave?'

'Mmmhmm.'

'I don't know anything about that, babe. Are you sure it was him?'

'Yeah, I'm sure.' I nod, fiercely.

'You've spoken to him about it?'

'Well, no.'

'So maybe it was someone else?' she quizzes.

'Like who?'

'Well, you said their names yourself.'

'Sam and Alex?'

Cassie shrugs a shoulder up to her ear and gives a cute 'I dunno' expression, prompting the make-up artist to straighten her head again.

'Why would they write it?'

'Just, Sam was a bit –' she thinks about her words – 'funny about you guys.'

'Funny?'

'Yeah, y'know. He didn't like you guys hanging around with us.'

Wait. So, he *did* hate Jade! Or both of us?

'Are you saying he did something to hurt her?'

'No, no! Nothing like that, babes. Sam wouldn't hurt a fly. Trust me!'

Her words trigger my brain to flood with Mum's favourite motto, one she used A LOT (about Dad) after the divorce. *Never trust a person who says, 'trust me'.*

'Maybe I'm not getting my words across right,' Cassie continues. 'Can we do this another time? It's good to see you 'n' all. Just, I need to crush today.'

'Err . . .' I jolt up as someone's body part digs into my spine as they push past me on the backless stool. 'Sure, what about Friday?'

'Ahh, can't do this weekend.'

'Oh, okay. Doing anything fun?' I find myself saying automatically.

As Cassie goes to speak the make-up artist does too, in perfect synchronicity, the two of them talking over each in unison – with very different sentences:

'Um, seeing my gran.'

'Get Lost, babyyy!'

The make-up artist grimaces, realising she's put her foot in it and revealed Cassie's fat lie.

My heart flops out of my chest like a dead fish, leaving me hollow inside.

'You're going back?'

Cassie shrugs, looking a little sheepish for the first time ever.

'I can ask Jonesy about that note thing if you like?' she says, trying to plaster over the big gaping wound she's just left in me.

'You're *both* going back?' I get the same feeling in my chest as when Mum's late home. How can they be so insensitive? Have they forgotten my best friend went to a festival on her own two feet and came home lying dead in an ambulance?

I can't deal with this. I get up and turn to go. I don't trust any of them.

'Hey! You should totally stay and watch the show,' Cassie shouts after me, but I've already escaped from Narnia with nothing to show but a gem tear.

CHAPTER 23

JADE

As if by magic, a lone firework flies into the star-spangled sky with a screech, exploding into cerise and gold sparkles. As soon as that one has died away, another follows it – emerald green and silver this time – and another – lilac and orange. The group of us stare up, treading water to take in the display.

The explosions rage on as we 'ooooo' and 'aaahhhh' in unison. I glance over to Lexi to see her sweet reaction and I catch the reflections bouncing off the water too. Eventually, the sparks in the sky fizzle out. I feel Alex's arms brush against mine as he swims closer to me, wrapping me around him like a koala as we bob up and down.

Out of nowhere, a wave of lake water comes flying over the top of us. It's Jonesy, splashing us with glee, Cassie soon splashing back. But then Sam seems to rise up out of the water, his arms locked out and pressing something down.

'Where's Lexi?' I ask, frantically. 'I can't see her, Alex. Where is she?'

Instinctively, I know.

He's pressing Lex into the water! Sam's dunking her!

Shit, what if this is what the tarot reading meant, about the 'end of something or a new beginning'? What if Psychic Sally was saying that Lexi dies in the water, just like Emily did . . . because Sam has been the Fool card all along!

'Sam!' I yell. 'What the fuck?'

Lexi pops up out of the water, wiping her eyes before opening them. 'Bloody hell, Sam!' she snaps, after catching her breath.

'It was just a perfect opportunity,' he replies, giggling.

'C'mon, I need another drink,' Jonesy announces, swimming for the shore. We all follow, the ripples lapping against my skin.

We clamber out, Cassie taking Lexi's hand to help her scramble over the rocks on the bank. Lexi shakes out her hair and scurries off to the pier, shivering. Without towels, we all air dry whilst scratching around on the floor for the right clothes. I wring out my hair and collect my headscarf as I shimmy past Cassie to check Lex is okay. I loop it round my wrist for a minute and slip a hair tie off the other one about to scrape my curls up.

'Jade,' I hear Cassie behind me as I rake my fingers through, 'd'you need a hand?'

"What, with Lex? I mean, if you wanna come check on her . . .' I reply.

'No, I meant with your hair, looks like you're wrestling it.' She giggles. 'Lex will be fine, Sam was just messing around. Here.' She gestures towards the scarf on my wrist.

Cassie opens the scarf out to its full size, assesses it and then manoeuvres me so I'm facing her. 'Flip your hair forward, so it's in front of your face,' she instructs. 'Okay, now just hold tight.'

'Will this take long?' I speak loudly towards the floor. 'It's just, I really wanna go see Lexi,' I insist.

She places the fabric at the nape of my neck, passes the length of the scarf over my ears and holds the corners together at my forehead.

'It'll literally be a second. Okay, pull your head up slowly now to face me.'

I do as I'm told. She ties and tucks and before I know it my curls are all wrapped up. Cassie takes a picture on her phone, flash on, and shows me.

'Oh my God! I love it – it's like a super 60s vibe. Will you teach me that back at the tents?'

'Sure. It suits you,' she replies.

Alex comes to wrap himself around me. 'Aren't you gonna get dressed? It's freezing now.' I feel the goosebumps on his damp skin.

'I'm not cold!' I protest.

Jonesy arrives back from the pier with a scuttle, clutching a bottle of wine.

'Sssshhh!' he mouths, with a finger over his lips. 'Pinched it from Kreep's minibar. We should toast to our Get Lost adventure!' He pops the cork to a cheer from Cassie and the others. Lexi's here again too and she looks okay, so I'm okay. Jonesy passes the bottle to me. 'Jade, good work getting us back here!'

I press my lips to the glass and tilt my head backwards,

readying myself for the acidic flavour that will follow. I quickly realise it's filled with something very bubbly . . . that creates its own firework, flying directly into my face! Bubbles catapult up my nose and cascade down my chin. I lurch forward, holding the bottle at arm's length. The juice fizzes over and out, as if I were a Formula 1 driver celebrating on the top podium. I think I'd be an amazing racing driver actually, so I'd better get used to bubbles like this.

I let out a gleeful, 'Oh my God!' I try to wipe my face with the forearm I have spare before taking another, more successful, gulp.

'Jade, babes.' It's Lexi. 'You should probably share that – don't drink the whole thing!' Is she worried? She doesn't need to be. My energy is strong right now.

'Nah, don't worry,' says Jonesy. 'She's got a taste for it now! Get it down ya.'

CHAPTER 24

LEXI

As we pull up outside, I unplug my phone from the Uber's car charger and immediately swap it for a power bar as I thank the driver, then climb out and stare at the ridiculously large home in front of me. You could fit at least three of my house into this one!

I managed to get the address from Mum's mate at the paper. I didn't want to ask him at first in case he told Mum, but I'm desperate now. Paul's helped me a few times, like when we made a magazine for a school project. He found emails for some record labels so we could contact them and ask for interviews about careers in music. Jade and I called our mag *TV Is Better* as a joke. We even won a prize for it. It's the only thing I've ever won. We got book vouchers, but we were so buzzing you'd think they'd given us a trip to California!

Now Paul's helped me again.

I tried to find Sam myself, but it was hard not knowing his surname and not being able to find him on socials. So I did the next best thing. I put *Sam*, our town *Roseville*, and *The Spires*, which was on the crest of his bag he had at Get Lost, into Google all at once. A link popped up from his school, so I started looking on their website and found a headline: *The Spires head boy wins top national science prize*. I clicked through and saw a photo of him clutching a trophy in one hand and shaking the hand of some old dude with the other.

I immediately sent Paul the school site link and asked him to find Sam's address. Within a few days, he'd replied with the number and name of the street.

The place has enormous gates that are swung open, which is kinda handy for me. The alternative is a fancy intercom system to the left that appears to have a camera, so it's not like I can lie and put on a fake accent to say, 'Hi, special delivery. I need a signature.' If I give Sam the chance to see my face before he lets me in, I'll be waiting here until I'm 100.

I walk through the open gates as confidently as possible, stopping to dip a finger into the trickling water feature. I wonder if it'd be weird if I throw a penny in to make a wish, like people do in the town centre fountain. Mine would be, *I wish we'd never gone to Get Lost*.

It takes me a while to reach the door, that's how big the front garden is. My fake confidence is fading. Anxiety is snapping at my heels, threatening to swallow me whole. I used to be so free, so chill, but it's impossible now since Jade's been gone.

Not just cos of what Cassie told me about Sam, or Jonesy's note and Alex's weirdness, but cos of somewhere deep down inside, in the pit where my secrets are buried.

The secrets that I can never tell.

Then there's Petra. Each session it's like she's hanging a fishing rod down my throat to fish my secrets out of me. She can see inside my memory and it's only a matter of time before it all comes tumbling out: bad things happen whenever I'm around.

'Hello,' a voice comes from behind me, making me jump. I turn and see a needle-thin man with bushy eyebrows. He's in overalls and holding a pair of shears. 'I'm the gardener, love.'

'Oh, hi,' I say.

'Visiting?' His Scottish accent is everything.

'Err, yeah. Sam.'

'C'mon on. I can let you in.'

'Thanks.' I smile widely at him. I know that living people sometimes think dead people come back as birds or stars or whatever to say hello. I think if any of that is even remotely true, then Jade has just come back as a fifty-year-old gardener to help me.

'Follow me.' He steps in front and types a number into a security pad to open the giant front door, which looks like a bank vault.

I follow my new fairy godfather inside to a huge hall. My heart is bouncing around like I'm a human pinball machine. I'm *so* out of my comfort zone. What if Sam throws me out as soon as he sees me? Or calls the police? Or worse, remembers more than I do?

I try to keep my cool on the outside even though I'm petrified on the inside. I hover politely beside the gardener as I look around the hall, so big it's like a cinema foyer. There's a stunning mosaic table in the centre with a vase bursting with fresh flowers. Jade would *love* it – she liked anything shiny. There's an umbrella stand to my right like I've seen in hotels. Light from the skylight beams down as if someone is visiting from heaven.

The gardener nods at me then voice bombs, 'Sam! Visitor!' through the air.

We stand waiting for a reply, or for Sam to appear, as thoughts speed through my mind. How am I going to ask him about what Cassie spilled yesterday and get him to 'fess up about why he never really liked us from the start? What did we do that was *so* bad?

The gardener walks towards the stairs and starts to climb. He only gets halfway up the staircase before turning around to come down again.

'He's in the shower, hen. You can go up and wait for him in his bedroom. Turn left at the top of the stairs, first right.' Then he pootles off down the hall.

I hesitate, every thought telling me this is a *bad* idea as my brain tells me to shush and just count. Right now, I'm fine listening to it. Cos today might be my only chance to find out the truth. I don't trust Jonesy, Alex or Cassie, and if I don't confront Sam, I may never know what happened. That's worse than anything he could ever do to me.

I close my eyes, dig deep for courage as the numbers bring calm to the thoughts swirling in my mind like flying objects in a tornado, and start to walk towards the stairwell.

I place my foot on the first step. The sound of my DM hitting the polished wood echoes around the house like I've just banged the drums in an empty cave. Jeez, Lex! I take extra care to make sure I put my shoe down more slowly on the next stair, not wanting to alert Sam to the fact that I'm here until I'm upstairs, when he won't be able to avoid me.

As I drift higher up, I hear running water. It's that pitter-patter of fake rain only a shower can give. I keep my remaining footsteps quiet just in case he can hear from inside the bathroom. Better safe than sorry. I eventually reach the top (going quickly and quietly is tricky!) and turn left into a long corridor with a mile of cream carpet. I feel like I'm on the decks of the *Titanic*, and it's only a matter of luck as to whether or not I'll survive this.

I arrive at the first door on the right. There's a sign saying, *Sam's Room: Keep Out*.

It gives me a funny feeling in my belly, like he's talking directly to me. But if I can sneak into a fashion show, I'm not gonna let a sign on a bedroom put me off. My arm reaches out and my fingers land on the door handle. I don't have much time, but I do know I must count again. Onetwothree . . . as quickly as possible to stay safe as the water still runs.

I open the door.

Inside his room, it's *very* Sam. If the bed wasn't here, it'd look more like an office. There are framed certificates on the walls boasting his achievements. There's a desk with a computer on it – a proper one not just a laptop – and a corkboard above with pieces of paper pinned on.

I edge over the threshold, from the doorway into his private space, and feel a little bit mischievous. I'm the one with the power now! I tread across his vast room and make my way over to the bed. I don't want to be standing by the door when he finds me. It needs to feel like he can't get rid of me easily.

I continue creeping over to the mattress, brazen enough to perch on it. I take a seat in the middle so that he'll see me as soon as he walks in. Something catches my attention out the corner of my eye – it's leaning against the bed. I turn my head to the left and peer down into the gap that was hidden from view when I entered.

It's a backpack.

I jump up and walk around the bed to discover the bag propped up by the side of the mattress. There's a head torch and camping stove on the floor beside it.

And four tickets!

They're incredibly colourful, just like last year.

My tummy flops like I'm made of slime as I see the Get Lost logo on them.

They're *all* going back. The snakes. How can they carry on as normal, like nothing happened? Don't they care? Or are they going to find new 'ideal victims'?

I hop about, counting and waiting. Do I go straight in with what Cassie said? Or play it cool and ask why they're going back to the scene of the crime without *any* remorse?

My legs are skittish, and I begin to pace. I glare at his festival gear then aimlessly gaze around the room. It's only as I turn around towards the door that I see the oversized canvas hanging from the wall.

It's a family photo.

I do a double take.

HOLY SHIT.

I've not seen that face for years.

The sound of running water stops. I need to run. NOW. It's not safe here. I've arrived in Hell. Only, instead of the Devil at the gates, it's Emily.

The energy inside me is extra-terrestrial. I dash across the room so fast I'm flying, scrambling out of the door and to the stairs as I hear another door creak open – the one to the bathroom. But my feet are already bombing down the staircase. I'm running like my life depends on it . . . because it does! I need to get out of here before Sam finds me.

My feet are tumbling so fast I can't even make sense of what they're doing. I race down, nearing the final steps, then take the last three stairs at once, jumping down to the floor. I feel a crunch and my ankle bends in a way that it *really* shouldn't. I go to yell out in pain but throw a hand over my mouth to stifle my cries. I limp as quickly as possible across the giant hallway. It never seems to end, as if I'm going down death row. Eventually, I reach the front door and twist the handle. But it doesn't open! Why isn't the door opening?

My heart is flapping like a trillion butterflies. I try again and still it doesn't open. There's a creak upstairs as footsteps come out of the bathroom. I look up and down the door, searching for clues for how to open it. There's a latch right at the top. The gardener must've closed it when we came inside. I stretch to reach it as the footsteps get louder. Praying, hoping, begging I reach.

It's stuck!

My hands feel alien, like they're too big for me. I have zero coordination, as if I've just downed a bottle of vodka, and my vision is staring to blur. What's happening to me?

I try again, hurling myself into the air this time. My fingers brush against the knob . . . And I dislodge it! It slides across as I hurtle back to the ground, crashing onto my sprained ankle. I think I hear someone say my name, but I'm already turning the handle, letting daylight spill into the hall. The front door opens. I leg it out of the house through the front garden to get back to the street. Then. I. Run.

The pain of my ankle is next level agony, but I still sprint so hard, feeling the slap of the wind against my cheeks. I keep going until I'm far, far away from that place.

I cannot believe Sam is Emily's brother. Emily Rathborne, which makes him Sam Rathborne. It wasn't Jonesy after all! SAM IS R.

Cassie was right. Jade was right. The drink over her head, the tripping me up, the weirdness, the everythingness! He knows who we are. He wants revenge.

HE KILLED HER!

Oh. My. God. The dunking at the lake . . . Was he practising on me so that he could do it to Jade later? I may have come up for breath, but Jade wasn't so lucky.

I feel like I'm in that lake again. I can't breathe. There is water instead of oxygen flying up my nose and mouth, filling every cell of my body. Now it's my turn to drown.

I keep running, running as fast as my feet will carry me, all the while thinking there were two of us there when Emily died, and only one of us is gone now.

Sam's clearly going to try and finish what he started!

CHAPTER 25

JADE

Alex pulls me to one side, clutching my clothes in his arms. 'Here, you're gonna freeze if you don't get dressed.' He offers the bundle towards me.

'I'm fine, honestly. I feel really hot actually!' I reply, turning to head back to the others.

'No, Jade, c'mon,' he insists.

'Oooh, I get it. You don't like that I've got my body out!' I accuse, playfully. 'You can't handle anybody else seeing alla this!' I giggle, wiggling my hips and running my hands over my soft tummy as I say the words. 'Well, Alex, you're just gonna have to deal with it. You don't own me!' I shout, sassily.

'What, no . . . I just,' he attempts, clearly shocked.

'What? *You're gonna freeze*, blah blah blah,' I mimic, rolling my eyes.

'Jade?' He's hurt.

'Oh, c'mon, Alex, I see you! Don't pretend – there's no point pretending. I know what you're thinking.' He looks perplexed. 'I mean, you're not the only one – you've been taught to think that you can own people and that girls being naked is a sexual thing. But it doesn't have to be, and honestly, I thought you'd know that. I thought you were a bit less of a dick, to be honest!'

'What? A dick? Are you honestly saying you think I'm a dick?'

'I mean, if it walks like a dick and it quacks like a dick.' I laugh at my own joke.

'Jade, what's going on? Who are you right now?'

'See, there you go again, thinking you know who I am. You just met me. The only way you would know me already is if you had a spirit telling you everything like I do. And to be honest, I know you don't, because mine would have told me.'

'Ooookay,' he replies. 'I think you're acting a bit weird, Jade. You're being mean. Maybe you need to just take a minute, sober up a little bit . . .'

'I don't think so. You're just closed off to the energy that's everywhere – the fucking powerful energy. Right now you're only tuned into the darkness! When you're tuned into the light and the power, it's impossible to not see everything for what it really is. Like you can't not cos the spirits talk to you – they guide you.'

'You've lost me,' he replies.

'Okay, so, take now . . . right now. My friend from the other side – you know, the one I told you about, after Psychic Sally?'

'Yeah, what was her name?'

'Doesn't matter.' I race on to the important part. 'Sometimes she comes to me – she tells me what you and everybody else thinks – and no one can hide from her. She's inside your head. Literally, in your head, in my head – she's everywhere! She's wise for someone who died so young too. I guess it's all that time spent around the other spirits. Anyway, she sounds a bit bubbly still, like from the pool water, but . . . you might be able to hear her if you were just a bit more enlightened.'

'Jade, I don't know what you want me to—' He breaks off and continues, 'Sam was right about you – this is nuts. You're being completely . . . nuts!' He shakes his head and turns to storm off.

'I'm not nuts, Alex,' I shout after him. 'You're just a closed off, uncentered, unenlightened dick . . . And I know that's the truth – Emily told me!'

'Jade!' I hear Lexi from behind me. 'What are you doing?'

I spin round to look at her.

'You told him?' she slurs, not waiting for an answer before carrying on. 'I knew it. Why can't you just leave it alone? We promised. I thought our promises meant something. We heart-hugged that we'd never talk about it, ever. And now you're blabbing to the first person interested in anything you have to say. Some fucking boy you've known for all of five minutes. I thought you were better than that!'

'Well, I tried to talk to you,' I reply, 'on the Ferris wheel. I've been trying for years actually! But now is really the time, because she's here – can't you feel her?' How can Lex expect a person to carry a secret like ours around for their whole life? 'Besides, how could I not talk about her when she's right here?'

'Jade, I don't care about all your hippy-dippy shit right now. You should never have opened your mouth! A secret is a secret. What I don't get is, it's been years. You've been just fine without telling anyone for all this time – I should know, I've seen you every day.' She's whisper-shouting, trying to control her volume in case anyone is lingering nearby.

'Fine?' I squawk back. 'You think I'm fine? Did you ever, ever hear what I said to you about having to start taking pills last year?'

'That's not the point, and you can't use it as an excuse for everything! It's been me and you, day in day out, doing what friends do. I trusted you. And you know, being a friend means there's some stuff you have to do and some stuff you can't ever do. And d'you know what friends don't do . . . ?' She's on a roll now. Despite the pause, I know she doesn't want me to reply. 'Take a wild guess.' But I don't, so she goes on, 'The most important thing that friends don't do? Friends. Don't. Tell!' She screams that last bit into the darkness, her body thrust forward for the full force of her anger to slap me in the face. It does. It echoes through my brain and across the lake.

CHAPTER 26

LEXI

I fumble with the key, my alien hands shaking so hard I can't get it in the lock. My fingers are sausages. There must be the screeching sound of metal on metal, but I can't hear it. I don't have any senses. Sight, sound, smell, taste, touch are all replaced by fear.

Suddenly, the door opens from the other side.

'I heard you rattling around. Thought I'd save you the bother.' It's Mum.

I grimace. 'You're here?'

'Yes, darling – it's my holiday, remember? I booked a few days off to spend with you.'

'Oh. Yeah.' I nod, struggling to think of how I'm going to get justice for Jade when the person I need to confront wants me dead too.

'Come through.' Mum ushers me in. 'Where have you been?'

'Nowhere.'

'Nowhere. Was it fun?' She smiles. 'I was just about to call to see where you were. I've got a surprise.' She tries to push me towards the kitchen while closing the front door.

But I push against her hand with my back, harder.

'Oi, missy.' She laughs.

'Mum, I can't.' I wriggle away from her touch.

'But . . . I made you a cake.' She sounds half cheery, half deflated, like she's not sure whether or not this is a game. 'It's Pop Tart flavoured!'

'I don't have time,' I reply, scurrying towards the stairs while trying to count my steps. But it's hard to focus as Mum keeps chattering.

'Oh, don't be a spoilsport. Come onnn,' she says. 'I'll cut us a slice?'

'I have to pack,' I say. My throat is raw like I've swallowed a beehive. My feet are already halfway up the stairs as Mum stands in the hallway still talking to me.

'Pack?'

I'm nearly in my bedroom when Mum clicks I'm not messing about, and I hear her footsteps scamper after me. She follows me into my room and sits on the bed, out of breath and watching me.

'I need to work on my fitness,' she pants.

I can't really hear; it's like she's talking to me with my headphones in. I grab a small rucksack out of the wardrobe, so that I can get ready to go back to the scene of the crime.

'Would you care to tell me what's going on?' she says, puzzled.

'Nothing,' I say.

'Doesn't look like nothing.'

I pull out a spare T-shirt and hoodie, then head to my chest of drawers for a bra, knickers and socks. There's a black wig in here that I wore for Halloween when I was Wednesday Addams. I wonder if I should take it as a disguise, so they don't recognise me.

Whatever it takes, I'll do it.

I just want the truth – once and for all.

And if they're all together they can't cover for each other.

I can't stop thinking about that photo hanging on Sam's wall. Her face frozen in time, a kid forever, while Jade and I got to grow up. Her beaming smile iron-branded onto my retinas; the smile I've worked so hard to forget over the years. If Sam already knew that Jade and I were friends with Emily when he met us at Get Lost, why not just say she was his sister? We could've explained. If he'd given us a chance, I would have owned up. Though if I told the truth, maybe *I'd* be the one who's dead.

Sweet Jesus. If he knows who we are, then he knows where we live. His family might've moved after it happened, but I've lived at this address since I was born. This is the house that Emily came to for princess parties to eat cupcakes and Smarties. In that documentary about killers, I'm pretty sure it said that most victims know their murderer – which means Sam's blatantly hurt Jade and he's coming to get me next.

'The ingredients!' I yell, snapping out of my thoughts and back into the room as I realise what this means.

'Sorry?' Mum replies, confused.

'Did you eat any of the cake?'

'Not yet, no.'

'Okay. Good,' I say.

I'm trying to think straight, but it's hard to remember what I'll need. Jade packed everything for us last time. I head towards my door and run out to the bathroom.

'Why?' Mum shouts after me, but I'm too focused on grabbing a spare toilet roll and deodorant, while looking for the mini suntan lotion that I know is in here somewhere.

I drop the items outside my bedroom door then sprint back downstairs to the hall, the pain of my ankle obscured by the adrenaline exploding through me. I hunt for Mum's handbag on the rack amongst the jackets. I can hear her calling me, though it's muffled, like I'm in an avalanche. I find her leather satchel and delve inside, feeling for my treasure. I know I should ask but I don't have time to explain – and I can't risk her saying no. My fingers find what I'm looking for . . . wrapping around her wallet. I pull it out, opening it up to see her bank cards all lined up and glowing at me like gold. I help myself to the one I know the PIN number for cos it's my birthday date, then dash back upstairs like a lightning bolt.

'Lex, why?' she asks again as I reenter my bedroom.

'Why what?'

'Something about the ingredients?'

'Promise me that you won't touch the cake!' I say, as I shove the toiletries into my bag.

'Is this a joke?' Mum looks at me like she's never seen me before.

'He could have been here.'

'Who could've been here?' Mum's frowning with worry.

'He knows where we live.'

'You're scaring me. Who knows?'

'Sam!' I wail, sprinting over to my bedside table so I can pack lip balm and gum.

'Sam?'

'Emily's brother!'

Her normally wrinkle-free face cracks with a thousand lines as she takes a moment to think. 'Emily? From primary school?'

'Don't touch anything!'

'Darling . . .' Mum stands up and comes towards me, putting an arm around my shoulders and steering us towards the beanbag corner. 'Why don't we take a seat.'

But I can't, not yet.

'What are you doing?' she asks, her voice sounding frayed, like a loose thread.

'Nothing.'

'You were . . . saying numbers?'

'No.'

'I heard you.'

'Fine. I have to! Okay? Before I can sit. Or else it's not safe,' I say, relenting.

Mum looks at me with wild eyes.

'PLEASE! Don't touch the beanbags, Mum,' I beg, desperate for her to listen.

'Why?' She looks at me, baffled.

'Anything could be contaminated,' I say. 'He could've touched things, put poison on them,' I add, as if it's the most normal, rational thing in the world.

CHAPTER 27

JADE

I hunt around for my shoes in the dark, tears streaming down my cheeks now. Lexi stares at me in disgust. Emily tries to comfort me from inside my head. If there's one thing I thought I could count on, it was that Lexi would always understand me. But maybe I was wrong about that. And maybe she was right – maybe I shouldn't have told Alex.

But Emily keeps saying I was supposed to trust him, that he understands, that he'd make everyone understand.

I hear a stick crack in the distance and jump out of my skin. 'What was that, Em?' She doesn't answer. Why would she leave me now?

'Lexi?' I hear Cassie. 'Y'okay? What's going on?'

'Nothing,' she replies, flatly. 'Jade's just being . . . well, the worst.' Ouch.

'It's okay, she doesn't mean that,' Emily comforts me.

'Jaaade!' Cassie moans. 'Don't poop the party! C'mon, Lex, let's go grab a drink.'

'Gladly!' Lexi bites, throwing something that bounces off me.

And just like that, she leaves too, wrapped under Cassie's arm.

'Who is it?' I shout fearfully into the night.

'It's Ryan,' Jonesy replies. I hear his voice drawing closer. 'Don't cry. It's all gonna be okay.'

I try to wrestle my foot into a shoe as my fingers sweep over what Lex just threw. My heart collapses. I sit wrapped in a little ball, hugging my knees. Jonesy stumbles out of the dark. He passes me a cup as he plonks himself down on the ground beside me, then throws his arm over my shoulder, his gigantic hand engulfing my bicep.

'You know what you need, don't ya? A big old drink! It'll help take the edge off.'

I turn my head to look up at him, and he lifts his cup to cheers mine.

'If you say so,' I mumble, wiping my tears with the back of a hand followed by snot from my nose. He starts to down his drink and I do the same with mine, placing it against my lips and tipping my head back to glug the whole thing without registering what it tastes like. I feel more tears fall from my eyes and race backwards towards my ears.

'You had a bust-up with Lexi?' he asks, whilst the liquid is tumbling down my throat. Once I'm done, I pull the cup away from my mouth. From nowhere the biggest burp I've ever heard comes careering out of me. I shake my head from side to side to try to relieve myself of the fizzing and bitterness in my mouth.

'Yeah . . . a big one,' I reply. 'How did you know?'

'Oh, I just saw her and Cassie on the way.'

'She hates me!' I say as I panic. I'm trying desperately to stop my mouth from running away with itself. If anyone else knows why, Lex will be even madder, if that's even possible.

'Keep quiet, Jade, keep quiet,' Emily whispers.

'So what was it about?' he asks.

'Sssssshhhhh,' Emily insists.

'I can't say, but I'm pretty sure she hates me forever now.' More tears roll out of my eyes again. There's a leak that I just can't plug.

'Jade, man, you gotta chill out. It isn't the end of the world. It'll all blow over by tomorrow.'

'It won't!' I wail. 'You don't know Lexi and you don't know me. She doesn't talk about things easily – it's why I don't push her on anything. And now, in her eyes, I've done the worst thing ever and she's never gonna forgive me. And the thing is . . .' I'm rambling now and Emily sounds almost as annoyed as Lexi was when she tells me to shut up, but I just can't . . . 'I'm not very good at getting over things like this. These horrible feelings sit in my tummy like a dragon in a cave, waiting for the night to come so they can fly out and breathe fire over everything!'

'What?' Emily's confused.

'What?' Jonesy is too.

It's noisy with the two of them talking to me. I wanna close my eyes and just let it be me and Emily for a minute – but then Jonesy will know she's here. So I just keep talking . . .

'But now it's not like night-time really, because you always know when the night is coming, and I never know when these feelings are gonna arrive.'

'I've never been good at riddles, Jade,' Jonesy slurs.

'Sorry, it's just I don't know how else to explain it. You know that feeling when there's something in your belly that's, like . . . growing?'

'Only after a burger,' he jokes, but I don't laugh. 'No.' He shakes his head. 'No, I don't get what you're tryna say, but it doesn't sound like much fun. D'you know what is fun?' He waits for me to answer but I can't. 'Booze! It helps every time. I promise. Why d'you think I drink so much of it?' He wiggles the cup in front of me.

'That's like my pills. They help a bit, but I don't know how or why.'

'Okay, Jade . . . I like you, but this is all a bit dramatic, innit? We're at a festival! You need to . . . I dunno, shake it off! Then come dance with us! Here.' Jonesy picks up a clear bottle of brown liquid with a shiny label that he brought over with the cups. He plonks it down in front of my feet, squeezes my arm and gives the top of my head a little pat. Then he heaves himself up and stumbles into the darkness back towards the party.

CHAPTER 28

LEXI

I'm squished beside a girl with pongy tuna sandwiches who could represent England in the National Chatty Competition. She's been FaceTiming her mate (on another coach cos she missed this one) for most of the two-hour trip, talking about what she's forgotten to pack, what bands she wants to see live and that she's busting for a pee.

I'm *insanely* jealous of her.

I would give my life savings to swap places. Okay, so I don't have any life savings. But I'd let someone have my entire band T-shirt collection. I want to chat with my bestie and eat Meal Deals instead of sitting here with a sickly stew of nerves and terror in my gut on my way to finally get answers. No one can hide from the truth anymore. Including myself.

We're off the motorway now and driving down twisty country roads with arching branches that look too small for this beast of a vehicle. It means we're nearly there.

Eventually, we begin to slow, soon bumping along the gravelly path as we pull into the site. The parking attendants in high-vis jackets wave the driver through, but there are coaches everywhere I look, so we go at snail's pace into the car park, worming around to a space. There's a whiff of mania in the air as everyone anticipates the weekend's adventure. No doubt they've been counting down the days for this – while I still count up.

362 days gone.

We begin to pile off the coach. People are pushing and shoving, desperate to be the first ones to touch the holy ground and not waste a precious second of their weekend. They're all snapping selfies, giggling and gassing away as they catapult into the Vegas of festivals. Excitement oozes out of every pore, gigantic grins replacing their stresslines from a summer of exams. They've earned this moment. They look like Jade and I last year. I want to bottle their delight and guzzle it down my throat so that I can feel free just one more time.

Instead, I'm here to confront my best friend's murderer.

I try to force a smile on my face so that I blend in. It feels totally unnatural. I must look like a toy whose dollmaker sewed on the wrong mouth, not matching my empty eyes. I reach into my belt bag for my shades and hastily put them on to hide my lies.

Luckily, my rucksack is small and fitted on the coach with me, so I don't need to wait for the driver to open the luggage storage. Instead, I make my way to the welcome cabins, weaving in and out of people who have no idea where they're going.

The queues for the late bird tickets are long.com, though I'm pleased really – it buys me time before I face the others. As much as I want justice for Jade, I'm also freaking the hell out. It's not like standing up to a killer is on my bucket list.

I bite my nails down past the point of soreness, and finally edge closer to the kiosk window. I reach the front of the queue just as the morning sun really starts to beat down and let myself check my phone for the first time since arriving. The juice bar is bulging with life and blazing green thanks to the USB port on the coach. 100%. It's a good sign.

'Hi,' says the kiosk woman, who already looks like she's worked an eight-hour shift. 'How many?' She's got at least six wristbands on, each colour allowing access to a different area of the festival.

The jitters are in full force.

I have jellyfish for legs.

But NO WAY am I chickening out.

'Just one day ticket,' I reply, handing over Mum's card.

Turns out, finding people in a crowd of 50,000 isn't so easy.

I've been wandering about, trying to spot them, while the cinnamon scent from the churros stand tries to tempt me. Everywhere I look, people are *so* happy. They've left all their troubles at home and are here for the best time ever, while I'm doing the exact opposite. I've left safety behind and am heading straight for danger.

My heart feels extra heavy as I pass *Glitter n Glam*, our henna stall. Only, it's not *our* henna stall anymore. There's no *our*. No *us*.

I stand staring as two mates link arms, vibrant henna rainbows splashed across their faces. They don't even notice

229

me as they pick up their backpacks and tents, ready to go and find a camping spot. That's exactly what Jade and I would've done this year . . . if we'd had the chance. Gone to get our glam on *before* bothering to set up the tent. I envy their priorities.

I distract my brain by reminding myself why I'm here. I need to get focused. Where could they be? If they got here yesterday as early birds, maybe they're just waking up. But if they only arrived today, they'll likely be trying to find a spot to set up their tents.

I look at my phone; the battery is still perfect and full as it's connected to one of my power bars. I'm surprised to see how long I've been wandering for. It's already 11 a.m. They could be anywhere by now. Maybe even in the arena waiting for the first band?

I begin to twist through the party animals in headdresses and sequins and tassels, without a care in the world, watching in awe. I decide to head for the main stage, following the signs. I don't really remember the layout from last year. Maybe it's changed.

I hike for ages, though my swollen ankle begs for rest. Everything here looks close by, and I can see things in the distance, but when I start making my way over to wherever I wanna go, it feels like I'm walking to France. That's why we had to be so careful last year not to forget things when we left the tent each morning – slogging back to the campsite was legit worse than doing the beep test in PE class!

After a megasaurus trek, I finally reach the main arena. It's starting to fill up and if it's the same as last year, the music'll start in less than an hour at midday. I meander around, examining the crowds with X-ray vision.

Left, right, turning in circles.

By the ice-cream van, near the bars . . .

Finally! There's a familiar sight on the grass . . .

She's in amongst a group of friends, sat looking at their festival itineraries. Her hair slinks down her back like a waterfall, the golden clasps on her braids catching the light as she moves. Her strappy silver top rises to flash her dark skin at the small of her back. Instinct takes over and I move speedily towards her, expertly dodging other people as I go.

My nerves are like rhinos colliding inside me, every bone in my body wanting me to charge in the opposite direction, but I count to stay safe cos . . . This. Is. It.

It's happening.

'Cassie.' I keep going forward. 'Cassie!' No one reacts, burying their heads in their Get Lost programmes. 'CASSIE!' I shout as I edge closer.

Still, no one is moving.

Yeah, nice try.

Ignoring me isn't gonna cut it!

'Cass.' I place my hand on her shoulder now, my heart spinning endlessly like a roulette wheel as I wait to lock eyes with her.

Her head swivels round, looking at me like she doesn't know me.

Then I see the braces on her teeth.

'Hey!' the girl who is very much *not* Cassie says. 'What?'

'Oh, I'm so sorry,' I say, pulling my hand back. 'I thought

you were someone else.'

'Yeah, fine, no worries.' She turns back round.

I skulk away and keep snaking around in 360-degree loops. I pass the churros stand and henna stall again, then find myself prowling past Psychic Sally's caravan. I stop, taking in its colours and floaty fabrics. I stare at it, willing for something to give me a sign.

Jade, if you're up there . . .

Throw me a lifeline!

ANYTHING!

I swear to the good Lord above, even though I don't believe in God, I think she heard. Cos I'm by the wooden arch and suddenly I overhear a group as they eat delicious dough, licking their hands clean of the cinnamon sugar. A guy in a Hawaiian shirt has just told his mates, 'We need to find the Blue Zone – it's closest to the stages.'

The Blue Zone. It's where we camped last year.

But . . . my day ticket doesn't allow campsite access. I need to latch onto the boys.

I follow closely enough so to others it looks like we're together, though not so closely that it's creepy for them.

We ramble, hot and sweaty, through the crowds, until we finally arrive. The security guard on the gate asks to see our wristbands, and my 'friends' thrust their arms into the air. I copy but keep mine a little lower, just waving my fingers instead.

The guard is doing his best to look, but I can tell he's having difficulty. He's trying to check us individually, but another group of people are now pushing from behind. I drop my arm even lower in amongst everyone's forearms and stick to them like honey.

It works. I'm back in the Blue Zone.

It pulls me in like a hug and a punch at the same time.

The heat is cranking up as I roam purposefully, pulling out my best acting skills to look as if I'm finding my tent. In reality, no one else cares what I'm doing. They're too busy pitching up and making friends with their new neighbours as they crack open breakfast beers. Pretending makes me feel just a teeny tiny bit more normal though, like maybe I am just here for a good time. My eyes dart from person to person, and tent to tent, but it's like being asked to find your friends' red car on a motorway with thousands of other red cars.

It's not long before frustration creeps in. I've been plopped into a party when I feel like I'm at a morgue. And I can't see Cassie, Sam, Alex or Jonesy anywhere!

I need a better plan. I head back to the Blue Zone entrance, towards the tents nearest the gate, and start to work my way along the rows. If I do this until the final row, I'll spot them for sure. That's assuming they're even camping in this campsite.

I'm getting sticky under my armpits and on my top lip. I keep clocking new campers arriving and settling into the gaps on rows I've already looked at. It's messing up my system – I'll have to keep going back to the beginning in case they've only just arrived.

Urgh, this is impossible.

Hot and bothered, I make my way to the Portaloos to pee. I plod along, wondering if this is all hopeless. I'd have more luck getting backstage again. I *know* they're at Get Lost though.

Somewhere. Cassie told me and I saw the tickets at Sam's with my own eyes.

Maybe I should phone Cass? I don't even know if she'd help me, but . . .

WOAH.

Hold on a sec.

Holy fuckaroni, IT IS!

Here, right here before my eyes, I'm seeing black splodges on white plastic, greeting me like an angel. An actual angel – attached to a red tent. It's Monty!

I've never been so happy to see an inflatable cow.

He's sticking up on a pole, just like how Jonesy attached him last year. I run over, forgetting about needing to pee. I can't believe it. Jadey, I've found them!

A whole year I've waited to find out what happened, and now the moment is here. Anxiety and excitement flood my bloodstream, a kaleidoscope of panic.

It's time for justice.

I sit on the grass, and I wait.

Then I wait some more . . . and some more . . .

I count for protection, though it's hard to focus. There's a throbbing on my nose from where sunburn is already attacking. I keep having to go back to start at number one cos I'm losing my place and the numbers don't work when this happens.

Where are they? It's been hours. If they're not back before the last DJs sets, it means missing my coach, and I don't have a tent or sleeping bag of my own!

I've been waiting so long, the temperature is starting to drop.

The mood around me is shifting, the innocence of daytime swapped for a different kind of euphoria. I get a stab of resentment, and I allow myself to daydream what it would be like if Jade were here right now with me and what we'd be saying . . . Wait.

They're HERE!

The squad are back. It looks like they're coming to collect their hoodies and beers for tonight's partying cos they're all linking arms for warmth.

I watch as they approach, wondering if I should hide. But I'm done hiding. I want them to see me and know there's no escape from the truth. I stand up, as boldly as I can, and wait for them to spot me. But they're ambling slowly, and I can't keep it in any longer.

All the courage I couldn't find to confront Sam at his house comes surging out of me, like a million party-poppers all exploding at the stroke of midnight on New Year's Eve.

'WHAT DID YOU DO TO HER?' bursts out of my mouth as I rush towards him.

'What the hell?' Sam laughs awkwardly.

'I KNOW YOU DID IT!' My hands are on him now, my palms folded into fists as I rain down thumps on his body.

'Careful, buddy.' Jonesy steps in, pulling me away from Sam. 'What's going on?'

'HE KILLED JADE!' I shout, not caring about the other festivalgoers gawking at me.

'I think she may've dropped some bad acid,' Cassie says to them, trying to nudge the passers-by forward so they don't stare too long. 'Come here,' she says to me afterwards, trying to get between me and the boys. 'Let's chill at the tent.'

'I don't want to *chill*,' I seethe.

'Get your hands off me, freak,' Sam says, his voice darker now.

'You did something to her. For revenge!'

'Revenge?' It's Alex, sounding confused. I can't tell if it's an act though.

'So you *do* know who I am then?' Sam's closing the gap between us that Cassie tried to make. I feel his breath on me as his eyes lock mine like a padlock. Even with thousands of people milling around, it feels as if we're the only two people here.

I nod, riled up and salivating, a pitbull ready to attack.

'Can someone please tell us what's going on?' Cassie says.

'Sam murdered Jade as payback,' I say.

'Riight, okaaay.' Cassie sounds like she's thinking I really did take mind-bending drugs. 'And why would he do that?'

I hesitate. 'Cos we were there when Emily died,' I finally say, unable to hide it anymore. If I want the truth from Sam, I need to be honest too.

I watch as Cassie's face contorts like playdough into a bewildered expression. She looks at Sam as if urging him to speak.

'Interesting theory,' Sam says. 'I hate to break it to you, but you're wrong.'

'YOU'RE LYING!'

'Christ.' He looks at me with contempt. 'You actually think I killed her, don't you? You're mental, mate.'

I move to grab him, but Jonesy is still by my side and intervenes for a second time.

'Lexi, take it easy,' Jonesy says, sympathetically. He's holding me back as I froth like a demon. 'Sam, d'you know what she's talking about?'

'Yeah,' Sam replies. 'Those two shit stains were there when Em died.'

'Who?' Alex and Cassie say in unison.

'My sister!' Sam says, angrily.

Three jaws drop at the exact same time as Alex, Cassie and Jonesy gawp at us.

'Wh . . . why didn't you say?' Alex asks, puzzled.

'Wanna try having a dead sister?' Sam bites. 'My *entire* life is defined by Emily!' He shakes his head as anger turns to upset. His usually perfectly gelled hair comes a little loose and a few strands spill across his forehead. He looks small even though he's tall. 'It's—' Sam breathes in deeply then exhales. 'It's like the day she died, I died too.'

'Bloody hell,' Jonesy says, clearly in shock.

'Dude, you should've said.' It's Cassie.

'Said what?' Sam replies. '"Hey! My sister died, my parents never got over it, and my mum's having a breakdown." I didn't want you guys to know me as "that dead girl's brother".'

'We wouldn't have, babes,' Cassie assures him.

'It's not like I planned it,' Sam continues. 'It's just, when I met Alex at football, it was easier not to say anything. Then when he introduced me to you guys a few months later, it felt like the moment had passed and, well, it was too late.'

'But . . .' Alex goes to speak but trails off. I'm guessing he doesn't know what to say.

Sam keeps talking anyway. 'I'm fucking invisible at home!

I didn't want to be invisible with all of you too.' He takes another deep breath, as if assessing whether it's safe to carry on. 'We tried the whole moving thing, away from the house where it happened, but nothing changed. Mum set up a bedroom for Em in the new place anyways. All her clothes hang in the wardrobe and her toys sit on the bed. Mum screams her head off if you go in and touch anything.'

'Oh, Sam.' Cassie tries to comfort him.

'Then Dad got Mum the "reborn doll"! Do you know what that is?'

Cass, Alex and Jonesy shake their heads.

'Mum calls it Emily. She sits in the bedroom talking to a piece of plastic all day. It even has dinner with us . . .' He takes a moment. 'And yeah, that's how it is . . . You think I'm smart cos I like studying. I don't have a choice. It's the only way they notice me. To get any kind of reaction . . . from my own mum and dad . . . Even then, it barely registers.'

I stare in disbelief, wondering how he kept this locked inside. He looks so 'normal', though I guess Jade looked 'normal' too and look what happened to her. Jeez, I look 'normal' and I'm a mess. Guess you never can tell what goes on behind closed doors.

'Look.' Sam turns back to me now. 'I *hated* you guys.' He spits out the word *hated* with extra venom. 'But not enough to kill Jade. Anyway, if that's what I wanted to do, why would I have waited so long to do it?'

'Why should I believe you?' I say, feeling mixed emotions after his revelation cos it doesn't exactly sound easy living in his house.

'Because the last time I saw Jade, she was alive. She was okay.'

'When was that?' Jonesy chips in.

'Yeah, when was that?' I repeat Jonesy's words, my eyes still like magnets with Sam's. 'What happened the last time you saw her?'

'By the lake, at the party. I told her who I was.'

'*Whyy* did you do that?' I groan. He should have told us when we were together.

'Cos you two didn't seem to have a clue!'

'We didn't!' I say. We'd met Emily's brother a few times when we were little, but he'd never been interested in hanging out with us. That was a long time ago. Besides, Em had always called him Sammy.

'What did you do, babes?' Cassie says delicately to Sam.

'God, not you too,' he replies.

'Look at her,' Cass says, pointing to me as I tremble. 'You have to tell us the truth.'

'You think I don't feel guilty?' Sam snaps. 'I'll never know if what I said made Jade jump into the water. But I *swear* I never touched her.'

'You would say that,' I say.

'Trust me,' he nips. 'All this time I thought I wanted revenge, like it was the right thing for Em. But Jade's gone, and it hasn't changed anything. It's like the whole thing has happened all over again. I couldn't save my sister but . . . maybe I could've saved Jade.'

I scowl at him, trying to read his mind, unsure if this is all just a performance.

'But how do I know you're not lying?' I add.

'Because we were all together when she died,' Alex says, 'including you.'

I spin to look at him. 'We were?'

He nods. 'Believe me, I've read *every* article and report possible. I've worked it out that at the time of her death we were at the afterparty back at the tents—'

'Afterparty?' I say.

'See,' Sam says, smugly. 'We've all got a watertight alibi. I *didn't* murder her.'

No. This can't be true.

It just can't.

I've come all this way for . . . this?

If they're being honest, then the open verdict is most probably right. The chances are Jade *did* take her own life OR got stuck in a terrible accident. While I was . . . partying!

'In fact, if anyone's to blame,' Alex continues, 'it's me.' He drops to the ground and hangs his head in his lap. 'I messed up badly.'

I kneel to get on his level. What's he talking about? 'What do you mean?' I ask.

'Jade wasn't right. Like, in the head.' Alex looks up to face me. 'The stuff she was saying . . . I dunno, it was weird. I didn't really know what to do, so . . . I just left her.'

'Alive?' I say, hesitantly, unsure if this is a confession.

'Yes! Alive. Jesus, Lex.'

'Sorry, I just—'

'I didn't *do* anything. That's exactly why I feel guilty.'

'But if you didn't do anything, why—'

'Don't you get it? I did *nothing*, when she needed me most!'

Cassie bends down to comfort Alex, settling herself on the ground to hold his hand.

'And I was jealous of that Dave,' Alex says. 'How can I compete with a rock star?'

'It's okay,' Cassie tries to soothe him.

'With all his money and fame! I couldn't tell Jade about my shitty, minimum wage job. When you found me in the shop, I was so embarrassed that you knew I'd lied about working there properly. Then when you started saying Jade was upset, I thought you had it all figured out. I thought you knew I'd abandoned her – I left her alone when she needed me most and never came back.'

'What were you meant to do?' Sam pipes up.

'I was an arsehole. It didn't matter whether she wanted to be with me or not, she needed a friend, anyone, to listen. As if dick Dave cared anyways – they were off on the tour bus again before the party was even over. And without the pills she lost, it made her mind a million times worse. Jade told me she saw herself as different. Like, powerful or something. She said when it happened, she thought she was capable of superhuman stuff.

'I should've taken her to the medical tent or something. If she thought she was stronger than she was without her meds to mellow her out, maybe she thought she could swim alone in the dark and be okay in the water?'

'But . . .' I want to tell Alex that it's not his fault. That *I* have the pills. *I'm* the reason she didn't seem right. That they're upstairs in my room and if Jade had taken them as she was meant to, she'd probably still be here.

'I'm sorry,' Alex offers. 'I'm really, really sorry. Don't blame Sam – blame me.'

'Pal, don't torture yourself. It's not your fault at all,' Jonesy says. He's sitting too now so we're all in an uneven circle. 'You weren't to know it'd end like it did. Besides, I . . .'

'Besides what?' I cross-examine him like a lawyer.

Jonesy looks at me then shakes his head. 'I didn't know it'd go that far.'

'*What* would go that far?' I push, nervously, as the sun dips in the sky.

'I thought she could handle it . . .' He stops himself again.

'Handle *what*?' I glare at Jonesy as the others watch on with mystified faces.

'I mean, what's a party without bringing the party, right?' He tries to chuckle, but it doesn't come out properly.

'I don't understand,' I say.

'I thought I was helping. She needed cheering up.'

'What did you do, Jones?' Cassie pushes.

'Just . . . she said she liked the stuff that Dave had given her during the DJ set. So I maaaybe took some rum from their rider when no one was looking.'

'I thought you took wine?' I say.

'Yeah, that was before.'

'And?'

'Well, I gave her the rum,' Jonesy says, his brow crinkling. 'I told her to have it.'

'What, like a shot?'

He looks at me with regret. 'The bottle.'

I grimace back. I knew Jonesy getting us wasted messed with my memory of what happened, but I didn't realise Jade was still knocking them back without me. She'd have been paralytic! Waay too drunk to swim to safety if she ended up in the water by accident.

'I thought it'd cheer her up. She seemed up for it. Then when I woke up on the final morning and saw she was gone, I . . . I . . . was bricking it. I wanted to tell you so badly, but I . . . well, I just couldn't. I even went to her grave to say sorry, but I still feel guilty.'

As Jonesy talks, I try to keep up. If *he* left the confession note, I was right first time.

R *is* Ryan. Not Rathborne.

'It's my fault,' Jonesy's whimpering now. 'I should've walked her back to the tents, got her some food, anything! I'm an idiot. I'm sorry. I'm so, so sorry.'

Everyone falls silent. The noise from the campsite seems to fade. Even the music and sound of people screaming on the fairground rides drifting over goes quiet. I'm sure I could hear a pin drop. All I can think of is Jade in the water, lost, not knowing where I was.

'Mate, I don't think it was you.' Cassie scooches over to Jonesy to comfort him, putting a hand on his arm.

'Sounds to me like it was,' I bite back.

'Lex.' She takes a breath before she says more, which is rare for her. 'I get how it looks, babes, but Jonesy was only trying to have fun.'

'Have fun! Are you for real?'

'Look.' She pulls apart from Jonesy. 'He may've given her

the bottle, but he didn't put a gun to her head to drink it.'

'Oh, wow, Cass,' I say, 'that's low.'

'Is it?' she asks bluntly. 'I didn't love the girl, but I didn't want anything bad to happen to her.'

'Sure.' I keep prodding. 'He practically spiked her to death!'

'He didn't spike her, Lex,' Cassie snaps. 'Jade was her own person – she was perfectly capable of making her own decisions.'

'Why are you defending him?' I say, hurt.

'I'm not defending anyone. I just don't think it's his fault, or Sam's or Alex's . . . it's mine.'

'What?' I say, surprised, as we all turn to face her.

'Yeah,' she says, coolly. 'That's why I hate thinking about it all.'

'What happened?' I ask.

'I saw how she got in your head.' Cassie's tone swings from that of a friend to that of a stranger. 'How the two of you couldn't exist without each other. It reminded me of my ex. So controlling! I needed his permission to breathe. I thought I was helping you, Lex, making you see that you could be you *without* her.'

'You were?' I say, weirdly flattered despite the inappropriateness of the feeling.

'You're a force, Lex, and you don't even know it. I feel guilty, just like Alex, Ry and Sam, every day. But I'm the one who left her – after Alex had gone and after Jonesy gave her the bottle. I stole Jade's best mate. I should've asked her to party with us. Should've, would've, could've. I can't change it. Doesn't mean I don't wish I'd done things differently.'

Just as I think Cassie's finished, she keeps going . . .

'Happy now? You have someone to blame. I'm sorry this shitty, awful, ugly thing happened to you. But you're not so innocent yourself, Lexi.'

CHAPTER 29

JADE

I glug some of the brown stuff from the bottle Jonesy gave me. It burns my throat on the way down, like I have a dragon in my lungs now, not just my belly. I pace around in circles, desperately listening to Emily to figure out what to do next . . .

'Find Lexi. Find her and talk to her,' she whispers, gently.

I walk towards the forest, me and my bottle of fire water. It's the way that Lexi went after our argument, I think. I pass tree after tree, but they all look the same. For perspective, I try to keep an eye on the clearing that frames the lake, but soon it vanishes. Now I'm lost, wandering around aimlessly for what feels like forever.

In the distance, I see a figure I recognise.

'Jaaaade, fancy seeing you here,' he says into the darkness.

'Yeah, fancy that. I'm looking for Lexi – you seen her?'

'I'll leave you guys to it,' Emily interjects.

Wait, what? Em! Don't leave now, I need you!

'Yeah, I've seen her but I think you and me need to have a little chat.' Sam's cool in his delivery as he steps closer.

'Oookay,' I say. What could we possibly have to talk about?

'You don't remember me, do you?' he asks as he takes my hand and walks me to a tree, sitting us both down on the grassy mound at its base. It's damp with dew.

'Remember you? From when?' I ask.

'A long time ago. C'mon, Jade, think,' he tells me firmly.

'I'm really sorry – I don't understand what you're talking about.' I look into his eyes, desperately trying to recognise them.

'Oh, that can't be true, can it? I always thought you were the compassionate one, out of you and Lexi. That you'd be so affected that you'd never forget my face. It would haunt you every night. Are you telling me you haven't seen this in your nightmares?' He draws his face close to mine, his outstretched finger pointing towards his chin.

'Nightmares?' What is he . . . ? Oh. Wait. 'You're . . .' No, he can't be . . . Sammy.

'You're Emily's brother? But why didn't she say something?'

'Well, she couldn't, could she? She's dead!' he spits. 'But you saw me. You saw me, and my mum and dad. You saw how that day destroyed us all. Yet, for some reason, our faces and our hurt isn't burned into your mind.' There's a strange calm washing over him now; I see the colour of his aura turn lighter. 'Are you really that self-involved, Jade?'

'No, I . . .'

'I think you must be. When we arrived, I thought, *Oh wow, this is gonna be rough, when they see me. It's gonna slap them round the face, all the guilt. And then it'll be awkward cos they'll have to tell the others and they'll spend the whole weekend apologising over and over and it'll be hard to have fun.* But . . . there was nothing. I thought, *Maybe it'll take a minute for the penny to drop. Maybe if they get to know me, it'll all fall into place.* But we've been together, day and night for a whole weekend, and you only realised when I forced you to.'

'I'm sorry, I . . .'

'Sorry for not remembering, or sorry for killing my sister?' Sam tilts his head to one side as if to say, 'I'm waiting'.

'Both . . . Not a day goes by where I don't think about her. I talk to her all the time. She talks to me!' I insist.

'What does that even mean? She can't talk! She's dead. She died because of you and your selfishness and Lexi and her selfishness and neither of you even care or show any regrets? Otherwise, surely, you would have recognised me!'

I don't know what to say. I guess he's right. How didn't I recognise him? And why didn't Emily say anything? Maybe deep down she's still mad at us too.

'You know, the thing that I've just never been able to understand is why wasn't it you two?' He's staring at me again, waiting for an answer. 'And there's no doubt it should have been! It absolutely 100% should have been the two of you.' He lunges for me, and I throw myself backwards, my back catching on a root beneath me. 'Don't worry, I'm not going to do anything. I'm not like you. And if we're all honest, I don't need to, do I? You're quite capable of ruining your own life. I'm off to have a little chat with your mate, Lex, if she's sober enough to stand still.' He gets up and shakes his head at me before stalking off into the night.

Once his silhouette has vanished, I cram my hands into my

bra, grabbing for my phone. I have to warn Lexi. I have to tell her who Sam really is.

I dial Lex but it's not ringing. It goes straight to answerphone.

Oh Emily, what should I dooooo?

I'm sorry, Em, I'm so sorry. I'm sorry for all of it!

I leave a voicemail asking her to call me back, then wait. I pace. *Where are you, Lex? Where are you, Em?* Maybe they're together. I call again – another voicemail. I repeat time and time again. Nothing.

I voice note Lexi instead, telling her to come to me immediately so we can be together and make everything right again. We can apologise to Emily and the three of us can be reunited.

'Emilyyy, where are you?' I'm shouting into the night now.

'It's okay,' she replies calmly. Thank the spirits she's back. 'He was always going to be angry – you'd be angry, wouldn't you?' She sounds kind, caring. 'But I'm not angry. Not with you. I love you, Jade. I know it was just a horrible accident.' I'm still waiting for the ticks on my voice note for Lexi to turn blue. 'I know you're a good person. You must believe that. It's a beautiful night – I'm having the best' time with us all this weekend. The lake is magical – come and take a dip with me. It'll soothe you a little.'

CHAPTER 30

LEXI

'But you're not so innocent yourself, Lexi,' says Cassie, but it shoots in one ear and out the other. It's like I'm skydiving out of a plane with everything whooshing past. 'Parties' by Kreep comes through the speakers from a nearby tent and it corkscrews inside my mind.

> *You and me, we'll dance 'til sunlight*
> *Carry on some more, again 'til twilight*
> *Never stop those dancing feet*
> *Just you and me, baby, to the heartbeat*

It was our favourite Kreep song. We'd listen to it in our bedrooms, in our gardens, in the park, through shared headphones on the bus. We wrote the lyrics to each other in birthday cards, on schoolbooks, on pencil cases, passing it on secret notes in class. The words are Sharpie'd on my bedroom wall. It would take us hours to listen to the album as we'd keep stopping the record to play 'Parties' on repeat. It was our song.

You and me, we'll be forever free
Carry on some more, just wait and see
Never stop your singing heart
Just you and me, baby, we're works of art

I'm caught between the past and present. Here, last year. Here, today. 0 days gone; 362 days gone. The sky scribbled black then, the lazy blue haze now.

'Parties' twirls in my eardrums. I haven't been able to listen to it since she died. I catapult back to last year . . . and she's right here! I see her face but there's a galaxy of space between us. Not just literal, physical space, but mental space too. We're disjointed, hanging on by taut string. It's threatening to ping apart and send us reeling in opposite directions.

I hold a hand up to try to touch past-Jade as present-Cassie says something. I think she's asking the boys if I'm okay, but I'm rooted to the memory, no longer in the real world.

'Fine?' Jade squawks. 'You think I'm fine!' We're in the same spot as I saw us in Alex's video.

'FriendsDontTell,' I slur, the words spilling from my mouth, splattering out like bulbous raindrops.

My heart shatters at the memory.

Jade told.

I don't know who walks away first, but I yank off my amethyst ring and hurl it at her. It bounces off Jade and she looks down to see what I threw. Suddenly, Cass's hand is around my wrist, leading me away. I say, 'I'm upset', but she says, 'Jade's a party-pooper'.

I follow Cassie blindly, tripping on discarded plastic pint cups and people chilling on the ground. They shout, 'Oi!' as if it's my fault I don't have laser vision to see in the dark. I say sorry without stopping; we jostle away like seaweed through the ocean. It doesn't feel right without Jade, and I want to turn back, but Cassie directs us away from the crowd.

We walk and we walk and we walk, Cassie guiding us through the maze of the festival grounds, cheering when she sees the Blue Zone sign. But I can't cheer . . . Jade *betrayed* me. I hear, 'Relaaax – it's time for fun!'

Soon, I'm flying.

High in the air, above the ground.

I'm a bird gliding blind.

Then . . . I crash with a deafening crack.

My feet have tangled in the ropes attaching our tent to the ground. Cassie helps me up. There's a broken bottle underneath me. Everything smells like Skittles. Jade's perfume is in pieces. I can't feel the pain though I feel like crying.

'You'll be fiiiine!' says Cass. I'm told to cheer up. I do. My new T-shirt is slashed – the one Cassie bought me before our tattoos. I see blood. My blood. 'It's okay. You're hardcore, babes! No good story ever started with a salad.' She laughs. I laugh too.

I need to stay safe. We find our door using the torch light on Cassie's phone. She messages the others – they'll meet us here. Time to fix drinks. Apparently, we need more.

Jonesy, Sam and Alex appear.

Hugs. Lots of hugs.

There's a huge roar of excitement.

Drinks, everywhere. Swigging from cans. I've lost count. Mum always said, 'Lex, count your drinks – stay alert.' But I don't know how many; I don't want to poop the party.

We need music. Alex doesn't want Kreep cos he says Dave's a jerk, but Jonesy begs 'just one song'. He scrambles into the tent for speakers. 'Parties'! It blares out across the campsite. My heart is full. Wait. Where did Jade go? I can't remember when I last saw her.

Someone grabs my hand.

'You and me, we'll dance 'til sunlight. Carry on some more, again 'til twilight. Never stop those dancing feet. Just you and me, baby, to the heartbeat,' Cassie sings at me. I try to stay standing, propped up by Sam, Jonesy and Alex bobbing beside me.

'Justyouandmebabytotheheartbeat,' I sing back, looking at Cassie with glazed vision and wondering why she's not Jade. Jade should be here! 'WheredidJadeygo?'

'Huh?' Cassie shouts back at me. She pulls her braids aside to gift me her ear.

'Idontremember.' I giggle, completely forgetting what I asked a second ago. She laughs too, taking my hand and placing our wrist tattoos together to make a full moon.

We sing. Sing. Sing. The night is ours. Cassie wafts her arms in the sky like the divine fairy queen of the night that she is. I try to dance too. Must keep upright. The boys laugh.

A pain. In my arm. I look down and see glass sticking out of my skin. Why am I bleeding? Jonesy wrenches it out for me. I'm told, 'You tripped on a bottle.' I did? Oh yeah!

I keep dancing though now I'm crying. Why am I crying?

I need Jade, but I don't know how to get to her. Where is my phone? Cassie doesn't notice until I wipe the tears and pull my hand away to see a monster eyeliner smudge on my finger.

'What's wrong?' she finally asks. 'You look hilarious!'

'Idontknow,' I say, crying and laughing.

'Come here.' She takes my hand, leading us towards the tents. 'You need to have some fun, guurl! I'll fix drinks.' Then it's in my hand. A plastic shot glass. Smile for a selfie.

'Whatisit?' I ask, confused.

'Just knock it back, babes!' Cassie sinks her drink. I try to copy her. Not so cool. Sticky black liquid drips down my chin. Cass lets out a wicked laugh. How many drinks? Must find my phone. I've lost count. Mum said I should count. Another one? Okay!

'Give it here.' Cassie takes the shot glass. It's full again. Jonesy's behind me. Grabbing the back of my head. Cassie pushes the rim to my mouth. I feel the tilt of my neck. The drink goes down in one quick motion. Fire in my throat. 'There you go – you're a pro!'

Everyone cheers for me.

Jonesy passes the bottle round, saying he 'borrowed' it from Kreep's rider. We all laugh. Take it in turns to glug, glug, glug. It starts to rain – really pour – but no one cares.

Wait, where is Jade again?

Suddenly, there's two of Cassie. Two mouths, two noses, four eyes. Her skin is moving like a magic-eye picture. My head spins like a carousel. I want to be sick.

I am sick.

I'm too late to get to a loo or find a bin. A puddle of mushy Pop Tart pools at my feet.

'Imsorry,' I say, forcing my head back up. I feel snot hanging from my nostrils.

'No drama, babes,' Cassie says.

'I love a tactical chunder! Chuck it up now so you can carry on,' Jonesy adds.

'Butmyheadstillhurts,' I reply.

Sam says I should change into non-vom clothes. Okay. Sorry, everyone. I lost count. I put on Jade's pyjamas. Where is she? My sleeping bag looks beautiful. I need to get in it. Right now.

'Lexi? Lex!' It's Cassie. Here, last year. Here, today. 0 days gone; 362 days gone.

I don't know if it's real or a dream. I lose Cassie's voice. Shrieks and howls of laughter from people close by as they cackle around campfires.

'Lex,' a voice says, 'we need to party more!' I can't bring myself to reply. The words won't formulate on my tongue. It's made of lead.

'Don't go dead on me!' the voice says again. A rustle of Kylie's door. It moves aside. Jonesy. He tries to sit down. There's a pop. Laughter. Something under the mattress. A stone? He lifts it up. Nope, no stone. Underneath, my sunglasses – snapped. 'Hey, what's this?' Something shiny. Tablets. For a headache, Jonesy says. Take these. 'La-mo-tri-gine,' he tries to read. 'I think it's aspirin!' he adds. I take the little metallic rectangle. Two rows of round pills neatly packaged inside. I can't find a drink. Another shot appears.

A Jägermeister to take the 'aspirin' with, Cassie says. They all want me to wake up and re-join the part-ay. I take the shot. Place the pills in the pocket of Kylie.

Where's my phone? Need to call Jade. No energy. Zapped away.

Sleep calls my name. I answer its call.

'Booooriiing!' Cassie shouts. She gives up. The boys laugh again. They party. I'm sorry. Too many. I lost count. Knocked out. I should've counted.

I REMEMBER.

CHAPTER 31

JADE

As I paddle my toes around in the water, following Emily's instructions, I hear her reminding me, 'Check your phone again.' The screen comes on brightly and I notice the ticks for the voice note still haven't turned blue. 'She'll see it soon – it's going to be okay. Shall we go and wait for her by the cove? It's so pretty tonight! Lex'll come and meet us there and we'll have the most beautiful reunion.' Emily sounds excited.

'I don't know, Em – how do we get there and how will Lexi know where to find us?'

'I'll show you and I'll tell her, silly!' Emily replies.

'Okay, I'm just gonna send her another message in case she can't hear you. I don't know if she really can't hear you sometimes, or if she just wants to pretend she can't so we don't have to talk about you so much.' I bring my phone up to my mouth again.

'Okay, and then just follow the sound of my voice.'

So I do, past tree after tree. I can smell all the pines so intensely now. Their branches bend as though they're waving at me as I walk by, one after the other. Maybe because I want them to, they can tell, and they're trying to make me happy.

Emily whispers to me every now and then, 'here', and she sends a little flash of light from her position ahead to guide me. Soon, it'll be me and Em and my Lexi, and we'll put everything right, finally.

Em's flashes of light draw me towards the bank of the lake. The moon's reflection looks beautiful on the water. 'Here,' she says softly again, a little silver flash bouncing off the surface. 'Get in,' she instructs, gently.

'It's cold, Em!' I squeal.

'Don't worry,' she replies. 'I'll warm it up.'

I walk closer to the bank, water lapping gently against it. I place my shoes I'm carrying down, putting Lex's ring inside one so she'll know where to find us when she arrives. My toes submerge again, followed by my ankles, shins, knees and hips.

I go a little deeper and just like she promised, it gets steadily warmer. Just me and Emily, our lake and our moon. I look up to see if I can spot all the constellations that Alex showed me, but it's hard to see the stars tonight. Grey clouds sit on top of the blanket of navy-blue, the twinkles trying to pierce through. I turn around to spot Emily and begin to swim in her direction.

'I missed being in the water with you, Jade. It was our favourite place, wasn't it? Splashing and kicking and doing handstands on the bottom.'

I feel a little speck of rain fall from the clouds and land on the tip of my nose. The current begins to pick up. It's rushing in exactly the wrong direction, trying to push me away from Emily, making the swimming harder now.

I squeeze my eyes shut and speak to the wind, picturing it blowing towards Em's voice, all wispy and fragile. I think of the calmest words I can muster. I tell her to relax, settle and rest, on repeat. And she does. I feel her racing over the skin on my back now, pushing me along. I feel her friend drip-dropping onto me, heavier and heavier. Too bad I don't know how to talk to the rain – we'll just have to put up with him, Em!

I paddle as fast as I can now towards Emily's light, hoping to reach her soon. I might not be able to talk to the rain, but I can race it!

The wind must know my plan too because she starts to blow me off course again. I get it – you must always choose your best friend. I find some strength from somewhere to push back and make good headway. I'll get to you, Emily, don't you worry about that!

They don't like it one bit though . . . The rain starts to really pour now, and the wind blows a gust, throwing up a wave that pulls me under. I bounce to the surface and tread water to catch my breath and my bearings. The Magician card appears in the air next to Emily's light; it's life-size, bigger than me, and I swim towards them both. I do my best breaststroke, pushing with my legs like a frog, like I was taught in primary. I was good at frog legs; Lexi was okay; Emily was even worse. That's why the birthday didn't go as planned.

Splash Saturday, that's what Emily's invitation said. The house was amazing – her very own pool in the garden! Me and Emily wanted to eat cake, but Lexi wanted to play. So we bombed into the water to see who could hold their breath the longest.

We took it in turns, timing each other . . . Lexi could do it for ages!

Me and Em tried to beat her, so every turn took longer and longer. It was tiring in the deep end treading water, waiting for your turn. Me and Lex swam to the edge after our goes and stretched our arms over the side to hold us up. Emily said she wanted to have one more try to beat Lex's time and dived under without warning.

Lex was timing her but then, out of nowhere, this beautiful butterfly came and landed on my arm. It was so pretty, covered in colourful splotches . . . I wanted Lex to see the patterns. She must've forgotten to keep count cos next thing, there was a massive scream. It shook me back to reality and I spun around to see it was coming from Emily's mum. At first I thought Em was in trouble for something, then I realised Lex had stopped counting and neither of us knew where Em was.

Someone rushed from inside the house, waving something shiny in their hands. Me and Lex were still in the water, frozen stiff. The shiny thing in that lady's hands were scissors and the lady was Emily's auntie. She jumped in the pool fully clothed. I realised Em was still in the water, under the water – she hadn't come up that whole time we'd been playing with the butterfly.

We were still frozen, but my mind raced – should I duck under and go to help? Should me and Lex get out? Why wasn't she popping back up? C'mon, Em!

A head bobbed up to the surface and I started to feel relieved, but it was Em's auntie. She only came back up for a breath before going back under again. Emily's mum was on her knees at the edge of the pool, her hands wrapped around each other, like she was praying.

Her auntie reappeared, pushing Emily in her little swimsuit – it was red – up onto the poolside, where her dad lifted her out of the water. She had no hair left.

Emily was blue. Not blue like a blueberry, or blue like a summer sky, but a faded blue like jeans that have been washed too many times. Blue cos she'd been in the water too long.

I just wanted to look at that butterfly. I didn't know her long golden hair had got tangled in the filter, and she hadn't been able to free herself. Neither did Lexi!

I still hear the sound of the ambulance arriving sometimes, piercing into my brain. I see the looks on our mums' faces when they came to take us away. They told us it was an accident, but I don't think I believed them really. No one ever spoke about that day again.

This time, Em, I'm going to do it – I'm going to make it up to you!

I can see you up ahead, with all my tarot cards around you like guardians, all of them apart from Death. I guess that makes sense – Emily said it was all going to be okay.

Just as I'm settling into my rhythm of swimming, I feel my head bash onto something hard. A log, I think. I'm pushed under again, and I try to swim to the top, but I don't know where the surface is now. A flash of light appears. Emily!

I race towards her. My legs are tired now and I'm not sure how long I can hold my breath, but Emily calls me, whispering, 'Keep going.'

I won't be long, Em! Then the three of us can be together.

You did tell Lexi, right?

'Of course I did. Relax, she's on her way.'

So I do as Emily says. I relax, I stop fighting the water, I close my eyes for some calm and I let my frog legs take a break. The cards hover in my mind's eye and sway for me, back and forth. I feel like a baby being rocked to sleep.

Em tells me Lexi's close, and she'll be here any minute. I can't wait to squeeze her. She'll be so proud of me for swimming all this way by myself. Em says she's proud too.

The water decides to join in with rocking me to sleep. He sways me; the cards swing. And then they fade one last time, so now it's just Emily's face up ahead.

Oh, Em, I've missed your face!

So kind and open and gentle.

She smiles as I drift towards her, taking my hand when I arrive, as if to say it's all going to be okay. Off we go. Into the calm, twinkling, navy-blue night together.

CHAPTER 32

LEXI

I chew what's left of my nails nervously, knowing that Mum called Petra after I declared Sam was going to kill us and then ran away to Get Lost with her bank card.

'Guessing you know everything?' I say, breaking the silence for a change.

'Your mum mentioned a few things; perhaps you can tell me in your own words,' Petra replies as I listen to the whir of a fan in the corner. It's a new addition to the room.

'I . . . I . . . I don't know what's happening to me,' I cave.

Petra watches me, her eyes filled with sympathy, and I begin to crumble; everything I've kept locked inside rushes through me, like a million little fish racing upstream.

And suddenly, they plop out of my mouth one by one.

'Even though I know what happened to Jade . . .' I'm confessing! 'I'm still counting.'

'Counting?'

'Yeah,' I say, 'if I don't count to the safe number—'

'The safe number?'

I nod.

'What's that, Lexi?'

'It changes. Today it's 369.'

'Okay. What's special about 369?'

'It's the number of days Jade has been gone.'

Petra bobs her head to signal she's following, like the toy dog on Mum's car dashboard that moves as we drive.

'In the beginning, I didn't realise I was doing it. It was sort of for luck, but now it's like I can't stop. I have to count before I do things . . .' I trail off.

'Can you give me any examples?'

'Umm, yeah. Like, before bad things can happen: turning the oven on, the toaster, the kettle, when Mum leaves for work, while she's on her way home, then, err, before crossing the road or whatever. Things like that – but now it's more often, it just sort of keeps happening even when I don't plan to . . .' I begin to unstitch the tapestry I've woven, amazing even myself at how long the list is.

'How does it make you feel when you do the counting?' Petra asks calmly.

'Dunno.' I squirm.

'Sad? Angry? Alone?'

'No,' I reply.

Petra looks at me with a gentle smile as if it all makes perfect sense to her.

'You might count for that very reason. So that you *don't* feel sad, angry or alone. To numb yourself. The numbers take away all of these feelings.'

I guess I'd never thought of it like that before.

'Does that sound fair?' she asks. 'That the rituals busy your mind so that you don't have to experience these difficult emotions – that they distract you somehow?'

'Sort of . . . but I need to count . . . to keep Mum safe.'

'Oh, okay,' she replies, 'and she'll be unsafe if you don't?'

'Yes. If I don't, she'll die.' I look at her, ashamed. It's so real inside my mind, but out in the open it seems completely ridiculous. 'I know it sounds crazy, but . . .'

'It doesn't sound crazy.'

'Why do you think I do it?' I look at Petra, pleading for her to tell me.

'Why do I think you do it?' she repeats, taking a breath as if to choose her words carefully. 'It sounds like someone who is in a lot of pain trying to keep everything together to stop herself from feeling more pain. I think the counting allows you to feel in control when everything else feels out of control. I also think it's your way of keeping your mum "safe" so that you don't have to lose anyone again, like you did with your best friend.'

I take a moment to absorb what she's just said. 'What about my phone?' I ask.

'Your phone?'

'I check that more than 369 times a day – like, a thousand times.'

'A thousand? That sounds pretty exhausting.'

'It is!' I say, grateful that she is hearing me. 'I have to check that it's on 100%.'

'And what happens when it's not on 100%?'

'The same thing as not counting. I'll kill Mum.'

'You'll kill your mum?'

'Not personally, but if the battery drops below 100% she'll die, and it will be my fault because I let it.' I drop my head towards my lap, embarrassed.

Petra nods again in acknowledgement. We sit in silence for a while. I watch all of what I've told her sink into her mind.

'Would you like to talk about what happened to your friend?' she asks.

'Err, okay,' I reply.

'It's just, I'm wondering – what was the last phone call or text you two had before she died?'

'We didn't. My phone ran out of juice on the second day.'

'Ahh, okay. So you had no battery for most of the festival?'

'Yeah, the queues to charge them took hours and I wasn't bothered. Jade was taking all the photos and stuff.'

'You were okay with not having a full battery then?' she probes.

'Yeah, I didn't need for it to be 100% ever before.'

'And what happened when you got home and charged your phone for the first time after the festival?'

'It was in the car when my mum collected us. Well, me. The phone turned itself back on and all of these voicemails and messages from Jade came flooding in.'

I can see myself in the front seat, crusty old glitter tattooed on my skin, smudged eyeliner from the night before, in shock from what had unravelled after waking up to discover no Jade at the tents. Waiting and waiting for her to return. Checking the Portaloos – the girls' then the guys'. Yelling her name. Waiting some more. Shouting at the marshals as they shouted

266

back at me to get off site as the festival was over. Missing the coach we'd been booked on. Calling home. The sound of sirens. Assuming they'd carry on past me as I stood at the exit. Seeing the ambulance slow. Driving into the festival site. Overhearing a voice on a walkie-talking saying a body had been found by the lake. Running. Dropping to the ground. Jade. Dead.

'You've been through a lot – *are* still going through a lot,' Petra says. 'From what I'm hearing, I think what happened then might be triggering what's happening now.'

'How do you mean?'

'The fact your phone wasn't charged meant that you didn't realise Jade was sending you messages, when perhaps you feel she needed you most. I think you are maybe overcompensating for that by feeling the need to have your phone charged at 100% so that what happened that night can never happen again? I also think your brain believes you are in real danger when the phone isn't fully charged in case history repeats itself and you lose someone else. Your mum also said you lost count of your drinks, meaning numbers are immensely important to you right now. So by doing your rituals, you feel in control, like no one else can die – after Jade at the festival, and the other girl you told me about at primary school. When you forgot to count in the pool? That's a lot of death for someone your age.'

'Thank you,' I say.

'For what?'

'For not telling me I'm crazy.'

'Lexi, you're not crazy. You're grieving.'

* * *

267

I must be feeling extra positive after my session with Petra as I decide to walk to Jade today rather than wait for the bus. And instead of being grumpy that it takes so long, I'm grateful for the little things, like the sun shining and a ladybird that lands on my arm.

Even as I make my way through the cemetery, I feel lighter, like maybe there is a reason to wake up each day after all . . .

I place the pink crystal speckled with black down on her grave at the end where I imagine her head is. I spent a whole day researching the best one to buy. Apparently, rhodonite means honesty, forgiveness and truth. When it arrived through the post, there was a little pamphlet that said the stone can clear away emotional wounds and scars from the past, and that it can release any lingering co-dependency patterns!

'So . . . do you wanna hear how it went?' I say, laying my hoodie down on the marble so I can get comfy. I fill Jade in about Get Lost and pretend to wait for an answer. I imagine her curious eyes spurring me on to reveal exactly what happened.

And so, I begin to tell her all about the confessions: how Sam hated us for the part we played in Emily's death but how bad he feels for spilling his true identity when Jade was alone; how sorry Jonesy is for giving her so much booze she wasn't safe; that Alex tortures himself for abandoning her when she needed him the most; how Cassie feels guilty for trying to drive a wedge between us as she thought it would help me be more independent.

We were *all* full of secrets.

Each of us carrying around guilt, blaming ourselves.

I relay everything I remember about being at the tent that

final night: how I ripped my T-shirt on the broken perfume bottle, cut myself and didn't even notice I was bleeding; I took her lamotrigine pills thinking they were aspirin; and I blacked out while she drowned.

All this time I was feeling guilty that I might have done something. Now, like Alex, I feel guilty I did nothing. I now know why that word 'guilty' fell out of my mouth when I started seeing Petra – cos I was lying in my sleeping bag, warm and safe, as Jade fought for breath and her lungs filled with water. And I guess I've always felt guilty for not keeping count for Emily all those years ago even though I tried to bury it deep, deep inside.

'I'm so, so sorry, Jadey. I wish I could bring you back.' A lump swells in my throat. 'It's messed up, right?! Everyone had a part to play. We ALL feel guilty – we all messed up in our own stupid ways – but, also, no one meant to hurt you. I really believe that now.' I pause, swaying between reality and illusion that she can hear.

'It's hard,' I continue, 'cos even though I got what I wanted from Sam, I still don't know what happened to you in your final moments, y'know? You must've been so afraid when he told you who he was – I would've been, especially alone by the lake like that . . .'

I pick up the rhodonite stone again and play with it, as if it might hold more answers as to how I'm going to move forward without my best friend. It catches the sunlight, and I realise just how beautiful it is. No wonder Jade loved crystals; they let you dream of a better place without problems and the twisted pain of loss.

'Just . . . was it an accident or did you really want out?' I place the crystal back and hug my knees into my chest, wondering if this hurt will ever ease. 'I hope you know that whatever I said during that row, I would've always been there for you, no matter what.'

I stop and twiddle with my amethyst ring, trying to connect with her.

'Your mind is what made you you. No matter how much shame you felt. You know I've always hated that line: "a broken brain is like a broken leg". A broken leg doesn't leave you seeing spirits, thinking you can talk to them! But I get now why people say it, cos telling people you take those pills should be the same as telling them your limb is in a cast.'

As the sun beats down, I look up to the sky. For the first time in a long while, I feel like Jade is with me again. Spiritually, if not physically.

'So, yeah, there's peace in knowing what I do about what happened that night, and I'm trying to make peace in the not-knowing too and . . . well, I'm feeling okay about that.'

Petra said it'd be strange to go through all of this and not change as a person. I still feel like me, just a different version. At first, losing Jade made me feel harder around the edges. I didn't want to get close to Mum in case I lost her too. I didn't want to feel *anything*. I thought that if I didn't feel, I could somehow protect myself. But now, feeling is all I have. Petra also told me that grief is just love with nowhere to go.

I go to take my DMs off to free my clammy feet and wiggle my toes, when I realise I've forgotten to do the great unveiling!

'Wow! How could I not remember?' I bend my leg to lean

on my knee, pull off a shoe, tug the sock away and thrust my ankle into view. *Jade* is inked in a heart tattoo. 'Told you I'd get one with you! I wanted it on my ankle so it's like every step I take, you're right there with me.'

I place a finger to my lips.

'Sssh, Mum doesn't know about this one yet. And she's being cool right now, so I don't want anything to ruin that. Petra's a bae too. She's going to help me get some routine back – apparently it'll help me "feel in control again". She even wants me to try meditation! I know, right? I thought you'd be happy about that one. She said it'd be good to shut up my obsessive death thoughts.'

I pause for breath before the next thing, wondering whether to say it aloud or not, even though if Jade can hear me I'm pretty she can *see* everything I'm doing too.

'I've had a few texts,' I say, 'with the others, since I got back. Jonesy wants to see me, if that's okay? I know it sounds strange, given everything that went down at Get Lost. I guess Cass just opened my eyes to see that it's okay to have other friends and it doesn't dilute what I had with you. If you don't want me to, you can say . . . Seriously, now is that moment to rise from the dead and prove to me the afterlife exists.'

I chuckle to myself, even though the agony still rips at my insides.

'I'm tryna take it one day at a time,' I say, kissing my fingers then touching the headstone as if to transfer it to Jade. 'Petra said that if day by day still feels a lot, then take it hour by hour, or minute by minute. Even breath by breath. Just one breath at a time.

'I think I can do that.'

I reposition the crystal, say my goodbyes and make my way back along the path.

But before I reach the exit, I stop for the first time at the grave with all the helium balloons and colourful windmills, beside the girl who will forever be eight years old. I wanted to buy a card but I got scared her family might find it, like how I found Jonesy's note, and get upset. Instead, I pick up a twig and use it to write in the soil so it can blow away . . .

We're sorry, L & J.

ACKNOWLEDGEMENTS

NADZ

Firstly, thank you Mum for letting me go to my first ever festival, at sixteen years young. It became a space where I had permission to be me; a home where I found my voice during a time I felt voiceless; and a place I'd eventually meet the boy of my dreams, years later.

Reading Festival, you have my heart.

To my big sister, Livi. Thank you for letting me gatecrash your tent that weekend with the cool kids! For being my partner in crime to all the countless festivals and gigs that followed, which shaped who we are today. Stay beautiful.

To my fellow sagittarius, Dad. Your words of wisdom will always keep me cool in a crisis and your endless optimism inspires me every day.

To James. My twin. To all the nights I'll never remember with the person I'll never forget. You are the summer I'll feel forever.

To Grace, through the twists and turns of our own friendship, we did it!

To Emily, for being an early reader and giving your

witchy wisdom to lend authenticity to Jade's tarot reading with Psychic Sally.

To Kat (my very own Petra), for helping me see the light when all I saw was darkness.

This book wouldn't be here if it wasn't for the incredible Chloe Seager, book agent extraordinaire. Thank you for championing us from the start. Special shoutout to Papa Seager too – without his matchmaking, perhaps none of this would have happened.

Immeasurable amounts of love and gratitude go to Polly Lyall Grant and Anne Marie Ryan, for believing in Lexi and Jade, and the power of their friendship. To all the Hachette team for making this dream a reality . . . they say not all superheroes wear capes.

And GIANT thanks to all of you amazing readers for picking up this book. I hope you enjoy getting lost in the magic of Get Lost as much as we enjoyed writing it.

GRACE

Chloe Seager – our wonderful agent who believed in us and brought out our best from the start.

Hachette – for trusting our voice.

Mum and Dad – for encouraging me to chase pipe dreams.

Jonny – for pushing me when I didn't think I could do it. And for digging out the frying pan when I couldn't stop writing long enough to make dinner.

Nadz – for letting me believe there might be a writer in me somewhere.

Joanna – for helping me to trust my brain again so I can be more of myself.

Martin Seager – for bringing both Chloe and Joanna into my life.

And finally, 'Viva' Brother – for hurling me head long into the chaos of festivals and gigs I'll never forget.

RESOURCES

If you have been affected by any of the issues in this book . . .
. . . we see you, we feel you, we hear you.

For help and advice, the following organisations offer a
non-judgemental ear.

OCD UK
01332 588112 (9 a.m.–12 p.m., Mon–Fri)
https://www.ocduk.org

BIPOLAR UK
info@bipolaruk.org
https://www.bipolaruk.org

PAPYRUS (SUICIDE PREVENTION)
Call: 0800 068 4141 (9 a.m.–12 p.m., every day)
https://www.papyrus-uk.org

CRUSE (BEREAVEMENT SUPPORT)
0808 808 1677 (Mon/Fri, 9.30 a.m.–5 p.m.; Tues/Wed/Thur,
9.30 a.m.–8 p.m.; Sat/Sun, 10 a.m.–2 p.m.)
https://www.cruse.org.uk

Want to be the first to hear about the
best new teen and YA reads?

Want **exclusive content, offers** and **competitions?**

Want to **chat about books** with people who
love them as much as you do?

Look no further...

Find your place

 @teambkmrk

SNEAK PEAKS

BONUS CONTENT

OFFERS AND GIVEAWAYS

See you there!

bkmrk.co.uk